Pride Publishing books by Kayleigh Sky:

Backbone

I0681187

BACKBONE

KAYLEIGH SKY

Backbone
ISBN # 978-1-78430-690-8
©Copyright Kayleigh Sky 2015
Cover Art by Posh Gosh ©Copyright July 2015
Interior text design by Claire Siemaszkiewicz
Pride Publishing

This is a work of fiction. All characters, places and events are from the author's imagination and should not be confused with fact. Any resemblance to persons, living or dead, events or places is purely coincidental.

All rights reserved. No part of this publication may be reproduced in any material form, whether by printing, photocopying, scanning or otherwise without the written permission of the publisher, Pride Publishing.

Applications should be addressed in the first instance, in writing, to Pride Publishing. Unauthorised or restricted acts in relation to this publication may result in civil proceedings and/or criminal prosecution.

The author and illustrator have asserted their respective rights under the Copyright Designs and Patents Acts 1988 (as amended) to be identified as the author of this book and illustrator of the artwork.

Published in 2015 by Pride Publishing, Newland House, The Point, Weaver Road, Lincoln, LN6 3QN, United Kingdom.

No part of this book may be reproduced, scanned, or distributed in any printed or electronic form without permission. Please do not participate in or encourage piracy of copyrighted materials in violation of the authors' rights. Purchase only authorised copies.

Pride Publishing is a subsidiary of Totally Entwined Group Limited.

If you purchased this book without a cover you should be aware that this book is stolen property. It was reported as "unsold and destroyed" to the publisher and neither the author nor the publisher has received any payment for this "stripped book".

BACKBONE

Dedication

To my friends who are no longer here — with love.

Chapter One

The man was bent over inside the gas station. Naked. Tied down.

Fuck. A slave.

Hank gave a tug on Trixie's reins and pushed on through scrubby brown hills. The sky was a high, flat blue and a dry, astringent smell filled the air. Hank breathed deeply, inhaling a faint tickle of dust. Below was a spit of a town—just a gas station and an unused diner.

All familiar.

His life now. But, fuck, he didn't want to see this. He was a cop, for godsakes. He was supposed to break up fights and put bad guys away. In his old life, he knew the homeless man who rummaged in the alleyway behind the Thai Palace by name. He guarded a social worker named Joy who came to take a five-year-old in pink barrettes out of a crack house where her daddy had knifed her mommy to death for forgetting to put ice in his Pepsi. He dodged a TV somebody tried to drop on his head out of a fifth floor window. He took complaints and made reports. He hauled in pimps, drug dealers and drunk and disorderlies. He went after bad guys.

Guys like Thom—who bounced and wobbled in the too-hot sun. Animated. A friendly salesman.

Laughter floated in the air.

Christ, he wanted to go get that naked man. Wanted to grab him and run off with him.

Save him.

Like he couldn't save anybody else.

He wanted his old life back. The life with the dance recitals, soccer, movies with Beth, game night with the girls, work, bills.

He liked that life. It was a good life.

Then a company called Bio-Gen Tech had come out with a vaccine called Pox Vac and for only pennies a shot, almost all viruses—flu, colds, HIV—had disappeared. Conspiracy theorists claimed that Pox Vac was really nanotechnology funded by corporations to control the purchasing habits of consumers. To them, that was the only way Pox Vac could make sense. Otherwise, it was un-American. There was no profit in cures. Hank scoffed at that. The girls had gotten their shots. Beth too, but he hadn't. Lazy, he guessed.

It didn't matter. Life had gone on—piano lessons, school plays, a trip to the Grand Canyon, work.

Then Beth's affair.

He didn't like to think about that, but it was a part of the end—like summer's last barbecues and early twilights.

Then people had begun to die.

They'd called the new virus Eve. By spring, shell-shocked survivors had scattered out of almost-empty cities. Now, three years later, he lived in a half-dead world with people like Thom Donnell, the bulbous, waddling former insurance salesman, because that's what Thom was before—a salesman. Still a salesman. Gesticulating avidly to his customers between slaps to the naked man's ass.

It made Hank's blood boil.

Brey didn't know where he was anymore. He thought he used to know. But now he wasn't sure. His face scrunched up, but he didn't feel it. All he felt was that bar under his belly, and he wanted to get away from it, but he couldn't. His position confused him. He didn't like it. He couldn't get a good breath in, and his legs shook. He was hot, too.

Lemonade, he thought. That would be good. Under the verandah by the pool. A ball game on TV.

"Giants an' Dodgers."

"No Dodgers."

He didn't like that voice.

Metal clanked.

Fuck, that bar hurt.

Sweat stung his eyes, and he blinked grit away. There was concrete beneath him. A concrete floor. Oil stains. *Oh yeah. A garage.*

His legs shook again. *Fuck. Fuck.* "I have to go!"

Nobody looked at him, though. His voice wouldn't come out. Only a raspy breath that he couldn't quite catch. Noise rang in his ears—booming, raucous, shrill.

Fuck!

He struggled, metal bit into his wrists, and the pressure on his belly made his head swim. He was tired. Too tired for this. He didn't want to do it anymore. Shame flooded him like hot water—itching, burning and stinging. Surreal. Out of nowhere. His memories of getting here swirled with images of swimming pools, orange and yellow leaves, a cell with bars, a blue strobe light, bare dry hills and a fat man smiling brightly.

Thom.

He couldn't remember coming here, undressing or bending over the bar. Panic fluttered inside him, and he began to pant again. *Please God, please. I don't want this. I don't.* But he wasn't really sure of that anymore.

"Stop!"

His breath rasped, and that laugh came again. High-pitched. Shrill. "Wakey-wakey."

He thrashed. *No!*

One of the men grabbed onto him and slammed him against the bar. Pain burst inside, and his thoughts scattered again. He tried to grab on. Imagined a pool, lemonade, Goldy chasing tennis balls.

Sunshine.

The drone of a TV.

Beautiful things like autumn leaves.

His breath exploded. *Oh please, God. Please. I wanna go home! Please, please.*

But all that came out was a rasp, a whisper, "Help me."

Followed by a voice that grunted in his ear, "Who's gonna help you, pretty boy?"

Him, he thought, painlessly now, floating away again. *Him.*

Wobbling in the shimmers of hot air outside the garage, Thom swung a look at Hank as Trixie clomped out onto the pavement. He squinted in the sun, an arm up to shield his eyes. Hank squinted too. The shapes in the garage were a blur—two men inside, one standing outside. Then the man outside backed up and gave the person tied up a slap on the rump. His palm landed with a loud cracking sound. The man swayed, legs collapsing before he could lock his knees and struggle back up.

Hank closed his eyes. He felt almost lucky for a moment, almost glad that his wife and daughters weren't here. Beth and Annabelle and Matilda... They broke his heart. They were gone, and he was here in this horrible place with Jack, Beth's brother. After Beth and the girls and Lacy — Jack's wife — had died, Hank and Jack had packed up and driven away through almost empty cities and towns. They hadn't been going anywhere. They'd just driven. Saw skittish people who ran, armed people who stood guard, random car jams, empty stretches of interstate.

And Waterfall.

A small city with people walking on the streets, living in houses again, with farms and a cannery.

And slaves.

The people of Waterfall were happy to have Hank and Jack. Hank still wore his uniform and carried his service revolver. They wanted law and order, and once he'd seen this place, Hank hadn't been able to leave. He couldn't just walk away.

Opening his eyes again, he pulled in a deep breath and looked below. A man laughed, high-pitched, giggling. All three men were walking away now, leaving Thom behind in the sun outside the auto bay.

"C'mon back," he yelled, throwing his hands into the air as they rounded the corner of the gas station and disappeared.

Hank swallowed bile. *Waterfall men?* Which didn't matter because he couldn't arrest them. *Or Younger's men?* That wouldn't matter either. The slaves came from Younger's group. They started it. A loose mob of people that Younger took over. Doomsayers, Hank called them. They'd been ready for the Armageddon called Eve. They'd taken over an empty vacation resort. A lodge and cabins scattered throughout the pines — cooler, isolated. They'd taken slaves at the beginning of Eve. By the time anybody else had known about it, they hadn't cared anymore. They just wanted to survive. It was Younger's idea to rent the slaves to Waterfall. At the time, the population of Waterfall had been too small to work the farms and cannery. Now they were stuck with the devil's bargain. But the slaves in Waterfall were better off, to be sure. They didn't wear shock collars like Younger's slaves. Dog collars, really. Modified for stronger shocks.

"Too easy to run up here," Younger had once told him.

The slaves in Waterfall wore tracking collars. Bright orange posts surrounded the town and fields. A collar on anybody crossing the post-line sent a signal back to Hank's police. No need to shock anybody in Waterfall because there was no way to run.

Before Eve, Younger had been an engineer for the Army — a puzzle to Hank. He'd probably had a home in the suburbs once, an Army pension he never got to use, a wife, children maybe. A man who'd barbecued in summer, mowed the lawn, washed the cars, lived a regular life.

Where people weren't tied up and sold.

* * * *

Brey was almost happy. There was no pain now. He was dreaming about dancing underneath a tree where leaves fell all around him — leaves that stretched out in a copper-red carpet, scattering under his bare feet.

He loved to dance.

Sweat rolled on his sticky skin. He smelled the sour scent — a clammy, oily smell too. Sex. Cum.

His hips swayed. Achy.

Strange.

He tried to blink the pain away. His vision blurred. He looked up. The sky above was gray with random oily splotches and the air was cold. His feet slipped on suddenly slimy leaves. He didn't like that.

"Patric?"

But he was alone — dancing alone. He couldn't stop dancing. His arms moved fluidly, his hips like liquid.

He was naked and cold.

Shivering. Shaking.

His chest hurt. Raw. The air in his lungs like fire.

Leaves flew, settled like slimy fingers on his skin.

He thrashed, stumbling, and fell into the copper-colored carpet — clammy wet, fecund, smothering him. He was drowning in leaves — Patric's leaves. He flung his arms out. Metal clanked, like bars — like a cell door slamming shut.

I wanna go home!

"Help."

* * * *

The smell of the man in the gas station was rank. The other men were gone now. Hank grimaced at the bitter, sour stench that wafted over to him. The man made no sound. He was bent over a metal U-shaped bar that separated the two work spaces in the auto bay — ankles chained to the support bars, neck to a plate in the floor. He could raise himself halfway up, but that was all.

Thom pasted a smile on his face, assessing Hank. Hank made no secret of his opinion of Thom.

"We were just playin' *Remember When*," said Thom. "There was a baseball series with an earthquake in the middle of it. Giants and the As, right? No Dodgers?"

Baseball, for godsakes? They were talking about baseball?

"Not my game," he said.

Thom squinted at him speculatively. "No. Hockey man, right?"

He was, but he wasn't about to start a conversation with Thom about it.

"Long time ago."

Thom nodded then rubbed his palms together and said, "Got just the thing to relax you. Better 'n a good game. Givin' out free samples. You like 'im. You buy 'im."

Hank's gorge rose. The inconceivability of that comment made his head swim. *Christ almighty.* Trixie skittered sideways, suddenly nervous. The smell, he realized—terror, hopelessness. Thom gave Hank an encouraging smile and patted the man's bare rump.

"C'mon up."

"Christ, Donnell, this is a new low, even for you."

Thom bristled. "This is legitimate business."

The smell was overpowering up close, growing in the heat. The man's legs were quivering, a fine tremor running through them. His hole was a puffy raw ring between his ass cheeks. Hank swallowed his bile back down. "Let 'im up."

Thom gave him a look of shock. "Can't. Violent."

Hank laughed, an ugly burst of sound. "I doubt it."

"You buy 'im. You can let 'im up."

"No thanks."

Thom's hand began a stroking motion over the man's hip, and Hank watched the tremors grow stronger. He wondered why he stayed here. *Leave, you idiot.* Thom was watching him carefully.

"Like I said, free samples."

Fucker. God, he wanted to hit him. Pound his face in — his happy salesman's face. Uncop-like, but Hank didn't care.

Thom smiled cautiously. Encouragingly. Because maybe this was the day Hank gave in and took up Thom's offer.

Hank's mouth went dry.

He tried not to look at that raw, weepy hole.

Christ, he wished he'd never come by here. He hadn't seen anybody this morning, but it had still been dark then. Maybe Thom and his slave had been asleep. He didn't like to think about the things that had been done to the man while he'd been drinking fake coffee with Younger and talking about water shortages and the next Council meeting. But those were talks they had to have. Their reservoir was going dry and rain was scarce. They were lucky to have a river about fifty miles away.

"We can divert it," Younger had said. "Channel it to the reservoir."

Younger's people wanted slaves to do the work. Younger didn't care either way. "I just want a guarantee. Slaves or no slaves, your people see this through."

"You have three votes on the Council already."

Younger's smile had turned slightly grim. "My people are free to vote as they wish."

But they won't.

Silent for a moment, Hank had looked down into his cup of coffee before fixing his stare on Younger again.

"And you need slaves?"

Younger had shrugged. "I don't. I need a commitment. I don't trust free people. They quit. They complain."

"Not to mention those pesky union issues."

That had gotten him a laugh. "I like you, Hank. There's not enough humor in the world anymore."

Maybe because there isn't a lot to laugh at anymore.

Now, at the garage, Hank forced his thoughts away from Younger and back on the auto bay in front of him—on that naked, quivering man and Thom, standing obliviously beside him.

"Like I said, Donnell, a new low."

There was thick skin and there was Teflon skin. Thom's smile just grew. He raised a palm, almost in supplication. "C'mon. You're young. Are you gettin' enough?"

"That's a man." Hardly a consideration, but he wasn't telling Thom that—nor did he want to think about the twitch in his dick.

Thom guffawed. "These days a hole's a hole."

Hank suspected that was true. Women were scarce, thanks to Eve. She stole them quickly and heartlessly— his wife, daughters. He'd seen no women after Eve until he'd come to Waterfall.

"As interesting as your offer is, I could smell 'im a mile down the road, an' another man's cum is leaking out of his ass."

The man jerked suddenly, startling Thom and Hank both. Then he groaned, "Help," and the grief in that voice churned Hank's stomach.

He gritted his teeth and nudged Trixie closer. Thom laid a hard slap on the man's ass and said, "Shut up, you."

A band of pain tightened around Hank's head. "Stop leaning on 'im. You're only causing more pain."

Thom sighed and started to straighten. "I'm tryin' to save 'is life, cause if I can't unload 'im, I'm puttin' 'im down. I can't afford 'im."

In the moment that Thom straightened up and took a step to the side, Hank saw it on the slave's skin, black and blue ink, a tattoo of a snake curling up his side—a tattoo the slave had gotten because he was born in the Year of the Snake. Hank knew that. A chill like a bucket of ice water drenched him. He sucked in air, swallowing the sound and tried to control his voice.

"What's 'e look like?"

"Pretty."

"I want to see. Let 'im up."

Thom frowned uncertainly. "I told you. He gets violent."

"Christ, Donnell. How long have you kept 'im like that?"

Thom shrugged but looked slightly embarrassed. "A while."

"How much?"

For a moment, Thom just stared, then frowned while the idea sank in. "You're gonna buy 'im?"

"How much?"

"Money?"

Waterfall used currency, but Hank didn't think Thom wanted money. He did little business here.

"Or trade."

Thom pursed his lips thoughtfully. "Your horse?"

Hank's laugh was genuine and loud. "I don't think so. You can have the saddle or two hundred dollars. I'll send a man up here tomorrow with payment if cash is your choice." Hank knew Thom had a horse but no saddle. He wasn't going to pick the money.

"I get to keep 'im till then," said Thom.

"No."

"My property."

"The saddle or the money. Pick."

Thom scowled humorlessly. "Saddle."

"Good."

Hank jumped down and Thom tossed him a key. "Receipt's in back. Be careful."

The man's tremors were almost shudders now. The black and blue snake moved sinuously over the man's ribs and coiled over his shoulder to poise long, curved fangs over a nipple. Hank had seen the tattoo before, years ago — a pair of pale blue eyes filled with despair. He shook his head briefly, tried to wash the memory away. Stooping down on the dirty, cum-spattered floor, he spoke gently, quietly, "You're okay. You're going to be okay now."

He wasn't entirely sure of that, though. Heat poured off the slave. Under the dirt, he could see the stripes from a belt, open cuts, deep purple bruises. He looked at the face, slitted eyes, cracked lips, more bruises.

"Can you hear me?"

Nothing.

"Name's Brey," said Thom, coming up behind him. "Spells it with an 'e'."

Hank wasn't sure why such superfluity should irritate him as much as it did. "How do you know that?"

"The paperwork. I'm a legitimate business man, Hank Kresnak."

Hank ignored that, bent down to release Brey's ankles then rose to try to help him straighten off the metal bar across his belly. Halfway up, Brey's knees gave out and his weight dragged him out of Hank's arms. On the pavement, he scrambled backward with a sudden burst of energy, eyes staring wildly.

"Told you," said Thom.

"That's not violent. That's scared."

Then, ignoring both Brey and Thom, Hank went over to Trixie and uncinched the saddle. Lifting it off, he brought it inside and set it down.

"Clothes?"

Thom blinked. "No clothes."

"Christ." He gritted his teeth against the desire to pound Thom into the concrete. "Well, get me something to cover 'im up with then."

"You got a blanket right there," said Thom, pointing at Trixie.

"Which I need so I don't chafe the guy raw. Don't be so fuckin' heartless, Thom. That sun'll fry 'im."

"Fine," said Thom, stalking off again. "You're a lotta trouble, Hank. You know that?"

Squatting down on the garage floor, Hank let a hand settle on Brey's shoulder and pushed a water bottle at him. Brey tried to crawl away, digging desperate fingers into the concrete beneath him.

"C'mon, Brey. It's just water. Take a sip."

His face was tucked against his shoulder, and Hank tried to press the bottle on him again. Brey didn't want it. He just laid his cheek on the floor and grew still.

"This was all I could find," said Thom, coming back with a square of tarp.

"Did he eat today?"

"No. I told you. I can't afford that."

Hank took a slow breath. "How long?"

"I had 'im about four days. An' don't ask me to apologize. I didn't make this world."

Thom's sudden defense surprised him. "Help me get 'im up."

Hank could feel Brey's fear, his rapid-fire breathing, but he didn't struggle. Once they'd gotten him draped over Trixie's back, Hank pulled one of Brey's legs over, pressing him down against her neck. Climbing up behind him, he laid the tarp over Brey's body. He thought maybe it would smother some of the smell but it didn't, and he almost gagged at every breeze.

Stepping back into the shade of the auto bay, Thom was all smiles again, waving him away.

"Enjoy!"

Hank felt sick. He knew the heat under that tarp had to be bad, and he half feared he'd be riding with a dead man soon. He spoke quietly about nothing at all, just a monotonous litany of things to soothe the man. In the twilight, he pulled the tarp away and gently rubbed his dirty back.

"You'll be okay," he whispered softly. "You're safe. I'll take care of you. We're almost home."

On and on, he made gentle sounds of comfort to Brey's soft, ceaseless crying.

In the dark, lights glittered, bejeweled and welcome. After the collapse of the grid, the dark at night was intensely deep, the blaze of stars almost unnerving. Waterfall was a small town, surrounded by family farms and home to the engineers, construction workers and planners who built the town as an experiment in small hydro self-sufficiency. Electric cars with long-dead batteries occupied the driveways of empty homes. A few of the SUVs and Jeeps became patrol cars, but otherwise, people saved energy for lights and industrial use. Bikes were plentiful, and Waterfall was small enough to walk from place to place. A fountain in the center of town had once gurgled with recycled water, splashing over blue tiles and the dull copper color of scattered pennies—dry now and spattered by bird droppings and crusts of pale dust.

Starbucks on random corners, the smell of coffee a trick of the memory.

Almost everybody who was in Waterfall now came from other places. Everybody except Nate Vallero and Issa Moran. Issa thought that Younger came from Waterfall too—one of the engineers brought on toward the end of the project—but Younger just smiled at that and said, "I come from a lot of places."

As they got closer to town, Hank cringed at the thought of Jack's reaction to Brey. He knew that Jack stayed in Waterfall only because of him. They'd gone to the same high school, played football together, had gone to the same community college before Hank had gone on to the police academy and Jack joined the Army. Jack had been best man at Hank's wedding, godfather to Hank's daughters—Annabelle and Matilda—and Beth's brother. Jack and Lacy had even given Hank a place to stay when Hank and Beth had split up. Hank never stopped loving Beth, and he knew Beth still loved him. Jack knew that, too.

Jack wasn't going to be happy about Brey. Slavery cut Jack in a different way than it did Hank because Jack never believed Hank could do anything about it. When Jack was in a good mood, Hank was the 'righter of wrongs'. In a bad mood, Hank was the 'idiot who thought he could fix human nature'. Hank couldn't explain to Jack that the man lolling bonelessly against Trixie's neck filled him with an inexplicable mixture of despair and hope.

He rubbed circles on Brey's filthy back and moved toward a pool of soft light. Other smaller lights rimmed the eaves of a long white building. Around the far side, a wide door was open and light came from inside too. Pulling up to the door, he gazed down the long row of stalls. Horses stirred, snuffling restlessly. A shape emerged from the shadows. A tall, wary boy named Josh. Hank wasn't sure where the wariness came from except that this was a different world than three years ago, but it seemed natural – a cautious distrust of everyone. Considering the boy's father, Hank wasn't surprised. He didn't like the man and wasn't entirely sure he liked the boy.

"Where's Chrissy?" he asked.

"I'm here."

A blonde in braids came out of the dim light in back. He always worried about her working on the outskirts of town where it was easy to grab her and run. But there were alarms in the building, making her safer inside than out, and she was twenty years old and could choose her own life. Plus, being a man did nothing to save Brey.

She startled to a stop and pulled in a breath at the sight of him.

"Oh, my God."

"It's all right."

"Is 'e dead?"

"No. Just hurt. I found 'im outside of town."

Josh came near, a tense look on his face. "Is 'e yours?"

Annabelle would have been near his age by now. He imagined those words in her mouth. The concept of slavery so calm and casual.

"Yes." He sounded curt – the voice he used to make people pay attention to him, the stare that froze others, but not Josh, who just stared coolly back at him. "I need you to follow me to my place an' bring Trixie back," Hank told him.

"Okay."

Then Hank pulled Trixie away, not waiting. A moment later, her hoofs were clomping on pavement, taking them toward the center of town. He felt movement under his hand, that fine tremor in Brey's muscles again.

"Almost home," Hank said and again rubbed circles on Brey's grimy back.

There were lights on, but he met no one. They emerged from the smaller streets to a wide boulevard, past forgotten cars, empty parking meters, dark storefronts. During the day, a few of those stores would be open. At night, a restaurant and two bars were open. One of the bars was close to his and Jack's place, one on the outskirts of town just before the post-line where Younger's people went to enjoy a place with electricity for a while.

Behind him, he could hear the clatter of hoofs. A moment later, Josh came up beside him. Quiet at first. Hank could feel his examination but ignored him.

Up ahead, lights rose higher in the sky. The tallest building in town was called Centre Park. Hank lived on the fourth floor and Jack lived on the second, and took the first floor for his clinic. These were offices, not homes, but for reasons neither one ever discussed — or maybe even understood — they didn't want to live in a house. Hank's floor was smaller than the floors below, like a pillbox hat on top of the building, with a terrace filled with empty clay pots in a ring around it. He could imagine the greenery out there once — ficus trees, fluttering palms — but couldn't justify the water now.

"What happened to 'im?"

Josh's voice was almost toneless. Hank didn't know if Josh cared or didn't want to let on that he cared. He didn't explain, just said, "Thom had 'im."

He squeezed Brey's shoulder, just a slight tightening of his fingers, experimentally, wondering if Brey could hear, if he knew he was being helped.

"He'll be okay," he added.

At the front of the building, he slid off Trixie and said, "Go get Jack. Tell 'im I'll be downstairs."

Hank couldn't see Brey's face in the dark but thought he saw a gleam of light reflected in his eyes. "Can you hear me? I'm telling the truth, Brey. You're going to be okay. We're home now. I'm going to take you inside, an' nobody's going to hurt you. I promise."

He heard it then. A faint exhalation of air louder than Brey's normal breathing. He pulled him gently until Brey's upper body came down on his shoulder, gagged again at the foul odor up close, then backed up to slide the rest of Brey's body off Trixie's back. His weight sagged, and Hank slipped an arm under his knees, hefting him up with a grunt.

Just then the door opened, and Josh stood back to let him by. He went across a tiled floor and past an elevator they never used. The entrance to Jack's clinic was at the back of the building where a light was coming from under a door. This floor had once housed doctors' offices, a lab and a physical therapy practice. Knocking down some of the walls, Jack had made a large and spacious clinic. It was comforting in its way, bright and white.

After he'd stepped inside, he paused a moment to blink, Jack's form coming into focus.

"What the fuck, Hank?"

"Just help me. I don't need a lecture."

"Put 'im here." Jack adjusted a light over a bed and muttered, "Holy shit," behind a hand he clapped suddenly over his mouth and nose.

"Yeah, not so good."

Hank put Brey down then backed up, looking expectantly at Jack, who gave him an angry, baleful stare.

"Well?" Jack asked.

"Well, what?"

"What am I dealing with?" He was already leaning over him, delicate fingers resting on the side of Brey's face, his stare boring into Brey's slitted eyes. He gently raised an eyelid with his thumb.

"I took 'im from Thom."

"Took 'im?"

"Bought 'im."

"Really?"

"I couldn't leave 'im."

"Raped, I'm assuming." He was running gentle hands over Brey's head.

Hank cringed at the thought of that greasy hair. "I saw three."

"Who?"

"I wasn't close enough. It doesn't matter anyway," he added, knowing he sounded defensive.

"No, of course not. No crime committed here."

"I couldn't leave 'im."

"I get that. What do you know?" Jack hooked a stethoscope to his ears and pulled a blood pressure cuff off the wall.

"No food for four days at least. I don't know about water. I tried to get 'im to drink, but he wouldn't."

Jack was quiet until he got a measurement, then pulled the stethoscope back out of his ears. "Was he coherent at any time?"

"I'm not sure. I think so."

"I think he's listening to us now," Jack said quietly, reaching for a blanket from the pile he'd set on a nearby chair. "Go fill the tub. You know where?"

Hank nodded.

Jack covered Brey up as Hank left the room, talking quietly, maybe the same silliness Hank had been spouting to him, as if strangers could comfort him after strangers had hurt him. Of course, Hank wasn't entirely a stranger, although he doubted Brey remembered him.

He stooped down, swiped his fingers through the running water then stood back up and went to a closet against the wall where he pulled out a pile of soft, clean towels. The tub was partially sunken, complete with whirlpool jets. He set the towels on a moveable metal table at the foot of the tub and watched the water rise.

Waiting, his thoughts went backward, back to the days when Eve had just been a name, and Beth, Annabelle, and Matilda had still been alive—alive like electricity. Alive like the blue lights that pulsed and strobed across walls and glass and bodies. The Blue Glow—a nightclub he'd never been in before. Music pounded in him. As he'd passed through the club, his partner following, people had parted curiously. Others, oblivious, had gone on grinding against each other on the dance floor, stirring raw nerves inside him. Upstairs, a man had been sprawled on his hands and knees, shirtless, a snake tattoo sliding over his ribs. Another man had lain on the floor, the first one's shirt under his head, sopping up a pool of blood. The first man's friend, lover, fuck-buddy. His eyes had been sightless.

"Fuck," Hank had muttered and had met a pair of eyes shooting up at him. A pale, freckled face. The beauty of it had shocked him. Light blue eyes, stricken, pleading with him, confusing him, wanting to be saved. Hank had felt a crushing rush of uselessness, of shame and regret that had brought out a sudden sweat and anger at the man for wanting a thing that Hank wanted desperately and inexplicably to give him. But he hadn't been able to. He hadn't been able to save him. By then, he couldn't have saved anyone.

* * * *

Steam came off the water, broke apart as they lowered him in. Brey groaned, the first real sound Hank had heard out of him since he took him out of the gas station. His eyelids fluttered and a grimace crossed his face.

"Easy," Hank murmured. "This oughta feel good, right?"

Jack rose, went to the closet where Hank retrieved the towels and came back with a stack of rags and a bottle of soap.

"Clean 'im."

Hank scowled at the order, but Jack was soaping up a rag too, starting with a foot that pulled out of his grip.

"None a that now," Jack said gently, pulling Brey's foot back out of the water. "We'll need to refill the tub. Rinse 'im."

The water was already a dingy brown.

Hank started on Brey's shoulders, squeezing the rag, soapy sheets of mud rolling through Brey's chest hairs into the darkening water. Straightening up, Hank tugged off his shirt, bending down again, moving on to Brey's stomach, circling the rag over his bony ribs.

Jack was scrubbing at a knee, moving over to the side of the tub. Hank was descending uneasily down Brey's belly. Maybe he tensed, gave off some signal that set Brey off, but all of a sudden, Brey was thrashing and kicking, spraying filthy water everywhere.

Jack jumped up. "Fucking Christ!"

Water flew. Brey arched and twisted, arms flailing, heels thudding against the sides of the tub. Hank got him under the arms, lifting him half out of the water, squeezing him back against his chest, booming into his ear.

"God damn it, relax! Relax, already!"

Wild fingers snagged in his hair, pulling. He caught a glimpse of wide-open eyes.

"Shit. Aubrey! Aubrey, relax!"

Jack shot him a narrowed stare.

"Relax, Aubrey. Relax. We won't hurt you." He tightened his arms around Brey's chest and a bellowing groan came out of Brey's mouth, then his head fell back on Hank's shoulder, fingers slipping loose. "Better now, right? You feel better?"

He lowered Brey back down, and Jack drained the tub. They re-washed him, scrubbed his hair, rinsed and washed him again. He was silent and pliant, eyes at half-mast. Hank could feel the burn of Jack's stare, but he ignored it, murmuring again as he carried Brey back through the door.

"You're doin' real good, Brey. Just a little while longer now."

He laid Brey down, and Jack picked up a glass of water on the table beside the bed, lifting Brey's head up. "Drink some more for me?"

He put the glass to Brey's lips, and Brey swallowed, some of it leaking out. Hank resisted wiping it away.

Brey drank a little more then when Jack let his head settle back, his chest heaved and a long sigh gusted out.

"Fucker's tired," said Jack.

"You have a way with words."

"We all have our gifts." Jack looked cautiously at Brey's face while he rolled him onto his side and pushed his knees up. "Can't get away from this," he said. Then he pulled a stool over and sat down. "Just try an' relax."

Hank took Brey's hand, felt his fingers tighten, the muscles of Brey's face clenching into a deep frown.

"Could be worse," said Jack, gently working at the raw ring of Brey's hole. He slid a speculum in, and Brey spasmed, jerking as Jack straightened up, waiting for him to settle down again. After a moment he did, and Jack leaned back in and said, "Good. No tears that I can see right now."

"Wesson oil," said Hank, feeling Brey's clutching fingers begin to rub the bones of his hand together. He saw Brey's teeth bite down onto his lower lip.

"Thoughtful," said Jack, pushing back his stool. "I have some tea for you to give him. We can save the antibiotics for now. A sitz bath for the next couple of days wouldn't hurt either." Gently rolling Brey back again, he began to palpitate his abdomen, pushing down, watching for any discomfort on Brey's face. "I'll come up to see 'im again tomorrow. You can rub arnica on his bruises—not on any open wounds, though."

"Me?"

"You bought 'im."

"You could cut me some slack."

Jack gave him a cold stare. "Aubrey, huh? I remember that name."

Hank sighed and looked into Brey's suddenly open eyes. "Aubrey William Jamieson," he said gently.

For a moment, Brey's stare held then his eyes suddenly rolled up in his head and his lids shuttered shut. Hank started.

"What the hell just happened? Is he okay?"

"I told you," said Jack, covering Brey with a sheet. "The fucker's tired."

Chapter Two

The warm, steaming water enveloped Brey like
arms. A groan swelled inside him and escaped. He
held his breath, wary, keeping to the darkness behind
his eyelids. He didn't want to look, to see, to feel. He
wanted the safe darkness — the feeling of floating like
rising from a deep sleep, the comfort of warmth and
softness. He made himself believe he was home again
where the muffled sounds of life stirred outside his
bedroom door. As he heard those sounds, a little
niggle of uneasiness made him burrow down deeper.
He felt a breath brush against his cheek, and he
struggled with a memory, pulling at it, dragging it up
against the faint unease. The breath was his mother's,
attached to an indulgent laugh.

"Daytime is fun, too, sweetheart. You might like it if
you try it."

Stealing into his happy, sleepy darkness were the
sounds of water — splashing, people jumping into the
pool at home. His mother's face was floating away. He
dug deeper into the darkness. Then he was in the
pool, and people were pulling at him, tugging gently

31

at his arms and legs. He wanted to play back, but he was afraid and tried to wriggle away from the hands. He saw the surface of the pool above him, but he couldn't reach it. A hand was brushing his belly. He wanted to breathe, but then he'd drown. Then the hand stroked lower, and he was thrashing, terrified, breaking above the surface of the water. Arms pulled him out of the pool, but he couldn't calm. There was no air in his lungs. They were all gone—all the people who loved him. His heart raced, breathing stopped then a voice, rumbling and growing in force.

"Aubrey! Aubrey, relax!"

The feel of home, of comfort, washed over him again, seeped inside like warm sleepiness, a strange jangle of familiarity, and he felt his body go soft and lax, almost insensate again, impossibly but surely safe. Arms hugged him gently, buoyed him. A heart beat against his back, regular and strong. He smelled the sweetness of soap—roses or lavender. The thrum of a voice working through the chest behind him. Another voice, stern but not unkind, not like the other voices that broke him—not those voices. He shivered and stiffened. The darkness began to lighten. He didn't want that—bright lights, air on his skin. Arms lifted him, cradled him. He scrunched his eyes shut, willing the darkness back, hiding from the hands touching him, hurting him again—the person's thumb on his eyelid, fingers between his legs. The light invaded. He squinted at it. A dark-edged figure rose, painfully delineated by that blaze of light.

"Aubrey, huh? I remember that name."

"Aubrey William Jamieson."

His eyes opened, focused slowly, fixing on a face, cool and remorseless, that floated up out of his memory—his unconscious, the lost place in his heart.

He couldn't look, couldn't think about this... Brey felt his eyes roll up, and that was all.

* * * *

Sunlight poured in, dry and heavy, soaking into Brey's blankets. It drew sweat out of his skin, but it felt good and cleansing.

"What's your plan? Unless you think you can stay under there forever."

The voice was mocking, dry — a voice he liked. It didn't indulge him, didn't pity him — the other man's voice, not the one who knew his name. He pulled the blankets off his face, focused slowly on the sunlit room. A picture window faced him, filled with nothing but sky. A bedside table with a lamp, pitcher and cup. A bookshelf under the window. He blinked at that, greedy, heart beginning to quicken. Then he focused on a chair, a dresser and mirror out of the corner of his eye. A man in the chair — late thirties with short salt-and-pepper hair, a tough and narrow face and amused gray eyes. He was rubbing his chin between thumb and forefinger.

"You aren't going to duck back under, are you?"

Brey found his voice from somewhere, cleared his throat first. "No."

"Good." The man sat up, reached for the cup beside the bed. "Drink this. You can have two or three a day for the next couple of days."

He got an elbow under him, pushed back against a pillow-strewn headboard, pulling the blankets with him. He shivered, despite the heat. He knew it was hot in the room. His bladder ached. He looked at the cup, took it grudgingly, eyeing the contents suspiciously.

"What is it?"

"Willow bark tea. Acts like aspirin. Are you in pain?"

He nodded slowly.

"Drink it."

A small spark of rebellion urged him to refuse. His skin twitched, fingers possessed by a sudden desire to fling the cup across the room. But the twitch of his skin awoke the memory of Thom's belt cutting through the air. It bit like it was edged in razor blades. Brey looked back at the man in the chair, who was waiting patiently for him, then slowly drank his tea. For a few moments, he kept his eyes on the empty cup, then looked over.

"Who are you?"

"Jack Clement. You might hear some folks call me Doc."

"Are you? A doctor, I mean?"

"Close as we have. How do you feel, by the way?"

Brey thought about it. The heat baking into him was like a drug. Shifting a little, he set his cup down, tugged the blankets back up.

"Sore. I need to piss."

Jack lifted his chin at a door across the room. "Go do that. Then I need to take another look at you."

Brey could feel his face shifting into resistance, the beginnings of panic again.

"I was a nurse in the Army," said Jack. "A family nurse practitioner after that. I really do have medical training. I take care of people. Let me do that for you."

Brey just stared for what he knew was a long time, waiting for Jack's irritation, helpless almost to stop himself—to make himself agree, comply. He felt his fear growing, chilling him in the heat of the room. But Jack just smiled, made no move of anger.

"Take your time."

His breath came out in a rattling wheeze of surprise. He nodded, wriggled out from under the covers. They'd put a pair of soft cotton boxers on him, and he blinked angrily at the stinging in his eyes, then went into the bathroom and emptied his bladder with a sigh of relief. The sight of a bar of soap in a dish on the corner of the sink caught his attention, and he remembered the bath from the night before and curiously, hesitantly, turned a knob, gasping as water gushed out. With a grin of delight, he washed his hands, then quickly ducked away from the glimpse he caught of himself in the mirror.

Still waiting, Jack rose as he came in, pulled a loose blanket off the bottom of the bed and said, "Lay on top. You can cover yourself up with this."

Just like that he could feel himself slow down again, grow heavy, the spark of life in him dimming to nothing. Shucking the boxers, he lay down under the blanket and stared up at the thin and watery shadows on the ceiling. Jack spoke calmly.

"You'll have a couple of scars from the whipping you took. No apparent internal injuries. Besides sore, anything else?"

"A little dizzy."

"That I can fix. How does chicken noodle soup sound?"

"Oh, God."

"That good?" He could hear the smile in Jack's voice then that slow, calm tone. "I need to check inside you again. You were pretty swollen. You're going to feel bare fingers. I'm sorry about that. We ran out of gloves about a year ago."

He swallowed and rolled sideways. There were shadows on the wall too, moving like water. He jerked at Jack's touch and thought of stream water over sunny rocks, slipping into shaded darkness. The odor of the summer sun, warm and dry. A burn underneath the fingers, making him grimace. Sun sparkles. The hum of insects in the air. Suntan lotion. Pine.

"Okay."

He rolled back, and Jack laid a hand on his belly, warm and pressing.

"Any pain here?"

"No."

He squinted. Jack's hand slipped away. "You can put your boxers back on."

He sat up, hearing Jack in the bathroom, washing his hands. Grabbing his boxers, he got underneath the covers, letting the heat bake into him again. A moment later, Jack came back out. "I want you to rest today. I'll bring you your soup in a minute. Just a little for now, though. I don't want you to get sick."

"You..." Brey stopped, and Jack looked back at him. He was surprised at the question he was about to ask because there were too many things he didn't want to know about. He just wanted to be quiet and forget. It came out anyway, awkward sounding, maybe not how he wanted to say it. He could feel his frown deepening. "You... You didn't buy me?"

Jack shook his head and turned for the door. "That was Hank. He'll be by later."

A name to a face. A name he didn't remember.

* * * *

That he wasn't the same man he used to be didn't surprise Hank. He didn't think that anybody was the same. Although, after a while, he wasn't so sure of that anymore. Younger and Thom? Maybe the same. He never saw any change in Jack either — caustic, wry, kind. Jack was the same, but Hank didn't think he was. Before Eve, only his family and friends had called him Hank. He'd been Henry to everyone else.

Now he was always Hank.

He wasn't supposed to hurt people. He wasn't supposed to let people be hurt. He was supposed to be a cop. His father had been a cop, too, but he doubted a very good one. Henry Senior had been as volatile as Hank's mother. The pair had been legendary in the neighborhood for the volume and duration of their fights. They'd battled in shouts and insults and seldom-kept threats. Logically, Hank should have been inured to it. He wasn't. Their chaos made the law a rampart of sanity for him. But they'd loved each other, too, even if they didn't know it. And that care, under the barrage of insults, had given him a belief in the goodness of people, despite all the evidence to the contrary. People were wrong-headed and mean all the time, but maybe underneath they didn't want to be. He told himself that. He'd believed it for a long time. He'd become a cop to help. He was still a cop. The sameness of that was a comfort. That he was losing his way because of people like Thom was something he tried to hide. In moments of honesty, he admitted he might have started to lose his way a long time ago, lost it in a stunning instant, the instant that he'd stared into Brey's desperate blue eyes.

Six years ago Hank had arrested Brey because he'd had no other choice. Brey had killed his boyfriend in a split second of anger—in a fight that could have ended up with Brey dead instead but hadn't. He'd been high and drunk and it had been an accident, but it didn't matter. Hank had arrested him. It was his job. But almost hypnotically, he'd found himself drawn to the courthouse where he'd sat in jeans and a sweater, a spectator like everyone else, watching powerful people wreck Brey's life and little by little, his faith in the things he'd believed in—like fairness and mercy— had bled out on the courtroom floor. Brey's father had been a senator who'd led a ruthless push against government corruption and had taken down a police chief, three judges and a district attorney. Hank wasn't an idiot. He knew life wasn't fair. But the law was supposed to make it fairer. And he knew he'd been a hypocrite in that courtroom because he hadn't cared about the law anymore anyway. He'd cared about Brey. Aubrey—a man who believed in him without reason or logic, with a belief that rose out of a place that nurtured a different kind of knowing and being that threatened everything Hank was.

He thought Brey had seen him there once, then again before he'd been led away, and he'd met Hank's gaze over the shoulders of the family that had come to hug him one last time. Hank hadn't been able to reconcile his feelings for Brey. He'd had an ironic tilt to his smile. Everything about him reeked of money and carelessness—arrests for indecent exposure, drugs, drunkenness, speeding tickets paid by his father. There had been society page photos of him snapped at nightclubs and charity events—photos at the nightclub where Hank had found him huddled over his friend, dancing with this boy or that. One of the photos was burned into Hank's brain. A picture of Brey grinding his ass back into a boy behind him, arms up and curled back, fingers in the other boy's hair, the other boy's arms wrapped around him, crisscrossing Brey's crotch. The smile on Brey's face glowed with pleasure. He was blissfully happy. A twenty-four-year-old whose love of life overflowed him, poured out, pulled others in. But he'd killed a boy, and Hank had been able to feel a hum of envy in that courtroom, the glee of people who are happy when others fall. He'd stood in the back that last day and had seen Brey not even sway at Judge Stevenson's condemnation.

"You've shown no gratitude for privileges you haven't even earned. You have squandered and misused your opportunities and shown an egregious disregard for the welfare of others. On the night in question, you were intoxicated at the very least and callously took another's life. You have been judged guilty by a jury of your peers, and I sentence you to not less than fifteen and not more than twenty years in the state penitentiary..."

Straight and true. He'd taken it silently, turned a grim face to his family, met Hank's stare again with eyes that had melted, pleaded, as he'd been tugged away and the world had begun its swift and inexorable decline.

The sun was sinking in the far sky, the shadows in the room growing long, but it was still ungodly hot. Hank sat uncomfortably beside the bed, studying Brey burrowed under the covers. Sounds didn't seem to bother him. He didn't move, breath coming softly through parted lips. He had shaved earlier. His prettiness was strained, worn out under bruises and violet hollows, but his beauty was still there, like sunshine on water, flickering and dancing with the wondrous lightness of his pale blue eyes.

God. Hank inhaled hot air, pulled at the collar of his T-shirt, looked behind him at the window, back at Brey, flushed cheeks and brow. Maybe he should just crack the window. Fresh hot air had to be better than stuffy hot air. The room—his room—smelled different now, not just of Brey, though, sweating under his covers, sweating out fear and pain. Brey's smell was strong and sweet, called to Hank to press his face into Brey's warm neck, breathe in his damp, clean essence—a thought that morphed instantly into distaste at himself, dislike. *Sleaze.* His muscles tightened, and he squeezed at the back of his neck, focusing on Brey's vulnerability, his responsibility to him—a responsibility that still irritated Jack. Unreasonably, he believed, but then Jack would have taken care of him where he was. Let him go. Faced the consequences. But Jack wasn't the law, and Hank was. He breathed in the other scents of tea, ointment, chicken soup. There was an empty bowl on the dresser, a glass of water.

Getting up finally, Hank eased open one of the windows and paused to breathe in a few lungfuls of warm, fresh air. This room was once an office in a suite of offices. Plush carpets, bathrooms, one with a tub and separate shower, wood paneling on some of the walls. His living room was an old conference room with a giant picture window that looked out over the town to endless flat land, green with crops, and the straight black line of the interstate.

Turning back, Hank saw Brey's open eyes and sat down cautiously. Brey stared at him with a flat, empty gaze. He didn't move. Even the covers were still, as if he had stopped breathing. Hank shifted up on his seat, resting his elbows on his knees.

"How are you?"

He wasn't certain Brey was going to answer. There was a long silence then the blankness in Brey's eyes gave way to something that looked like surprise, maybe even confusion. His mouth opened and closed. He swallowed, then tried again.

"Better."

"Good. Sleep's good for you."

"I was tired," he said, and his voice sounded heavy with more than fatigue.

But there really wasn't a lot Hank could do about that. This wasn't his world, he told himself. "There are things we need to talk about."

The flinch was obvious even under the covers, the heat flush fading to a clammy pallor. But Brey nodded, pushing himself up. He was wearing a T-shirt with the boxers now, one of Hank's. Settling against the pillows, he glanced nervously at Hank, licked his lips with a grimace. Hank knew they were dry, mouth dry. It surprised him. He wasn't sure where Brey's sudden nervousness came from. He was being taken care of. Hank watched him run a hand through his hair, dampened at the edges with sweat. The smell reached him again, slightly sour, slightly sweet.

Christ. Hank reached over to the dresser and picked up the item he'd placed there earlier. "I have to put this on you."

It was a collar composed of sections of metal linked together. The segments gave flexibility. It wasn't uncomfortable to wear, light even, but it wouldn't come apart without a hacksaw, and it lay close enough to the neck to make that difficult. The metal was a cool gunmetal color with a key latch in back. Brey stared at it, swallowed dryly, nodded.

"You won't be hurt," Hank said. "I promise."

Brey nodded again, but there was no agreement in his eyes.

He dipped his head as Hank stood up and came over. Damp strands of hair clung to the nape of his neck. Hank felt his heart jump. Arousal fought with his despair. He wanted the despair to win, to be the man that Brey's eyes reflected back at him so long ago — to be the man who could stand up for what was right, save people. *You saved Brey, didn't you?* He lowered the collar under Brey's chin, fastened the latch in back then moved back again, sitting down slowly.

"There's a tracking device in one of the segments. You can't leave here."

Brey nodded, eyes distant. The muscles in his face worked. For a moment, emotion arose in his eyes then slipped away again. Hank thought he saw grief there. *For his freedom?*

"I'm sorry about this. I don't like it either, but I can't let you go." Brey stared at him. There was that surge of emotion again, this time anger, bitter, swallowed with difficulty. "I'll show you around tomorrow. Explain things. We'll convert one of the offices here into a bedroom for you."

Brey startled a little at that, a look almost of dread on his face. "This is your room?"

"Yes."

"You don't want me here?"

"I didn't say that."

Brey ran his fingers over the collar, staring sightlessly across the room. Again that strange mix of emotions — grief, anger. *Panic?*

"Do you remember me?"

Brey's eyes shifted over. He nodded. "Your name is different."

Hank smiled. "I went by Henry then."

"Oh."

"Are you okay, Brey?"

"Sure. I'm fine now. A lot better. I can do whatever you want."

"No rush."

Brey shivered. Hank was sweating. He noted the pallor of Brey's skin, the heat flush gone. Watched him fold his arms across his chest and stare with a look so much like the one from before—desperate. His gaze dropped, eyes lowering. Hank frowned, watching him. Brey's gaze settled, and he swallowed audibly. His voice was a whisper. "Do you want me to?"

He was staring at Hank's crotch, and Hank's cock jumped in sudden excitement, jolting him half out of his chair and startling Brey, who pressed back nervously into the pillows. Hank sat forward, hiding himself. He knew he was flushed in anger. His voice was harsh in his ears. "No. Never. Do you understand? I will never ask that of you. *Never.*"

Brey's eyes grew wide. "I'm sorry," he whispered.

"You have no reason to be sorry." Hank's head dropped suddenly, and he pulled at his hair. "Christ, this is a fucked-up world," he added after a moment. "I won't hurt you like that. I won't take advantage." Though he imagined Brey's mouth on him anyway, the feel of his hot, wet tongue and he almost groaned. "I promise you that."

Brey's lips moved, lifting up in a quick smile— grateful, trusting. Hank felt a pain in his chest, a hand squeezing his heart. *Could I die from this?* From the strain of his own gratitude. Grateful that after all these years he could earn back some of that gentle, gracious trust in a world where there was little he could do right anymore.

He wouldn't hurt Brey. Not ever.

Chapter Three

The stew was rich, scented strangely with lavender, bits of meat, potatoes, carrots and onions. Brey ate the bowlful, sitting in the chair by the bed, hands shaking. The spoon kept clattering, his mouth filled with saliva, but he didn't care. He was alone again. He stuffed his mouth, swallowed with closed eyes. The room was dim and shadowy, no lights until dark. He sighed, the empty bowl on his lap, eyelids growing heavy. His belly was warm, and the warmth spread out—a reminder of Thanksgiving, contentment. He was almost grateful. Thinking that stirred his anger again, dissolving into a panic that he'd never get away.

The collar.

He pulled on it, and it dug into the back of his neck. The feel of Hank's fingers when he fastened it unnerved him. He struggled not to bolt, to run, but he didn't even try to get away—sank into the helplessness that kept pulling him back to sleep, even now. He just wanted to sleep. He gave up his freedom. Just bent his neck and gave it up, like he had with that man in the city when he'd been trying to get back home after Eve. He was afraid, but he didn't try to run. He just took off his pants and lay down. He even liked it, for godsakes. With his family still out there... He knew they were alive, waiting for him. That was all he wanted, everything he lived for—to be with his family again. His father had promised they'd wait for him, and now this. God, he was tired. His limbs went slack, body sagging until the clatter of the falling spoon roused him. He caught the bowl, set it down and got up. *Fuck.* All of him was sore. His head swam as he made his way around the chair.

At the window he rested his head against the glass, staring forlornly outside. A few shorter buildings then a sprawl of homes—empty streets. No. Two people... A pair stepping off a distant curb, disappearing down a side street. Almost normal. He could almost pretend... Almost pretend he didn't open his eyes onto that face, a half-hidden softness underneath the strong jaw, the cool, detached gaze—handsome, hard. A face that couldn't be the face he thought he saw, a face he'd dreamed of, conjured up out of the misery he was drowning in. No, this wasn't pretend. He was never going to wake up to the world he'd lost.

Might as well sleep.

Then a gust of almost cool air blew in, and Brey hooked his fingers around the edge of the window and slid it halfway open. He was afraid of heights. He wondered if he could make himself go to the edge of the terrace. *Close your eyes? Let go?* After all he had gone through, with the one reason he was living still out there—his family, a place to go home to—and he just gave in. Bent his neck, too tired and worn out to run.

In that gas station, dizzy and sick with pain, he'd floated off into strange places. He guessed he'd been sleeping because he'd known he was dreaming those places. Awake, he'd felt fear slither in and curl up because he'd wanted to die. Wanted to go away and never come back. He'd never felt that way before— thought it was something about the way they had just talked over him. When he'd finally broken and had begun to cry, they hadn't paid attention. They'd just talked mundane, everyday conversation. It had made his tears dry up and his sobs taper to a struggle to breathe. It hadn't been until Hank had pulled him up onto his horse and tried to soothe him that he'd begun to cry again, angrily and helplessly, at the hope building back up inside him.

Shifting around to return to the bed, he eyed the room, absorbing the details, things that might matter later. He'd bent his neck, heard the click of the lock, but he didn't have to stay if he didn't want to. He'd think about it for a while. He didn't want to die right now, but he didn't have to stay either.

* * * *

The next day Hank went downstairs and brought Jack back up with him. Brey was hot and feverish, strangely talkative, and there was something furtive in his eyes. He licked dry lips and flicked wary eyes at the door, then at Hank and Jack, pushing himself back into his pile of pillows.

"You should stay away," Brey said.

But Jack ignored him, sitting on the side of the bed, pressing close to Brey's leg. "Why is that?"

"I don't want to make you sick."

"You won't."

"You don't know that. Nobody does. I don't want anybody to die because of me."

"We aren't going to die. This isn't Eve. You have a low-grade fever, a few aches and pains, no swollen glands. You're tired, Brey. You've been through a lot."

"My cellmate got it—in the same cell with me."

His cellmate had been Carl, and Brey didn't think Carl had ever done anything really wrong, not like him. Carl had just been an unlucky con artist—a man who'd played card games with a wry smile because he'd played in a cell with a cellmate who wouldn't play with him. Carl had never tried to cheer him up and had barely given him a glance every time Brey had come back from his father's visits, desperate and bitter. He'd just dealt his cards with his usual smile.

Then one morning Carl had begun to flop under his blankets, and all Brey had done in response was bolt back into a corner of his cell, muttering, "Fuck. Oh, fuck," because Carl was going to die, and maybe he was too.

He didn't want to die like that—dissolving, liquefying inside. He'd been thirteen when Pox Vac had first come out, and he remembered all the celebrations like New Year's—champagne and confetti, bits of colored paper on the streets for days. In prison, he'd heard rumors that it was the vaccine that caused Eve. Not that he cared about that. He just didn't want to die like Carl and he'd cowered in a corner of his cell as Carl had thrashed, flinging blood and spit through the air. Then a guard had run up, stared at him with a reflection of his own horror and run away again. Carl had flung himself up and down, slipped half off his cot and had grown still.

"Fuck... Carl?"

Grief welled up in him. The sound of pounding boots had come closer. White hazmat suits. The first guard had stood out in the corridor, staring at him—

worried. Then he'd gestured for him to come out, taken him to another cell, vacant and cold, with a rolled up mattress on each bunk. Vacant because its prior occupants had already died. Seeing that, he'd begun to laugh, and he hadn't been able to stop laughing for a long time.

Was he laughing now, too?

Brey wasn't sure. Hank and Jack were staring at him. He tried to focus. He was thinking about things he shouldn't be thinking about. Things he couldn't change. Things that made his heart hurt. His eyes found Hank's, met Hank's slight frown as Hank gripped the footboard of the bed, staring at Brey.

Brey felt lost. He tried to focus again, but his thoughts scattered. He stared back at them helplessly. "I—I was..." But he couldn't even remember what they were talking about now. His face burned.

"Eve?" Jack asked gently. "Your cellmate died of Eve?"

Oh, yeah.

He nodded. "I didn't get sick, though—not then. They took him away. I didn't get sick until later, almost a year later."

Jack nodded. "Okay. Tell me about it."

"I was with a couple of families," he said, fading back again. Back to that first winter.

* * * *

Two years ago

He was looking for food and went into a store with its windows punched out. Shelves were tossed onto the floor. There was nothing to eat. Then the glass behind him crunched, people coming at him, pushing him back. A man chased him toward the door, but then a woman stopped the man and gave Brey a packet of nuts. Her name was Mileka, and she let him come with them. They had a van, and they drove until the van ran out of gas then they walked.

Then it snowed — ethereal swirls, melting, slush and cold. Brey noticed Mileka shooting him quick, worried glances even before he began to feel sick. She put a blanket over his shoulders as they walked, and he gave her a look of confusion at first. He was pretty sure they stopped because of the snow, not because of him. They came upon a small apartment building, only two stories and only three bodies inside. His head began to pound as he helped drag the bodies out and opened up the windows. They took the rooms on the top floor, Brey alone in his.

Mileka had her two little boys with her, plus her brother and father and her father's neighbor, the man who'd chased after him. The man's name was Robert, and he looked at Brey with a wary dislike, although he also never spoke against him. He was a quiet, dark-skinned man who had lost his three-month-old daughter and his wife of only two years to Eve. His sister and niece had died, too, but he had his two nephews and two of his cousins with him.

Brey never told his story, but he suspected Robert knew it anyway and decided that there was still something criminal in Brey's heart. But Brey didn't have the energy to do anything, criminal or otherwise.

He didn't remember that snowy winter. Mileka said that occasionally he woke up and talked to her, but he didn't remember those conversations. Around springtime he began to stay awake and keep his recollections. Mileka fed him soup and fruit cocktail from the cans they found in a school cafeteria.

He didn't blame them for leaving. They had children. They wanted a safer place than a city still partly populated with skittish, shell-shocked survivors. They stocked him up with food, water and a couple of water purification tablets and barricaded all the doors. He wasn't sure why they bothered, but maybe it made them feel better.

On the day they left, Robert surprised him. Brey was sitting on the side of the bed, wanting to sway, but he held himself upright, not wanting to make them feel bad.

"Use the fire escape to come an' go," Robert said. "We boarded up everything below. An' this..." he added with a deep frown. "Keep this with you." Robert's arm came out from around his back, and he very slowly set a pistol on the bed. "It's loaded."

Brey stared, the room growing suddenly a lot colder than he knew it was. Every once in a while, he forgot about prison or viewed it as a nightmare. Then something would remind him of what he'd done.

Slowly, he shook his head, edging away. "I can't. Thank you, but I can't."

The frown on Robert's face stayed, then softened a little, and for the first time, Brey felt a little connection to him.

"Are you sure?"

"Yeah. You keep it. You have the kids."

Robert nodded. "Okay then. The Lord keep you safe, Brey. I'll pray for you."

"Thank you."

He felt wounded by that for some reason. Mileka held him close. She was younger even than he was. A girl with plans—like his, like everybody else's—that suddenly became laughable in this new world. But she was strong and kind, and she had saved his life.

After they left, he lay in bed for days, only getting up to eat cold food out of a can. In bed, he lay looking out of the window at the apartment building across the service alley. Curtains moved in a half-open window. A bathroom window, he guessed. Over the passing days, he became certain that there was a body in there, and fear began to uncoil in his belly and spread through the rest of him. Sometimes he'd shake, waiting—just waiting—for that body to rise up and turn this nightmare into an inescapably terrifying one. A nightmare out of every horror movie he'd ever seen, and he couldn't run, couldn't escape. God, it haunted him, every sound, rustle, strange unnerving silence. His heart raced. The room was a trap. He hated that room, the closed, panicked feeling worse than any he'd ever felt in a cell, and he began to pace in the hallway, building up his strength, and pulled the mattress to the front door so he could keep his waking eye on the hallway, the stairway.

He questioned his sanity, didn't trust the reality of anything he heard or saw anymore.

In the heat of summer, he left. He was stronger, calmer in the open. He kept away from towns and cities. In winter, he needed a place to stay again, hid in an empty mobile home until he heard voices, then in empty stores—shivering, achy, waiting for heat to return.

His loneliness was agony.

* * * *

Present day

The next night Brey wanted to sleep on the couch. Hank was surprised because Brey was still sick, but he gave him blankets and pillows and said, "We'll set up the office for you."

"Couch is okay."

"You can't sleep on the couch."

"Why not?"

"Brey, this isn't temporary."

Brey's stubbornness exasperated Hank. He felt guilty for his tone, though. Lying down, Brey just quietly pulled his blankets up and said, "I'm okay."

"Fine," Hank answered back.

Later on, a faint noise woke him up, and he lay quietly, listening. This happened night after night. He knew Brey was in the hall outside his door, but he never came in. Eventually, Hank would hear a sigh as Brey slowly sat down on the floor, settling in for the night. He felt resentment at Brey's attachment—felt guilt at his resentment. Hank didn't blame Brey. He'd lost his life in painful chunks—his freedom, his body, his hope. Brey had reasons for his restlessness, for needing to be safe. It was Hank who wanted to be his savior and resented himself for his failure to be that. He wanted to get up and go to him but was bizarrely convinced that he'd be violating Brey's privacy, witnessing his insecurity. *His loneliness, maybe?* Hank had Ken—nobody special, a body, occasional oblivion. Brey was alone. Special. Hank's obsession.

He didn't want to think about Brey. Hank needed to give him a place to be—a place separate from each other. A room, at least.

On the nights he heard him in the hall, he found himself staring through the dark doorway, imagining Brey's pale blue eyes meeting his.

* * * *

Brey'd told him that he didn't want a room. He'd balked at converting the office—a stubborn, furtive look on his face that he didn't, or couldn't, explain. It'd confused Hank.

"I don't need any space," was all he'd told Hank. "I'm not used to it anymore."

Then he'd given Hank that look Hank recognized as the one that made everything right, even though he was certain that he never did, and instead of the office with its view of trees and corn and wide open space, they'd put a bed in the large alcove off the hallway. There had even been room for a dresser against the wall and a lamp by the bed.

And it hadn't been like Hank knew what to do with that alcove anyway. He wasn't even sure what to do with Brey.

Hank walked him over to the Starbucks across the park, and Brey lagged in shock at the sight of the place, but he also had a look of giddy delight on his face.

Hank stepped back to retrieve him.

"No real coffee, of course. Just chico. Teas. Apple fritters, though."

Brey's eyes lit up at that, and he couldn't get inside fast enough. A ridiculous spurt of pleasure lightened Hank's step behind him. He thought with a twinge that it was a bad idea to view his good fortune through the eyes of the unlucky. He pictured Ken's broad grin. *You think too damn much.* Ken, the counselor before Eve. *Wasn't introspection a good thing?* Besides, the life in Brey's eyes was infectious, the same glow in some of the photos Hank had seen just after his arrest. Images of a spoiled boy—irresponsible, impetuous, shockingly happy. Following Brey inside, he remembered his dislike and felt a coolness come over him. Brey's eyes flickered with a brief uncertainty, then with eagerness again.

"Well, like I said, no coffee, only chico."

Hank longed for coffee, bitter, fragrant, floral coffee. Only Jack knew about his small supply at home. The coffeemaker behind the counter at the shop was shiny and clean—a treasured relic. Cubbyholes that used to house jars of various coffee beans now displayed tea cups instead. Cookies filled the old glass jars on the counter. There were pastries in the display case, and the air smelled of herbs and sugar.

"What do you want?"

Brey looked suddenly stymied. He stared at a few of the patrons sitting at the tables, staring back at him with the quiet reticence of small town people everywhere, at a space familiar and strange, at the pastries and chalkboard menu, then at Hank with a faint panic.

"Why don't I order an' you sit down?"

"Okay."

Hank got them both chicos with steamed milk, apple fritters and cheese pastries. Brey sat at a circular table in a far corner, his chair pushed back against the wall, looking almost gray. Hank winced. *Idiot.* Brey was rattled, of course. This was probably surreal. A joke in comparison to the last few years of his life—a life he wasn't born for. Coddled, vulnerable—eyes wide open on him as Hank crossed the floor—overlaying an invisible steel Hank was certain was there. Every time Hank wanted to feel sorry for Brey, he reminded himself that Brey was a survivor. He could be rough on him because there was something tough in Brey.

Pulling out a chair, he set the pastries down, then returned to retrieve the chicos, frothy with bubbling clouds of milk.

Brey eyed his with greed, took a long, slow swallow. "Oh, my God," he whispered, and Hank smiled, nudging the plate of fritters closer.

"You want a religious experience? Try these."

Brey grinned, broke off a piece and filled his mouth, eyes rolling, setting off a camera flash in Hank's brain, stilling a sweet, frozen picture of Brey's face, loose and wanton with lust, half-lidded rolling eyes, parted lips, bruised and swollen with kisses. *Fuck.*

Grimacing at himself, Hank fixed a stare into his cup. After a while, blanking out his mind, he looked back up, and Brey was frowning at him.

"You okay?" Brey asked.

"Thinking. We have a lot to talk about."

Brey sank, growing smaller in his chair. He had a way of enticing people, Hank thought then reddened, angry at himself because Brey hadn't done anything wrong. He'd been hurt. He deserved to be rescued. It wasn't Brey's fault that he fell into every fantasy that Hank had ever had about him — fantasies at odds with what Hank had believed he should feel about Brey, about the self-indulgence and privilege. Things that should have left a bad taste in his mouth and never did, because underneath it all he had felt the radiance of Brey's joy. Looking into his worried eyes now, Hank wasn't sure that joy was anywhere inside him anymore.

"Eat up. I'll show you around, and you can ask me anything you like."

Brey nodded, and there a quick flash of humor across his face. Not a good kind, though... A rueful, slightly angry kind, and Hank felt peculiarly caught out in a lie. They ate their pastries, drank their chicos without any more words then went outside.

Even in spring the sun was strong, bouncing off the pavement, the day hot. Sun glittered on the empty fountain, the clear white sides of mostly abandoned buildings. Still, there were people out, a vague normalcy. Hank noticed that Brey kept close to the buildings, and a fine coating of perspiration popped out over his upper lip. He understood somehow that Brey didn't want him to notice this, so he ignored it, talking as they walked.

"A virus didn't take out the power system. That was a bunch of crazies living out their doomsday prophecies. Just a couple of attacks, that's all it took. Waterfall was an experiment in zero-emission living — green, self-sufficient and self-sustaining, hydro-based. Luckily for us, we have power. We conserve where we can. No daytime lights. No private vehicles. Unluckily, we're running out of time. Our water source is well and reservoir, the same reservoir that powers the hydro system and irrigates the farms. We aren't getting enough rain anymore, though. A lot of ice and a little snow."

"I know. I couldn't travel in winter. Too cold."

"Where were you going?"

Brey stopped in midstep on the street Hank was leading him across, and Hank caught a curious kaleidoscope of emotions on his face — shock and anger floating to the surface. Hank steeled himself against those emotions, against keeping Brey here against his will. Brey was moving again, his face blank.

"Big Sur." His voice was calm, almost disinterested.

"Where's that?"

"California."

"Your family?" Brey nodded. "Brey, you can't be sure they're alive."

"Yes, they are. I know they are. Only my brother died. My father came to visit me right before the power went out. They were still alive."

"That's a lot of hope to keep up."

Hank could hear the discouragement in his voice, but he wanted to discourage him. This was the world they lived in. Discouragement was a shield against mortal blows. Brey was strong but not against hope. He needed not to hope, not to risk that loss. But the face in front of Hank's was inflexible, determined.

"I won't give up."

"You can't leave here," Hank said. "I have no choice in that." Hank's voice was chopped because he didn't like the belligerence that appeared on Brey's face. "You better get used to not always having your way."

Brey's belligerence turned into outrage. "*My way?* I haven't had my fucking way for the last six years!"

"Stop yelling. An' whose fucking fault is that?"

He regretted putting that look on Brey's face. The hurt. A bitter smile slowly replaced it. "You don't like me."

It was matter-of-fact, the realization that Hank could tell had grown in him over the years. Money and looks couldn't save him. Hank was supposed to. He was looking into eyes that were still swirling with that certainty, and it made him frown. He believed that there was some gap of logic here that he couldn't cross and Brey could, a vision of a future that was dark to him.

"I don't know you, Brey. I only know about you. I don't like or dislike you. But I don't want you hurt either. I have a responsibility to you now."

They were standing a block away from the police station where Hank was taking him — where he worked, where he felt at home, where he still had a part of his old life — and thinking that, he realized Brey had nothing of his old life left. He felt an itchy, uncomfortable need to make him feel better, to make him happy, to make him forget everything that had happened and everything Hank had said.

Brey looked away and rubbed tentatively at his collar. Then he looked back again with almost grief-stricken eyes. "I really don't like this, Hank."

And Hank felt himself give in a little, lose a little of that certainty of Brey's failure that he needed to hold onto, careless and lousy with money and things, a rich kid who always got away with murder. Until he didn't, and that wasn't murder anyway. He got away with nothing. He was just spoiled and callow and full of life.

"Fuck, Brey. I don't like it either."

They walked a slow circle around the center of the town and came back to the park with the dead fountain. A sense of the surreal fell over Brey — open stores next to dark windows and shuttered doors. Avenues led out from this hub like spokes into virtually empty neighborhoods, blocks of abandoned houses with dead cars at the curbs. There were business and farm owners, other slaves Brey didn't see, the mechanics and factory workers. Hank pointed out a long, rectangular building, tiny windows, two stories — a cannery. Cops like Hank. It felt like time stood still, except the moment picked to fix in time felt off. It wasn't quite right, and the little off things pricked at Brey's nerves. He was sweating, and his hands trembled. Hank gave him a gentle push against a scrubby tree in a corner of the park.

"We'll rest a moment."

"I won't break," Brey said irritably.

Above him, dry leaves rattled as a bird hopped from branch to branch, unperturbed. He felt inexplicably jealous. Then the leaves made him think of Patric. *Patric.* The caution in Hank's stare fed his irritation. It was growing into anger, mixing up with panic. People were looking at him—a handful, as big as a crowd after all these years—barely curious, more wary, flickering the same expression to Hank, who ignored them. It was noon. Two men sat on a bench, ate their lunches. A vaguely hysterical laugh burbled in his throat. He swallowed it. Hank put a hand on his arm.

"Brey?"

They were all men, all looking at him, veering off at Hank's stare. Any one of them. Any one of them could be one of the ones.

For a moment, he thought he was going to throw up. He could hear his breathing. It made a whistling sound. A little while ago, he'd been at the police station, had sat in Hank's office, had seen the communications center in back, a screen that flashed with occasional red dots. Slaves near the post-line. After that, he'd seen the hardware store, a sewing shop, a shoe store, a fruit and vegetable stand outside a small market. He was interested, just a flutter of nerves. Now the short buildings seemed to rise up and lean in. The sun pushed through the tree branches with a brutal heat, reflected like a radioactive blast off the sidewalks. His heart raced, and he felt Hank's arms going around him, adding to the heat—but a good heat. He was melting into it, staggering against Hank's body as Hank pulled him back across the park to a colorfully painted gazebo and sat him down on the steps. Shade under the roof, cool, smooth wood beneath him. He felt the roughness under his palms and sighed in relief.

"Don't move."

He didn't. The air here, only marginally cooler, felt arctic to him anyway. His muscles went wobbly, and he leaned against a post. His eyes closed. He sensed people but didn't look. They weren't there, weren't the people who hurt him. Weren't *those* people.

"Brey..."

Hank's voice floated into his space. Warm and strong. He opened his eyes. Everything blurred for a moment. They were alone, nobody staring.

"Drink this."

A glass of water, dripping with cool condensation. He gulped it, felt the spread of coldness inside, numbing him from the inside out. He sighed in relief. Gave a short laugh. "Phew. That was weird."

"Are you okay?"

"Yeah, fine. I just got dizzy. Too hot, I think."

Hank's frown was skeptical, but he nodded anyway. "Can you make it home?"

He wanted to reiterate—*I won't break, Hank.* But now he wasn't so sure. He blushed and the embarrassment turned to anger again, followed by that panic, the one that came with the realization that he was stuck here while his family was waiting—waiting for him. He could hear his father's voice, *'I'm coming back for you, but if... Well, if I can't...we'll wait for you, Brey. You come to us.'*

And he had to. He had to escape, but all he could see now was a wall of bushes he ran through, hurling himself away from the men running after him, chasing him. In the gray behind his eyelids, a ribbon of water ran by, shallow and sluggish, soundless over his panting breath, the pounding of footsteps behind him. He remembered the rip of dry branches against his skin again, the water, the thought pumping in him to his pulse beat — *Which way? Which way?*

He knew in his heart he ran the wrong way. The other way was freedom, away from his captors and away from Thom — the way he didn't run, the way he could never run now.

Finishing his water, he grabbed the stair rail and pulled himself up.

"Can we go now?"

"Sure. I'll take you home."

Home. He didn't want the laugh to come out, but it did anyway. Bitter sounding.

Chapter Four

Once the memory of that stream came to him, Brey couldn't stop the replay of his capture. The scene looped over and over, and his head filled with sound. He saw flashes of water, burned green leaves. The stream was really almost dry, its banks cracked and friable, a thin pale rivulet the sun would soon burn to oblivion. In his memory, water burbled and bubbled over a twig-strewn drop...

He was high in the foothills, still scrubby, but he could see pines not far above. Alone, walking through dry weeds — pale blue sky, a plain of dry, flat land below, treeless, a smudge of dark faraway, almost green, a ribbon of pavement.

Then a voice.

"Hey, you!"

He bolted and heard the scrabble of men in boots chasing after him. He ran for the treeline. The faraway pavement he'd been following for days stayed in the corner of his eye. He broke into the trees, running awkwardly on the slope, slipping on the scatter of leaves and branches. Gasping breaths sounded behind him.

"Fucker's fast!"

He was slipping, though – slowing, speeding up on level ground, running pell-mell down a slope. He heard the stream, burst through the bushes and came stumbling to a stop, head whipping side to side. Downstream led to the interstate, the pavement, the way home. He ran again, and one man came out behind him, one in front. He darted away from the one in front, and the one in back tackled him, laying him out across the thin trickle of stream.

A wheezing voice behind him, a rotund, jiggly shape blurring above him. "That's my property."

"We caught 'im."

"I claimed 'im. I'll pay you later."

"You bet your ass. Otherwise we're keepin' 'im."

That was the replay he didn't like, so like a tape he could rewind, he played it again, but this time he ran upstream. There, the trees crowded together, hiding him. He scrambled higher and higher, reaching the hilltop, gaining speed as he plowed downward again, reaching another copse of trees, losing them altogether, running until it was dark and they never found him.

This was the replay that put his mind at ease for a while. After he let it play its loop, he could sleep a little or read a page or two from one of the books on Hank's bookshelf. Hank's worry was like a vibration in the air, and his nerves started to itch.

At night, he crept out of his alcove bed and quietly eased Hank's door open. Hank left it ajar, but Brey pushed it all the way in so that he could go back to bed and see the gray outline of the door from where he lay down the hall. He shifted to the edge of his mattress and bunched a pillow under his head, staring.

He pretended to read when Hank came home, turning pages he couldn't focus on. He loved to read, loved school, wanted to teach one day. Now he pretended. During the day, he sat on the couch and stared out of the window. He could see the stretch of the interstate. The loop replayed, and this time the stream was a swelling river. He plunged into it, pinwheeling his arms, dragging himself into the frigid froth until the current pulled his feet loose and dragged him away. The men broke out of the trees, pale angry faces disappearing as he whirled and sank and bobbed. Always escaping in this loop until the truth yanked him back to the real memory, and he felt hands pulling him up off the ground. Ropes on his wrists. A fat man in a white T-shirt and black pants, circling him.

"That's a pretty one, boys. Real pretty."

He couldn't shut it out. The panic that he'd never escape short-circuited his brain, started up the replay again and again—the chase, the stream, the ropes or the river that carried him away. A hot sunny sky above. The loop he escaped in so he never saw the gas station with its oily floor, the metal bar and the metal plates on the floor—the fat man named Thom. In real life Brey had kicked Thom in the knee, made it back out into the sun, onto the crumbling pavement before the bottom of a boot had connected with his spine and sent him sprawling. A hand in his hair had yanked him back up. They'd stripped him. But he didn't want that to be real. He didn't want the kneeling to be real or the hands holding his arms wide. Or Thom pulling his belt off and coming at him with a cheerful smile. He didn't like that, didn't want it to be real because he couldn't bear it. It couldn't be real. The other was real. The stream. The trees. The cold water carrying him away.

The pavement under his feet, running, running.

Over and over, captive and escape. No sudden scream that shocked even him, blood-curdling. No pain. No panic. Only the escape was real, he was sure of it. All he had to do was wake up because this was a dream. He was sure of that, too, until Hank came home. Then Brey looked into Hank's carefully cool face, the distance in Hank's eyes, clutched a book he wasn't really reading, then looked away and it started all over again. He relived it, running the other way, downstream — the way that freed him — until a whisper, mean and ruthless in his head, always reminded him. *You ran the wrong way. You didn't escape. You'll never go home.*

* * * *

Waterfall was home now, a movie set version of a perfect small town — a place with curving sidewalks where children once played catch and rode their bikes on the streets with shade trees that were once lush and green. Brey even saw a church spire in the distance one day. Homes and cars where most of the people in Waterfall lived, close to the center of town in houses with shiny windows and clothes on the clotheslines out back.

The sight of these houses sent Brey's thoughts back to prison and the days of waiting for release. He'd wanted to see cars and parks and stores again. Church spires and movie theaters. He'd wanted to go home...

* * * *

Three years ago

When the power went out, the prison generators kept the lights on for a few days, then the doors rolled open with a booming metallic echo in block after block. He swung his legs to the floor, put his feet in his shoes and waited. The lights outside the cells flickered. Louder voices followed the murmurs.

"Fuck's up with this?"

"Hey! Guard! Guard!"

"C'mon!"

Now he was afraid to go. Afraid of the empty parks and looted stores. They saw it on TV while they still had TV—panic, riots. He sat through the clamor of a handful of cons bursting out of their cells, barreling past his, a rush that trickled to quieter, softer steps. A con in the corridor outside his cell paused and looked in, his dark face worried.

"Are you comin'?"

The sound of concern stirred him. He rose slowly, moved toward it. Then the man nodded and disappeared. His heart pounded. He ran down steps, past empty cells and guard stations, a lounge, vending machines, another corridor empty, another door with streams of pale sunshine coming through until he exploded outside, gasping for air.

Above him a cold sun flashed, and a blur of shapes scattered and ran. A man shouted in the distance.

Below him was an empty parking lot with washed-out dividing lines and weeds in the cracks. He went down a flight of steps and walked away. The soles of his shoes crunched across asphalt, a sound he'd almost forgotten. He walked for days then he found a bike. He made it home, but the house was empty, although his family couldn't have been gone for long because he'd seen his father for the last time only a few weeks earlier. But his sister was pregnant, and he knew they couldn't stay.

There was a car on the roundabout by the front door. He didn't recognize it, but he'd been gone for over two years by then. Why would he?

The house was two stories with six bedrooms, ten baths, a kitchen, a living and dining room, a media room, a lounge, a library and an office. There was a pool house, a caretaker's cottage, and rooms over the garage. He hardly knew what luxury was because luxury was all he knew.

He let the bike he rode fall onto the driveway. The gardens were slightly overgrown, and a set of tires had dug furrows into the grass. Looters. New blades of pale green were already springing up in the dark scars, but it bothered him anyway. *Assholes.* There was a fucking driveway right there for godsakes.

Emptiness swirled around him.

He remembered the exhaustion on his father's face the last time he'd visited him. "I'm still working on your release," he'd said.

Government lumbered on. A skeletal police force patrolled the streets. People went to work in grocery stores with empty shelves, and buses drove aimlessly from stop to stop. On TV, they saw a picture of a high school with a banner out front — *WE'RE STILL OPEN!*

Acts of crazy, sad defiance.

"Dad — " he'd murmured.

"For compassionate reasons if for no other."

"Compassion for me?"

"You're my only son now." His brother had died in the first outbreak of Eve. "We'll stay as long as we can."

A week after that visit the buses stopped. Nobody came to work in the grocery stores anymore. It was over. Everything they knew. He never thought then how silly it was to think that there might be a safe place.

At home, the front doors opened, unlocked. Cabinet doors hung ajar, the contents off the shelves, drawers yanked out. He went through the long hall over the glowing pumpkin pine floor to the kitchen in back of the house. Silverware and broken china lay scattered across the black and white tiles. He went across to the French doors. The pool pump was solar, and the water in the pool was leaf-strewn but clear. Stripping, he went out and jumped in. The water swallowed him, slid against his skin like gentle hands. He broke the surface with a gasp. His eyes filled with the sky. He felt grief shake him. That night he slept in his bed, found clothes to wear in the morning, packed a bag, filled bottles with water from the water heater, took a car out of the garage and drove away.

* * * *

Present day

The circles under Brey's eyes were a dark purple.

One morning, Hank woke him up and said, "C'mon. I have something for you to do."

The air was gray and dotted like a snowy TV screen. Hank swam in the misty pallor. "I'm tired."

"Get up, Brey."

He didn't want to. Pain squeezed his body in a vise. He wanted to bellow, to hit, to run. *Fuck!* But he'd never hit. Never again. He pushed the blankets down, kicked free sluggishly. Got his clothes and took a shower. He stared at his face in the mirror, swiped a hand across the glass.

"You aren't pretty anymore," he whispered.

Perversely, though, it didn't make him glad, and he felt sick about that.

Untangling the waves in his hair with his fingers, he walked slowly down the hall into the kitchen—a lunchroom once, with a white, wrap-around counter and a wide open, gray vinyl floor. The walls were yellow, and Hank had added a big wood table and wood chairs with red leather seats. It was a cheerful room but sent a sliver of pain through Brey's eyes.

"It's early," he said.

"It's nine, Brey. Sit down."

He looked without interest at the bowl of oatmeal in front of him. Hank was eating his, chewing slowly. He shouldn't like somebody who didn't like him, but he couldn't help it. It bothered him when Hank went out to see Ken. Just a friend Ken. *Fuck-A-Friend Ken.* But Brey wanted to please Hank so he picked up his spoon and took a reluctant mouthful, eyeing Hank from under his brows. Hank's skin was sun-flushed, and his eyes were clear and focused. His face was strong, and he was unafraid. Brey frowned, staring at his oatmeal, losing his interest in it. The anger and distress that prickled under his skin like a living thing was beginning to flare again. He hated his weakness, his dependency, the view of the interstate out of a room that wasn't even his. It was all Hank's. Hank's town. Hank's apartment. Hank's control. The light grew brighter. He squinted, rubbing a hand over his eyes.

"You stopped eating."

"I'm not hungry."

"Christ, Brey, you're skin an' bones."

Was he? He let his eyes come up, met Hank's scowl. "I'm sorry," he mumbled. "I don't mean to be trouble."

"You aren't trouble. Just…try."

Hank's voice didn't match Hank's eyes. The voice didn't seem in control. Brey ate another bite. It was sticky in his mouth, hard to swallow. He looked at the pitcher of milk blankly. His swallow was audible.

"I have a friend named Ken," said Hank, and Brey's stomach plummeted. He wasn't supposed to know about Ken. But he'd seen him once in the coffee shop. Seen the nod Ken and Hank exchanged. The flash of amusement in Ken's eyes—intimate amusement. "Ken was a counselor. I was thinking maybe you'd like to talk—"

"No!" Brey was shocked by the sharpness in his voice. His eyes widened on Hank's frown, and he felt a flutter of panic. "Please."

He could see the irritation on Hank's face and the feeling of pressure that made his panic grow worse came as the walls seemed to close in on him.

"I just wanna help, Brey."

"Help with what?" He whispered it, truly unsure.

"Help you feel better."

Brey barked a laugh. "Feel better? I can't feel better. I don't want to talk about it. I don't want to fucking remember." His voice was rising. "I don't need you to help me. I want to go home."

"You're a slave, Brey. You can't go home, an' you can't forget just by not talking about it."

"You don't know anything about it."

"I know that every day I come home you're sitting on that couch out there, and I know that you're thinking about it. I'm not stupid, Brey. I know that there's no way for you to get away from it."

"You *don't* know that. You don't know a fucking thing about me! I think about going home! That's all I think about! You can't keep me here. I can fucking leave any time I want. You can't stop—"

"Brey!"

He froze, his breath stuck in his throat, sound wheezing out. Hank's face was red, his lips thin and white.

"I... I didn't... I didn't mean..." Brey sucked in a breath, a useless gasp for air, eyes rising as Hank got up, poured a glass from a pitcher in the refrigerator and sat back down, pushing the glass over with his fingertips.

"Go on. Drink it."

Brey pulled the glass over, almost spilling it. His fingers shook. He sniffed it, then said, "Oh," and drank it down.

The beer was spicy, sour and warmth chased away the coolness in his stomach. Setting the glass down, he took a slower, deeper breath.

"Better?"

Brey nodded. "I'm sorry. I didn't mean any of that."

"I think you did, an' I'm okay with it. I have no expectations of you, Brey. I'm worried about you. I don't like this either. I know that probably doesn't mean much, but I'm sorry you're unhappy. I won't make you talk to anybody. I won't push that. I want you to get outside, though. You're just getting worse sitting by yourself all day. You need something to do. Everybody does."

Brey's mouth grew dry. He swallowed and said, "I know what I was sold for."

Leaning slowly against the table, narrowing the space between them, Hank said, "You barely know me, Brey, but I know you know me better than that."

Brey swallowed again, nodding slightly. "What then?"

Hank rose, and there was a rare smile on his face. Inexplicably, Brey wanted to smile back, could feel the loosening of his jaw.

"C'mon. Put your shoes on, an' I'll show you."

* * * *

The sun blazed off walls and glass and pavement and bleached the sky and trees of color.

Lifting his face up, Hank closed his eyes for a few steps, enjoying the feel of hot air on his skin. He could sense Brey behind him, keeping close to the buildings, seeking out slivers of shade. Glancing back, he caught a wary stare before Brey looked away. His eruptions of anger didn't surprise Hank anymore. At first, he'd tense up too, waiting for a fight that seemed barely contained in Brey's fists, white knuckles down at Brey's sides or pushed under his arms, shaking that slowly settled into a strained nervousness. Getting up to pour Brey the glass of beer was a reflex motion to distract, to upset the edge of Brey's hysteria. His soft "Oh" of surprise pulled a sudden tenderness out of Hank that he didn't want to think about.

Brey didn't walk beside him. Hank listened to his footsteps. Then the footsteps faded. Stopping, he looked back and saw Brey on the street corner, gripping the metal pole of a street sign, the fingers of his other hand hooked in his collar. His eyes were half-closed, and his lips were moving. Hank returned slowly. No sound was coming out of Brey's mouth. Hank's shadow fell across the sidewalk, and Brey looked startled, coming back to himself.

"You okay?"

"Where are we going?"

"We're almost there. Give me a chance, okay? I can make this better for you."

He hadn't hurt him but wasn't sure he had any right to ask for Brey's trust anyway. The look on Brey's face was shrewd, his eyes thoughtful. His fingers moved on his collar, fell to his side.

"Okay."

Hank smiled. "You'll like this. I promise."

A small smile moved Brey's lips. Hank found himself wanting to see that smile often. Sweat beaded the sides of Brey's nose, and he could smell him. His lust for Brey annoyed him.

"C'mon."

He couldn't get past the frivolity of Brey's old life, castigated himself for judging him at all, but he couldn't stop the replay of memories of Brey's arrest, his cavalier partying, the bloody boy lying on the floor. Everything in Brey's face defied Hank's judgments. He was mostly compliant, but there was iron in him, something that brought him through all this. Hank didn't want to like him and wasn't entirely sure why he didn't want to—almost didn't trust himself, as if he were purposely subverting some truth he could barely even remember.

At night he heard the whisper of his door, almost soundless, pushing open. That, or some stirring in the air, always woke him, disturbed him in a way he didn't understand. It wasn't surprise or nerves. Brey had been doing this since Hank had brought him home. It was an annoyance really, but not at being woken up. He realized now that he felt burdened, felt the weight of caring. He didn't want to care about Brey. In a way, Brey had ruined his life—with that first look six years ago Hank had realized that he'd never feel for any woman what he felt in an instant for a man he didn't know—a boy he didn't know, barely twenty-four. A boy on the cusp of a life he didn't get to live. A man he'd bought. At night he made himself not go to him when he heard the sounds of Brey through the open door, thrashing himself awake.

Focusing on him again now, he saw the flush on Brey's cheeks, shadows under his eyes, weariness and that god-awful trust, and said, "We'll get you a hat later on. You're gonna burn to a crisp."

Then he was climbing a sunbright set of wide stone steps, Brey following behind him, face lighting up as he saw the sign over the door.

WATERFALL LIBRARY

Chapter Five

Sunlight bounced off the bright white stone of the tall building. Double doors of dark glass were inset into the front of the library at the top of the steps. Inside, coolness descended, pale light drifting down from high windows set into the side and back walls. A short lobby with glass display cases on one side and a water fountain between bathroom doors on the other led into a cavernous room. The ceiling rose high above the small windows, decorated with a mural in muted colors of the small town of Waterfall surrounded by farmland and the distant rise of mountains. Bookshelves and tables filled the room around a center of heavy wooden desks set in a three-sided square. Books, notepads and pictures hid the surfaces of the desks, except for a patch of cleared space on the desk facing the door. A nameplate for somebody named *Issa Moran* faced outward. Voices murmured in the distance. In a world without computers or TV, the library rose to ascendency again.

Hank smiled at the look of reverence in Brey's slowly wandering gaze. At the time of his arrest, Brey had been working on his doctorate in American history. He'd wanted to teach. It always struck Hank as incongruous—a staid plan from such a feckless boy. Everything had been easy for Brey until that one irrevocable mistake. Hank knew he'd like it here.

Brey looked at him, let out a slightly choked-sounding laugh. "Wow."

"Yeah. We're lucky. Think you could work here?"

Brey's eyes lit up, then dimmed again. Hank was almost confused until he recognized the way Brey was crushing his own hope. But this was the hope of real life, of the things he could really have. The things Hank wanted him to have.

"Work here? I can't. I know about the contract. I was being sold for sex. Thom told me."

"Thom Donnell is an ineffectual, immoral, underhanded son of a bitch. You have my permission— No, I'm telling you to dismiss everything you ever heard from him. You get to make the decisions about your time, an' I'm asking you. Do you think you could work here?"

Brey didn't want to believe him. Hank watched him struggle with it, let his eyes sweep over the mural, the shelves and books with that hope so beleaguered it made Hank grit his teeth in anger. Then Brey let out a breath, drew his shoulders up in a shrug, and drawing a sudden laugh out of Hank, said, "Fuck, yeah."

"Language, young man."

Brey spun, and Hank smiled at the light and cheerful voice floating out from the shadows thrown by a pair of shelves. Issa emerged, sandals slapping on the travertine floor. She wore baggy jeans spattered with paint and an oversized T-shirt. Her silver blonde hair was tied in a spiky ponytail at the top of her head, and she had black suns inked on the back of both hands.

Her blue eyes had the bold happiness of a twenty year old.

Hank whispered in Brey's ear, "Issa painted the mural."

Brey gaped back at him. "No way."

"Kindred spirits, you two."

That got him a bewildered and curious frown. Then Issa was there, hands on her hips, leaning in. "This is a library. No cursing allowed."

"Unless it's coming from you," Hank said dryly.

"Stuff it," said Issa, looking from him to Brey. "Is this my new assistant?"

"Yes. Brey, this is Issa."

Smiling, she took Brey's hand, and Hank saw her eyes rove his face, the brightness of her gaze softening. "I'm glad you're here, sweetheart."

Brey blushed, but he didn't pull away from her. "Thank you."

Issa winked at Hank. "I think I can keep your boy busy."

"Good. I'll be back with lunch in a couple of hours."

Brey frowned, and his blush turned into a flush of anger. "I don't—"

"Yes, you do. You have to eat—lunch, in a couple of hours."

Hank didn't wait for his response. Brey's trigger-happy emotions wore him out. The soles of Hank's boots barely made a sound on the travertine. Silence followed him. He resisted looking back and pushed through the doors, back into the sunlight.

Brey sighed as the doors closed, relaxing—nervous, though—even as his anger passed, stuffing his hands in his pockets with a slightly embarrassed smile. "What can I do here?"

"Exactly what I do, sweetheart. Everything."

She gave him a bright smile, tapped his arm and said, "C'mon. I'll show you around."

Her feminine energy, so rare now, soothed him. He thought of his mother and sister and pushed down a sudden stab of pain. The light of Issa's eyes seemed to absorb him. He felt known and wondered if Hank had told her everything about him. There was no pity in her eyes, though, nothing that made him feel less.

"I'm an original resident of Waterfall," said Issa. "I've lived here for almost fifteen years now. My husband was one of the project managers hired to help build the town. Our children were young an' this seemed like the perfect place for us."

"I'm sorry," he said softly.

Her smile never faltered, but she took his hand again, patting it. "Hank says you think your family's still alive."

He nodded.

"That's something to hold onto. I know Hank wouldn't agree, but personally, I think Hank needs a little more whimsy in his life."

She swung her arm backward as they passed out of the large room. "Our main book room, obviously. We're back to a card catalog now. You can help out with that. Still a work in progress. You'll have to record every book people check out on paper. Cross-reference that with the card catalog an' add anything not already there."

From the main room they went into the reference section, still with its racks of periodicals, shelves of encyclopedias, cushy chairs and round tables.

"You know," said Brey, "even back in the day, this was a pretty old-fashioned library. You have a lot of books. The libraries I went to didn't have many books anymore."

"Pretty short-sighted, eh?"

A door in the back of the reference room opened into a hall that led to conference rooms and offices. A large room up front for collecting and sorting books led back into the main room through a door behind the book counter. The automated checkout machines were still there, shiny and silent. Issa was taking him back down the hallway, past the closed doors to another door with an exit sign over it. She pushed out onto a stone stoop with steps on one side and a ramp on the other. A strip of empty parking lot lined the back of the library. On the other side was a chain-link fence with the middle section cut away. Weeds grew in the cracks of the pavement. Another building beyond looked older than any of the others in Waterfall. It was single story with a flat roof that extended over a walkway. There were no windows in the building that Brey could see. The parking lot here looked even older, bubbled and lifted in places with deeper cracks. Waves of abandonment and later reclamation came off it.

Pointing as they walked toward it, Issa said, "This was a supply store for restaurants. Plates, plastic ware, napkins, takeout containers, that kind of thing. There was a sort of business complex here before Waterfall was built, in decline. Most of the buildings were razed but a couple were kept as warehouses as the town was built. I don't know what this was used for after that, but we use it now for our collection."

"Collection?"

"You'll see."

Brey loved the crumbling asphalt, the strange smell of decline. Not the finality of things now, but the smell he remembered of failed businesses, bankrupt industries, ways of life abandoned, forgotten in the buildings that stayed, emptied monuments, darkened, disintegrating, fragrant with dust and mold and stillness. He could smell it again in the sunbaked asphalt, the bitter weeds, plaster dust, staleness. His heart picked up, eager to look inside.

Issa flipped a switch just inside the door. Old fluorescent lamps sputtered. "Take a quick look before I turn the lights back off." Underneath the lamps were rows of tables on chipped and peeling linoleum.

"Christ," said Brey. "Are you having a garage sale?"

Issa laughed, and it sounded like bells, cheerful and full of reverberation. "All my treasures."

He walked the aisles between the rows of tables. Glasswork, Limoges, a Hermann teddy bear, champagne flutes with the year 2000 etched in gold. A Belleek vase. Baseball caps. Piles of greeting cards — birthday, Christmas, graduation. Letters, even diaries. The tables extended down the long dark room and most were bare.

"You took this from people's homes?"

"Yes. I take things that talk about who we were, but I can't give it the time I want to. I was hoping that you —"

He shot her a look, and he knew there was something like horror in it.

"Would think about taking over for me."

"I'd feel like a looter." Then he blushed and stammered, "I mean —"

"I'm not offended. I can never go into anyone's home without feeling their lives there. These people were my neighbors and friends. That's why this is important to me — to remember for the people who can't tell their own stories anymore. I have a lot of other things for you to do, though. You are going to be a big help to me either way."

The fact was that Issa's project appealed to him, but he remembered days of hunting for food in stores and warehouses, pushed by hunger into people's homes only to run out again, ashamed and sickened—homes with bodies, homes with a strange stillness, with cups or plates in the sink. A pair of shoes by a door, magazines on a couch... Waiting for people who thought they'd come home again.

"I dunno."

He began to sweat, thinking of Hank, that he'd be disappointing him. But Issa just shook her head and said, "C'mon. I have a card catalog waiting for you."

* * * *

Hank brought him a cheese sandwich and a canvas hat with a wide, floppy brim. Brey put on the hat and grinned at him. "Fly."

Hank chortled, eating his own sandwich. They were sitting in the room behind the checkout counter. Hank wasn't deluded enough to think that Brey was any better than he was that morning, but his grin was the most spontaneous and carefree he'd yet seen. Of course, the moment he thought that, a look of bewilderment and shame crossed Brey's face and that duller, pulled-in look took over again.

Hank repressed the sigh he wanted to let out. "Think this'll work for you?"

"Yeah. I like Issa."

"I thought you would."

The first few bites of Brey's sandwich seemed to go down eagerly, but now he was eyeing the rest of it with reluctance. Hank watched him, gaze roving the pale face, the slightly flushed cheekbones. He wanted life in Brey's eyes, wanted to kiss the corner of his mouth, the skin under his ears. Teeth gritted, he berated himself. *You're a sick fuck.* Because there was nothing Brey could do to prevent it. Not only was Hank bigger and stronger, he also had the law behind him. He could do whatever he wanted. He had every right to and had vowed never to touch Brey. He vowed it again watching Brey take a slow bite of his sandwich. His teeth crunched the toasted bread, and the cheese oozed slightly. The problem was, with every articulation of that vow, Hank wanted Brey all the more.

Christ.

He inhaled deeply, smelling dust and old books. Then he grabbed the container he had brought the sandwiches in and stood up. "Be back for you later."

"Okay."

Brey's stare was curious. Hank could feel the weight of it following him. The feel of dependency again, the thing he resented. Not the responsibility part of it. He always had that. Waterfall Chief of Police. Council member. People came to him, depended on him. Waterfall was small enough that most of his time was free. He went out, visited with people and stopped off to talk to the shop owners, formed the relationships that helped defuse conflicts long before they became real problems.

Hank's role in Waterfall was the role he'd taken in his old life. He led with the slight emotional distance that gave him credibility. That was not the sense of responsibility that made him tense and angry. He was responsible to Beth, never burdened by the dependency of his girls. Brey filled him with impatience. Images in the back of his brain of Thom's gas station never faded far enough away, filled him with guilt.

His teeth ached, and he focused on relaxing his jaw. Halfway back to the police station, he turned away and walked to the park instead, following the meandering pathway that once led through cool green grass. Through slitted eyes he could imagine it, the splashing of water in the dry fountain, a string quartet in the gazebo or a jazz band on a Sunday afternoon. In his mind's eye, people sat out on blankets and Beth was beside him, the girls at the fountain, flicking water at each other, squealing in high-pitched joy. Curly brown-headed girls like their mother with brown eyes and rosy cheeks. Their mother's daughters. But they had his lean face and strong bones, a sorrowful softness that in him clashed with his sternness, the tense emotions under his surface.

"You are a bottomless pit of repression," Jack had once said.

Hank had just countered, "You dunno jack, Jack."

That's where he was headed now, crossing the street over to Centre Park and Jack's clinic where gray stucco was darkening in the shade. The sun shone ferociously on the other side, sending out deceptively cool shadow in front of the building. The glass doors were dark and mirrored. He pictured all the emotions, all the memories Jack said he hid, behind those doors. Real, but invisible to him because he didn't want to look. *Was that true?* Pushing into the lobby, he found nothing there out of the ordinary and felt a certain vindication. He didn't hide anything. He released it all because there were things nothing could change. Still, there were times the sight of Jack's face brought Beth back vividly.

Just like now, an angle of light maybe as Jack sat in a chair in his waiting room, slowly sipping on a glass of his homemade beer.

"Not waiting on a patient, I hope."

Jack grinned at him. "Nope. Done for the day."

"Banker's hours."

"Don't knock it." He lifted his glass. "Get you one."

"No thanks."

Hank sat down too, sighed, and rubbed the bridge of his nose. Jack's patient awareness of him was a vibration in the air. He calmly drank his beer, but he was waiting. Beth's dark hair—with gray in Jack's—her eyes, her dimples and sly humor.

"I got Brey off to work today."

"Was 'e happy?"

"I don't know about happy. Almost happy. I saw a glimmer, I think."

"Give 'im time."

"I have to."

He was sitting at an angle to Jack, staring across the small waiting room at a collection of botanical prints hanging on the wall. Strange, Jack left them there. They were so normal. But maybe that was why.

"You okay, Hank?"

"I was thinking about Beth an' the girls today."

"Sorry."

"Why? You know."

Without looking, he knew Jack nodded. "Sure. I think about Lacy all the time. Issa can't take her place."

A chill froze him. He thought it was shock, but he wasn't shocked. He was angry. He kept Beth in a special place—a place nobody could go near. He pulled his eyes from the prints. "Take her place?"

Jack's eyes had an almost merry light to them. "Don't come to talk unless you can take the truth."

"What are you talking about?"

"You know what."

"I bought 'im to save 'im," Hank muttered.

"You have feelings for him."

"No. I just remember him. I like that. It's a connection — the same I have with you."

"You don't wanna screw me."

"Jesus, Jack."

"I'm tellin' you, Hank, the things people do to each other are un-fucking-believable. Yeah, Brey's dealing with real damage. I'm not gonna minimize that, but the guy's tough too. He wants his family." Hank watched Jack wave a finger in front of his eyes. "Never loses sight of it. Never looks away from you for very long either. The guy's got a definite thing for you."

"A thing?"

"Yeah. Like you have for him."

"I don't have a thing for him."

Jack shrugged. "Okay."

"That's sick."

"No, Hank. Sick is Thom. Sick is everything that sonofabitch did to him. Sick isn't Brey. Sick isn't anything he feels. Or anything you feel. You didn't hurt 'im."

"I won't either. Fuck. I barely know 'im."

"I know you never stopped loving Beth, but you stopped being *in* love with her. You went to that kid's trial every chance you got. Beth told me."

"I was interested."

"I know. An' you need to know that Brey's going to recover. People get over things, even really awful things. An' then they start caring about the things they thought they'd never care about again. We're living proof. Brey's got a thing for you, an' he's going to want to start to do something about it. You need to not fuck that up, Hank."

Hank gave a huff that might have been a laugh and pushed up. "You dunno jack, Jack."

"Probably not. Could just be the beer talkin'."

"Yeah, well, you enjoy it. I have to get back to work."

Outside, the heat enveloped him again, and it felt good, blunting all the cooler edges of things.

Chapter Six

Hank blamed Jack for putting thoughts in his head.

He dreamed about Brey in Thom's garage.

He was alone with him, coming up silently, hearing the whistling gasps of Brey's fear, alone in the shadowed garage, not knowing who was near. Hank saw the tremors in Brey's legs, came up quietly, drawing his fingers up the pale skin, and Brey drew in a breath, a soft wail coming up on the exhale.

"Shush," he murmured. "I won't hurt you."

He trailed his fingers up Brey's hips, ran his palms over the muscles of his bowed back, pulled his fingertips down over the nubs of his backbone. Brey jerked against his chains, and his groans grew guttural and panicked.

Then, with the suddenness of judgment, the sun darkened, and outside there was only a still, silver light.

Hank grew uneasy, felt the ominousness of the desire growing inside him. Still, he stroked Brey's sides, pressed up against his pale ass, frowning at the feel and sound of his fear. His hands shook, fingers on Brey's bottom, pulling him open, thumbs sliding slowly to his hole.

Then the inarticulate sounds Brey was making took form and his voice was deep and grief-stricken. "God! No! No!"

Hank yanked his hands away from Brey's skin, fingers slick and oily, coated with the feel of shame, sickness. "Stop! Stop! Please!"

Bolting upright, Hank came scrambling out of his dream, kicking his way out of the sheets. *Fuck.*

"Stop! Please!"

"Brey!"

He got up, staggering, and smacked at the light switch, blinding himself for a moment. Brey was on his knees on the bed in the alcove, rearing back, thumping against the wall, pushing back off it. Hank grabbed him.

Brey's eyes were wild. He kicked and bucked, and the strength of his wiry muscles slammed Hank back across the hall into the other wall. Hank let the force of the impact push him forward again then bent his knees and dragged Brey down to the floor with him. Brey rolled and reared up, trapped in Hank's arms. His head smacked the floor, and pain came into his eyes.

"Brey! Aubrey! Wake up! C'mon, sweetheart, wake up."

Then the thrashing eased. Brey's head rolled slowly, eyes blinking, focusing. Hank lurched up and back, slumping against the wall, Brey still in his arms.

"You're okay, Brey. You're right here with me. You're okay."

"No."

"Yes, you are. See where you are? You're home, yeah? You're home with me. You're safe." The panic in Brey's eyes faded, but the doubt remained. He grew stiff, and Hank sat him up, let him go, looking carefully into his eyes. "You scared me, Brey."

"I was dreaming."

"I know." The memory of his own dream brought a cold, sick sweat out on his skin. He'd never touch Brey. Never.

Brey ducked his face and covered it with trembling fingers until Hank tugged his hands away and got up. "C'mon."

Brey let Hank sit him back down on the bed and followed his motion to lie down. He was stiff, breathing with a conscious slowness. "Stay there."

A few minutes later, Hank returned with a jar of homemade bourbon and two glasses. Brey followed his movements with a sort of dazed attention. When Hank gave him his glass, he pushed himself up on his pillows and drank it down. Hank poured him another glass and sipped his own while Brey took a long swallow, shuddered it down, drank again then blinked, looking clearer. There was confusion on his face, as if he was returning to a place he used to know and was different now. Maybe, in a sense, he was.

"Better?" asked Hank.

"Yeah. I'm... I don't even remember it."

"Good."

"I guess so."

He gave Hank a slightly uncertain look that made Hank flush as he remembered his own dream again. He gestured at Brey's glass. "Want another?"

Brey shook his head, finished his last swallow, and gave his glass back. "I'm okay."

"Okay to sleep?"

"Yeah."

Hank nodded and got up. "I'll be right here."

He took the jar and glasses with him, switched off the light and lay down, staring at the ceiling as he tried to relax. He didn't think he slept, but he must have, because he woke up when he heard Brey come into the room. Rolling onto his side, he saw a shape in the corner made by the dresser and the wall. The faint moonlight outside was caught in the mirror above the dresser, otherwise he would never have seen him. Brey was utterly silent, just hunched there with his knees up.

"Brey. You can't sleep there."

"Please."

Hank sighed. "Okay. Get in with me. I won't touch you. I promise. Just so you aren't alone."

He gave him a moment, then there was a faint grunt as Brey pushed himself up. He got underneath the covers and rolled his back to Hank without a word. Hank sighed and fell back asleep.

* * * *

Every morning Hank walked Brey to the library, leaving him to sit on the stone steps and wait for Issa. Hank always took the first shower and let Brey stay in bed for a few more minutes. Waking up was a struggle for him, but it surprised him anyway when Hank came out of the shower one morning and said, "Stay and sleep in. You don't have to come with me. You have an extra hour."

"I don't mind going in early," he lied. He liked to sleep, but he didn't like being alone more than that.

He could see a faint urge in Hank to argue with him, but then Hank just shrugged and said, "Your call."

Brey didn't think it was. It was just that Hank didn't really care that much. He could let it go. Brey's smile hid his hurt. The hurt embarrassed him, made him anxious, and he knew from the expression in Hank's eyes that Brey's emotions confused him.

At night, Brey got into Hank's bed, lying on his side on the edge of the mattress by the window, and Hank let him. The first night, Brey could feel Hank's stare, and his body grew so stiff it hurt. Then he felt the bed shift, Hank rolling away on the other side of him. They didn't touch, didn't talk. In the night, if Brey woke up lying too close, he rolled away again, cold and panicky. He'd stare blankly out of the dark window, trying to calm, aware of Hank's warm body. He breathed in the memory of dusty books, pictured the mural, farmland, green grass, haystacks. He ran through dry weeds, sunburned bushes, saw water, fell sprawling to the sounds of footsteps behind him.

Dreaming, struggling, kicking.

"Okay, Brey. Okay. C'mon now. Quiet."

Hank's arms squeezed him close. Warmth surrounded him, comforting and safe. He sank into it. A dimly remembered feeling like happiness rose in him. Then he stiffened, and his voice came out in a whisper he barely heard. "Get off me."

Hank let go. Cold instead of warmth. He shivered.

"Are you okay?"

"Yes."

"Go to sleep then."

He rolled away, bundling under the covers in a room that made him sweat. The air at the windows was still and warm.

* * * *

Three years ago

After he got out of prison, Brey met a man in the city on his way home. A man he gave sex to because he was afraid of him. Other people scared him too.

Random gunshots rang out. Explosions. He was hungry. He didn't have any food, but he had half a bottle of water and bleach to purify it. He ran away from voices and footsteps. Once a man ran after him, and he skittered around a corner, his bag of water and bleach swinging sideways, pushing himself between cars at the curb, up across the sidewalk.

"Wait!"

He didn't. His heart pounded. Grabbing onto an iron railing outside an old stone apartment building he flung himself around another corner and kept running. He knew where he was going then. The place where his life had stopped. He came out onto a wide boulevard, crossed it quickly and turned another corner. Near the end of the block, he paused to look down an alley. No litter, just grimy pavement, a blue door in a black painted wall. The door opened with a push of his fingers onto a landing and steps that led down to a bar and dance floor. The Blue Glow. Lights in the ceiling used to strobe rapid-fire shades of blue — sky, water, heaven. He looked back at the door and twisted one of the locks. Functional. Glasses covered the bar and tables. A few of the chairs lay on their backs, but otherwise it looked as if everybody just stood up one early morning and walked away.

"Wish that was me," he whispered and his voice sounded loud.

They had to know they weren't coming back, the last ones here. The end didn't happen that fast. He closed his eyes and swayed, let his imagination fill the room with people again, crowded at the bar, jostling each other, laughing, grinding against each other on the dance floor. Music pounded inside him, his heart keeping the rhythm, filling him with energy.

He pictured a farewell party. For tomorrow, we die.

Then he opened his eyes and faced the dark room.
Went down the steps. On the other side of the room,
stairs led to an office and a few other rooms in back.
One of the rooms was doorless, closed off by a blue
velvet drapery panel on a plastic curtain rod. He
didn't want to think about that room. Instead, he
pictured Bernard, the club's owner, lumbering up and
down those stairs, surprisingly agile, an enormous,
rosy-faced, kindly man. In the office upstairs, Brey set
his bag of bottles under the window, wrenched open
the bottom drawer and fell on his knees, muttering,
"Thank you... Shit... Thank you."

Oreos, Ritz, Snickers. He ate blindly, leaning back
against the wall, eyes closed in bliss. Warmth stole
over him. He didn't feel himself falling asleep, but he
must have. When he opened his eyes again, he grew
cold all over and stared motionlessly at a man in the
doorway.

"This is my block."

The fact of the man speaking to him seemed to reach
him from a distance. He blinked uncertainly. "What?"

"This is my block. All the buildings in it are mine."

He struggled up woozily as if he'd drunk and eaten
himself into a stupor. "Sorry," he mumbled. "I'll go."

But the man didn't move out of the doorway. Brey
was trapped there—scared. He felt his heart pound.
The man stared pointedly at the cookie and candy
wrappers on the desktop.

"You ate my food."

"I didn't know."

The man kept staring at him, eyes dipping down.
Brey looked down too. His stolen jeans hung low,
hoody unzipped, a strip of skin showing between his
waistband and the hem of his T-shirt. He looked back
up. The man was staring fixedly at his face again. His

clothes hid his body, but he knew what the man saw — wavy, light brown hair, light blue eyes, pale skin, pale freckles.

"You need to pay me," said the man.

His mouth was dry, but he shrugged easily, pushing his hands into his pockets. The man smiled grimly at the gesture. He was offering no resistance. He could do this. "Okay."

"Money's for crap," the man added.

He shrugged again, watching as the man approached, grabbed a handful of his hair and pulled his head back, examining him in the dim light. His heart raced. He thought briefly of bolting. Maybe he'd get away.

"You're pretty, but you're not pretty like a girl."

His smile was mild. "There's a reason for that."

Dropping his hand to his shoulder, the man pushed him down. "Suck me."

He didn't want to, but he didn't have a lot of options, and the slight roughness excited him. The hand on his shoulder went to the back of his head as the man pulled his face to his crotch. The smell was strong — urine, unbathed skin. He jerked away but didn't rise, just lifted his eyes to watch the man's face as he undid his pants, pulling at his thickening cock.

"C'mon," the man said.

The hand was on the back of his head again, pulling on him. Almost robotically, his hands came out of his pockets, one bracing on a steely thigh, the other gripping the man's cock. He licked the oozing tip and felt a shudder under his palm. His mouth filled with spit, and he took the tip inside and let his spit wash away some of the smell and taste. He let the cock slide deeper, laved it with his tongue, squeezing gently with his hand.

"That's right."

He felt a little sick at himself because he was excited now, too, throbbing and aching in his jeans. Removing his hand from the man's thigh, he yanked his fly open and pulled his dick out, stroking as he sucked. His cheeks hollowed, and he slid his tongue all around, flicking at the ridge under the tip. The man dug his hands in Brey's hair and began rocking.

"Yeah... Good."

He pushed closer, letting the cock slide against his tongue, bump the back of his throat. He opened for it, moaning against the feel of stiff flesh filling his mouth. The man above him moaned, too, grinding closer. He gripped the man's thigh again and pushed away, letting his cock slip free. The man's hips continued to pump. Brey looked up into glassy eyes and licked his lips.

"You can fuck me," he said and watched lust flare in the eyes above him.

Then the man looked quickly around the room, nervously almost. Brey waited. His heartbeat deafened him, a rapid, panicky sound. Close to shaking, he saw disgust fill the man's eyes and looked to the door again, ready to run. Then the man said, "Take off your pants," and he struggled up clumsily, kicked off his shoes, slipped out of his jeans.

The man made room for him in the open space of the little office and he lay down on his back, waiting. He didn't want to lie face down. Didn't want to turn his back. He covered his cock and balls with both hands, arching up a little, while the man considered what he was about to do. Then, with a twist of his lips, the man was between Brey's legs, pushing at his hole with hot, desperate fingers. Brey bucked and squirmed away.

"Ow... Shit."

"What?"

"That hurts."

"You want it or not?"

"Yeah. Just…" He rolled his head back, viewing the upside-down door beside the upside-down filing cabinets. "Check out the bathroom."

"Fuck," the man grumbled, getting up. "You better be worth it."

He put his feet flat on the floor, heart still racing, heat coursing through him, rolling his fingers over his balls, wanting this. Always wanting it. He bit his lip and pushed his dick up against his palm. A cabinet door slammed, and the man came back.

"Lotion."

He let his legs fall open. He was panting, writhing in excitement. The man stared at him with darkened eyes.

"Fuck, man, you're a slut."

"Yeah," he answered with a grin. "I used to be, anyway."

The stab of grief at that came out of nowhere. He felt tears in his eyes and groaned at the insertion of the man's fingers, grinding down, remembered pleasure surging through him.

"Christ, you're tight."

"Just fuck me. I'm ready."

He wasn't. Pain knifed through him, and he cried out, "Fuck!" The man froze. He felt a surge of gratitude. "Just a minute. Gimme a minute," he whispered.

Slowly, his body relaxed, and the man slipped his elbows under his knees, lifting him gently. "Okay?"

He nodded, eyes washed with tears, biting hard on his lower lip. The man pushed in, pulled back, pushed in again, rocking slowly, deeper and deeper, opening him, filling him, and those waves of pleasure slowly started to roll through him once more—warm as bath water, tingling in his thighs, sparking at the base of his spine. His cock, shocked to softness, began to fatten again, and he stroked it in time to the thrusts rocking him across the carpet. He lay with his face sideways, no eye contact, just this wondrous, mind-numbing sensation washing through him. His moans reverberated inside him, the man above gasping into the air. The thrusts went deeper, harder. He squeezed at his cock, his balls pulling up. The dull throb of pleasure filled his belly. He felt his body curl as the man rose above him, pulling his knees higher, pounding down in relentless thrusts. His breath burst out of him in frantic groans. The tingling raced down his spine into his balls. He pulled on his cock, opening his legs wider.

"Yeah... Yeah..."

His balls boiled, and he slammed his head back, spurting hot ropes of cum over his fingers, onto his belly and T-shirt, ass muscles clamping down.

The man yelled, "Fuck!" and began jerking erratically, shooting inside him. A moment later, the man fell over him with a gasp, breathing heavily before he rolled away and struggled up. There was a shuffling sound as the man pulled up his pants. They didn't look at each other. Brey rolled up painfully and sat still, waiting—scared again.

"This is my block," the man said.

"Okay," he answered.

He waited for the footsteps on the stairs, pulled on his jeans, picked up his bag of bottles and followed slowly.

* * * *

Present day

Now, in Waterfall, Brey thought about that man in the club. The man he didn't fight. He wondered about Thom and the men he did fight too. He thought about Patric. Then he remembered his old life and he grew quieter as the days passed.

He still liked sitting on the library steps in the early sun. Sitting there relaxed him.

He leaned a shoulder against the step enclosure, hidden from anybody walking by. The sun wasn't hot, and the sky was always a deep, hypnotic blue, like water he could sink into. He could smell the sun on the stone. He sat with his hat in his lap, enjoying the sleepy feeling, smiling at the sound of slapping sandals.

"Mornin', honeybun."

He loved her endearments, felt his smile strangely falter at that realization.

"Hi, Issa."

He stretched and got up with a yawn. He ate because Hank wanted him to, but sleep was a torture and his eyes were still hollowed and shadowed with purple. The freckles stood out on his pale skin. Issa was sun-flushed with lines around her eyes from laughing and squinting. She quirked a smile at him.

"You sure you don't camp out here?"

"That's an idea."

She went past him with her key out, an appraising look angling out of the corner of her eye. "No reason to go home, is there?"

He shrugged and followed her in. "I like it here."

Gray air filled the room, drifting cool and calm. Quiet and familiarity washed over him.

He took a stepping stool and a pad of paper into the stacks, jotting down notes for the card catalog. Later on, he would fill index cards with more careful script. It depressed him that he couldn't even type it.

Issa had grinned at the suggestion. "With what ink, sweetie?"

"Fuck."

Dried-up ink cartridges. Computers that didn't work. Printers that didn't print.

He turned pages with remembered devotion. Collected books to take home with him.

On other days voices drove him down the aisles. He sweated and his heart raced. The room swam around him, dissolved and reformed into the dry weeds where they brought him down—Thom's garage. Sounds whistled in his ears. He hated being afraid. He was ashamed and angry. On another day he remembered the man he didn't fight, and he stayed where he was, staring out past the end of the aisle into the open room. Empty tables, three men crossing the floor.

"Hey, Issa!" The booming voice faded, then grunted, "Damn."

All three men wore khaki trousers, dark T-shirts, boots and ball caps.

Two of the men moved off, one staying where he was, younger than the others—a boy really. His gaze drifted, meeting Brey's stare. "Hey. You know where Issa is?"

Casual. Interested. He came closer. Brey's fingers rose, hooking in his collar. The boy followed his movements, gazed back at him. "Can't you talk?"

He swallowed. "I don't know."

The boy frowned, then said, "You don't know where Issa is?"

"Outside maybe."

Another man appeared. "C'mon."

"In a sec."

The first man came closer and fixed on Brey's collar, then squinted at Brey's face. He put a hand on the boy's shoulder. He didn't look anything like him. Probably not related.

"What's your name?" the man asked.

"Brey."

"You're Hank's."

"Yes."

The man nodded, an expression Brey couldn't read crossing his face.

"You here by yourself?"

"I'm working."

"With Issa?"

"Yes." His voice had a dry, whispery sound, like dead weeds, like the wind through the auto bay.

"Well, I can't wait around. Tell Issa that Aaron Mason wants to talk to her about the Council meeting."

"Okay."

Alone again, he shook and let out a low wheeze of air. Closing his eyes he could remember the way he used to be. Lively. Cheerful, with an almost constant laugh. A flirt. The green-brown eyes of that boy didn't stir him at all. Shaggy, walnut-colored hair. Brey wasn't the shameless boy he used to be anymore, happy to wear down any reluctance, take advantage of any interest, devour any experience. All of a sudden, he was sick of himself and sat down on the stepping stool, staring sightlessly at the wall of books in front of him.

At lunch he gave Hank a stack of books and said, "Can I have these?"

Hank nodded and set the pile down beside him. Brey had no rights. He couldn't even check his books out himself. Hank had do it for him. He tried to relax and ate a mouthful of his noodles. Jack's noodles — slippery, chewy ribbons with bits of chicken and a fragrant, golden gravy. Over this he'd salivate, fill his belly. He grew warm inside.

"God, this is good."

Hank nodded. "My wife made these noodles all the time. Reminds me of her."

Brey frowned. "The same recipe?"

He caught Hank's perplexed stare, then it cleared with a look of surprise. "I didn't tell you? Jack was Beth's brother. We all grew up together."

Family... Hank had family. The jealousy that flooded Brey's body shocked him. Heat flushed his face and tingled his skin. He took a deep breath and let go of his spoon, his fingers in his collar again, pulling it against his neck, feeling the cool bite of metal. He stared sightlessly, and the sound of his blood rushed in his ears. He liked this. Anger was good, liberating. It burned his fear away.

"I hate this fucking place."

Hank's voice echoed in a distant space, shocked. "Jesus, Brey. Where'd that come from?"

"I just remembered," he said bitterly. "I just remembered that I hate this place."

Chapter Seven

Days passed again. Hank gave Brey money that he kept in a box under the bed he didn't sleep in anymore. Occasionally he sat and stared thoughtfully at the little pile of bills. Growing up, he'd barely ever wanted anything because wanting had been a transitory thing. Wanting had flowed easily into having. He hadn't saved, hadn't worked, hadn't struggled. He hadn't been grateful, and he hadn't been greedy. All his life had been easy, abundant. The things from that life he thought about now were sounds—laughter, the splashing of water in the pool behind the house he'd grown up in, the chatter of voices in the kitchen, Goldy's happy, yappy bark, his brother's amiable pontifications, his sister's exasperated refutations—the feel of his mother's fingers in his hair, pulling him in for a quick kiss, the smack of his father's hand on his back, the colors of roses and dahlias, the smell of the lavender that followed the curve of the driveway.

The money that touched his fingers was dry and lifeless.

* * * *

On their way home from work, Brey felt Hank's stare.

"You okay, Brey?"

He hated that question. It came all the time. "Fine."

He stole his own glances at Hank, his cheeks flushed with sun, sun-bleached hair. Calm. Brey felt that calm, the pull of its quiet, safe place. In the explosion of his life, in the spray of all his shattered pieces, he stilled under that calm stare that didn't like or dislike him. Felt for him, though, Brey could tell that. He shot sideways glances at Hank's mouth, firm without tension. A warm smell came off him, warm in the sun.

Brey couldn't be happy. *Could he?* Panic stirred in him at the thought. He dug his hands into his pockets and planted his gaze on the sidewalk.

"Wanna listen to the band tonight? Issa an' Jack will be there."

An' Fuck-A-Friend Ken?

"You go. Is that okay?"

"Of course. You're welcome to join us, though."

He nodded, felt cold in the shade the building cast. Glancing back up again, he saw a sheen of sweat on Hank's forehead. Brey's tongue moved restlessly against his lip. Hank's gaze shifted sideways, and his eyes seemed to darken. Brey looked away.

At the door to their building, Brey darted up the stairs ahead of Hank.

The sound of the music that night drifted in through the open bedroom window. It stayed light outside for a long time and a soft, warm air blew in. Earlier, Brey had found packages of Top Ramen in the cupboard. He knew Hank had bought these from Thom. The supermarkets and department stores in Waterfall had been cleared out years ago. The thought of Thom made his stomach clench. He shook the package of noodles, considered the expiration date with more curiosity than worry. He didn't eat, though. He lay down on the bed in the warm room, the sound of banjoes and fiddles drifting in, thin and distant. He imagined Hank sweating in the warm air, the smell of him, Fuck-A-Friend Ken's tongue on Hank's damp skin. Then he remembered that boy in the library with the man who wanted to see Issa. The boy had come back a few other times, looking for Brey, staring at him with intense, calculating eyes. *Great.* A teenage stalker. *Just what I fucking need.*

He should be flattered, but he wasn't. He wanted the boy out of his brain—Thom out of his brain. Running away, the garage, the pain out of his brain. He just wanted Hank. The warm feelings he thought he'd lost. The gentle lapping of pleasure.

He lay in bed with the light off, listening to Chrissy's faraway voice—just sound, soft and bell-like, carrying on the twangy notes of a fiddle. He breathed in the memory of Hank's scent. Imagined sitting next to him on a blanket on the dead grass, leaning into him, feeling his heat. Brey's mouth watered, and he pushed his hand down his pajama bottoms, his heart jumping in time to the pulse in his cock. He hissed in a breath and slowly stroked his dick. A teasing touch. The scent of Hank surrounded him. He wanted to taste him, brush his lips against blond stubble. Behind the lids of his eyes he saw Hank's head slowly turning, gaze meeting his through the distance, darkening, lips curving in a smile. Heat pooled in Brey's belly. He humped his fist, the slide of his dick against his palm igniting his flesh. His heart was pounding, sweat beading his skin. It felt sticky, itchy. His balls ached.

With a gasp, he gave his cock one hard pull, then let go to kick his pajama bottoms off. He spread his legs, gave a wet lick to his palm, rolling his balls in the fingers of one hand, squeezing his dick with the other. Sensations — pent-up, half-dead — swamped him. His skin tingled. His ass clenched. He licked his lips, and it was Hank's hand on him, Hank's fingers tightening, slick and slippery with lube, stroking, twisting over the head, thumb dipping down into his slit.

"*Jesus… Fuck,*" Brey whispered.

He sucked his bottom lip between his teeth and bucked up, smearing his cockhead with pre-cum, lightly squeezing his balls. His fingers grew slick, slipping and sliding, faster, faster. He panted, electricity building in his spine as he saw Hank lean over him, darkened eyes on his, mouth opening, hot and wet on his face.

"*God, yes… Please.*"

He choked. Gasped. His balls pulled up, sparks racing down his spine. Hank's fingers squeezed and pulled then he arched his back and felt other hands on him, hurting him.

He cried out in grief. His body shook and cum splashed his belly, pain burning him, burning out his pleasure. He jerked and spasmed, fingers milking out the last warm drops of his release. Waves of shame and misery washed over him. He sank into the darkness and swung an arm over his eyes, lying there for a long time, letting his spunk grow cold and sticky.

After a while he couldn't hear the music anymore, so he got up, washed and climbed back into bed. When Hank came in, he pretended to be asleep, lying with his back to him, feeling the slow depression of the mattress, the warmth he ached for and pulled away from.

Hank put up a wall he couldn't climb, a judgment he deserved, a dislike he shared. He had no right to happiness.

That night he dreamed of Patric.

Lights pulsing, techno-rock pounding into him. He was happy, buzzed on tequila and Ecstasy. Colors kaleidoscoped, noise drummed and echoed inside him. He was dancing between two men, a pair of hands on his hips, lips on his neck, crotch to crotch, a cock pressing into his ass. He swayed with his arms in the air, hips liquid, undulating. A drop of sweat ran down his cheek and the man dancing in front of him licked it off. The room swirled around him. Then the man behind him tugged him away. Laughter burbled out of him. He looked behind him at the man following him and saw Patric at the bar then, trying to catch his eye, worry on his face. Patric followed halfway, then stopped in the middle of the club, a motionless figure in a sea of motion. All around him people danced with their arms in the air. Sinuous waves. Skin and leather. Denim and silk. Reds and blues and yellows, a sea of color floating in the air like party balloons.

He giggled, and Patric moved again, his eyes messaging distress. Brey slowed on the stairs and the man behind him gave his ass a push. He grinned at Patric down below, saw Patric's mouth moving – "Aubrey!"

He waved. "I love you, Patric."

He did and he didn't—at least not the way Patric had wanted.

Chapter Eight

The boy was at the library again. Brey felt his stomach lurch and grabbed an armful of books out of the book drop, ducking through the door behind the counter. He wasn't alone. Issa was out there, and he heard chairs scrape, people sitting down. Sometimes they came in to eat. Issa didn't complain unless they didn't clean up. They wouldn't help him, though — only Issa would. He wasn't anybody. They didn't sell people in Waterfall, but they followed the laws. They grew comfortable, adjusted — even Issa. He couldn't check out his own books. Slaves worked the farms, in the cannery. He hadn't seen any yet. They didn't come into town. They didn't try to run. Runaways were whipped. He didn't count, really.

Coming back to the door, he glanced out. The boy pinned him with a stare and looked him over. His body prickled, hot and cold. He shivered. He took back another armful of books, looked out again, and the boy was gone. Brey was constantly aware of him. Even at home, he dreaded seeing him. Waking up was a chore. He wanted to plant his face in his pillow and never move, but he didn't want to walk to work alone either.

One morning he lay curled up, struggling, then the bed sank, and he peeked out. "What?"

"You wanna sleep or get up?"

"Get up."

Hank gave him a mild look, no worry yet, almost friendly. They were settling into their lives together — connected but apart. Jack was teaching Brey how to brew beer. He wanted to dislike it, but he didn't. He enjoyed his lessons, enjoyed Hank looking on. Game night with Jack and Issa. Monopoly. Scrabble. He warmed to every faint smile Hank gave him. Quiet breakfasts. Apple fritters on Saturdays. Bourbon and ice before bed.

Still sitting there, Hank said, "You can tell me if anything's wrong, Brey. We act like this is normal, an' I know it's not. If you're having trouble, you can tell me about it."

"Trouble?"

"With anyone."

"You know I want to go, Hank."

"An' you know I can't let you." Hank's voice was quiet.

Brey grinned at him. "Well, then, I guess I'm just fucked."

"Is that really how you feel?"

He made sure there was no malice in his voice when he said, "What a dumb question," and Hank expelled a breath that was half a laugh.

"Well... I keep trying to help."

Brey was quiet for a moment then said, "I want to know about you."

His comment brought a look of confusion to Hank's face. "Know what?"

"About you. Your life. The way you were. Your story."

"My story?" He seemed to roll the words around in his head for a moment. "I guess I keep things pretty close to the vest."

"Yeah."

"That's just me."

"You asked what you could do. I could use a friend."

"Okay. I can work on that." He stared for a moment into Brey's eyes, not smiling, making Brey nervous, then he got up a moment later and said, "C'mon then. We're running late."

* * * *

At the library, Issa went next door, and Brey wheeled a book cart down one of the aisles, sliding books into place. Soft voices carried, the scrape of chairs. The hazy light floating down made him sleepy.

"Is that your real name?"

He jumped, heart pounding, and wheeled around. The boy stood close, fingers of one hand resting on the book cart. Brey's mind struggled to grasp the situation, to hear the words. The face in front of him was smooth and young but not soft anymore, the barest hint of stubble on the jaw and chin. Wide eyes with a shadow of lust hiding inside.

"It's short for Aubrey."

The boy nodded. "I'm Josh."

He flicked his tongue over his lips, and Brey felt his anger grow, burning out his fear. He hated this, being afraid. He gritted his teeth and said, "Whaddo you want?"

The boy shrugged, but his eyes narrowed. "I don't want anything."

"You're always here, always staring at me."

"This is a public place."

"What are you, fifteen?"

"Eighteen."

Liar.

"You have no business staring at me. For crissakes, isn't there anybody your own age around?"

A red blush spotted the boy's cheeks, but there was no embarrassment in his eyes. Confidence. Sureness.

"Yeah. A couple, but I'm talkin' to you."

"I want you to leave me the fuck alone."

His anger had grown to rage, but underneath it, he could hear panic. Maybe the boy could too. He wasn't angry, wasn't afraid. He looked around slowly, cautiously, and Brey was scared. His vision constricted, and the room started to swim.

"You better not talk that way."

Because he had no rights. He didn't even have the right to refuse. Ice water flooded his veins. His anger was gone. His eyes darted, looking for Issa, but all he saw was the boy, his face looming as he came closer, curiosity in his eyes. Brey swallowed. He grappled for the book cart to hold onto, but it was out of reach. He stammered. He hated his fear. He hated his life.

Anguish squeezed his throat. "I'm... I'm sorry. I... Please..."

The boy was reaching up, a finger on Brey's cheek, lightly brushing against his skin. Worry in his eyes.

"I was just being friendly."

"I... I wasn't..."

"You have to be careful," the boy said quietly then he backed away.

Brey couldn't breathe. The boy's shape dimmed, then disappeared. He swallowed and blinked, aware of a ringing in his ears that was slowly quieting. Finally, he took a breath, let it out slowly. *God, please. Please.* The begging in his head made no sense. Nobody was going to help him. He had to get away. He had to get away or die.

* * * *

Hank watched Brey drift further and further away — not just in silence. A distance grew in his wonderfully pale eyes, clouded them over. He drank Hank's bourbon every night, and Hank wanted to stop him but didn't. On game night at Jack's, Brey stayed home.

In the mornings he lay groggily, got up with a clumsy, sluggish reluctance. He kept dropping the toilet seat with a bang, grating on Hank's nerves.

"Leave it up, for godsakes. It's just us."

That always got him a sour scowl, and Hank wondered if Brey didn't like the reminder that their lives were entwined. For a while, Brey's attraction to him was obvious, although Hank wasn't sure Brey actually realized it. It surprised him after what Brey had been through. Except for him and Jack, men intimidated Brey. But he couldn't get away from them, and he wouldn't go out by himself. Then, all of a sudden, Brey's strange attraction to him seemed to vanish. All that was left was dullness, flashes of anger. Quick, frantic awakenings at night, rousing Hank enough to murmur, "Okay, Brey?"

Hank knew not to touch him.

It was strange, to sleep in the same bed with a man he didn't touch. Ridiculous. He felt like a ten year old on a sleepover. But there was something deeply intimate about it too. He felt a closeness to Brey that Brey's withdrawal made painful. Hank made tea one day feeling the echo of tension like a band tightening around his heart. Feelings of helplessness brought out memories that felt like knives in his chest. He struggled to keep his expression blank.

Out in the living room Brey sat sideways on the couch, bare feet up, knees slightly bent, a book resting against his legs. He gave Hank a quick glance out of the corner of his eye.

"What are you reading?" Hank asked.

"*The Plague.*"

Hank almost laughed. "Seriously?"

Brey lifted his book, turned the cover to him.

"Is it realistic?"

"I don't know. I was locked up. I never really saw, except on TV."

Hank nodded toward the book. "What's it like in that?"

"Sad."

"Well, that pretty much sums it up," he said, hearing the bitterness in his voice.

"It's about what people do, not just about dying. Choices."

"I know a little bit about that, I think, from the things I saw. I used to think a thing like Eve would change people. Now I don't. People are who they are—good or bad."

He watched Brey's slow smile. "Things changed me. I work every day. I don't do drugs, and I don't want to. I'm celibate. You used to think I was a junkie slut."

Hank met bluntness for bluntness. "Weren't you?"

"I wasn't a junkie. And I don't regret it either. Not the slut part—or the celibate part. I'm really a monogamous type." He grinned one of his old grins at that, and Hank was happy to see it even though he knew there was nothing but disbelief in Brey's monogamy showing on his face. "I am," Brey insisted. "But I wasn't going to refuse sex with some hot guy — or guys — until I fell in love either. Hell with that. Life was too fun. I loved it. I just... I never saw this coming."

Hank felt his mood turn then and looked out of the window where the clouds hung in the sky, and the heat was like a weight. "The last time I saw my wife an' girls was through a sliding glass door."

Brey didn't say anything and after a long moment, Hank looked back over to him. "You wanted to know my story?"

Brey nodded.

"This is my story..."

* * * *

Three years ago

For a long time they tried to keep up. Robberies increased. Muggings. Tempers flared and fights broke out in office buildings, on street corners, in stores, doorways, apartments, even on the steps of a church near the precinct. The hospitals filled up. Bodies collected in mass graves. The streets grew empty, and people grew furtive.

Patrolling in his car, Hank could some days think that there was nobody living. Other days he could see the shadows on the other side of the windows he passed. Were they sick, waiting, hopeful, afraid? It didn't take long for the world to end. He was living at Jack's, sleeping on the couch. Jack never blamed him for leaving Beth. They were all three friends, and Jack knew Hank didn't stop loving her. She was seeing somebody else, and he guessed Jack knew that too. Hank didn't know who the man was, and it didn't matter. That she was lonely enough to start an affair shamed him. She was his best friend. He should have been the one she came to. He'd meant his vows. She gave him the stability he never knew growing up—a calm, happy home, a mortgage, car payments, weekend barbecues, summer block parties and his girls. It was enough at first. Not everything. No life was everything. There was always a sacrifice.

For Hank, the sacrifice was his desire. He loved Beth's smile and the freckles on her nose—but he didn't desire her. He ached to stroke bristly cheeks and a hot stiff cock. In his fantasies he felt cum spurt against his belly and the body that shook underneath him was a man's. His heart broke because he wanted his love for Beth to be enough. He wanted to love her the way she loved him.

But after a while the walls he'd built against everything he believed he could never have began to crack.

Images invaded his thoughts, pummeled him, knocked him silly. Christ. Everywhere—an ass in snug jeans, an Adam's apple bobbing in a strong throat, strong wrists, long-fingered hands, deep voices. The rumble of a laugh.

His throat was constantly dry, cock straining. The cracks in his wall grew wider. Desire leaked out.

And he knew Beth could tell.

Her smile was a pale glimmer of itself, but he couldn't talk to her. His mother and father never talked. They fought. He didn't know how to talk. Instead he fucked men he never saw again and knew that Beth had fallen in love with someone else. His life became a lie he couldn't live with anymore.

They were at a neighbor's house when he decided to move out, not exactly a moment of clarity — more like acceptance. Children were playing on a giant play set in a corner of the yard, and he stood outside with the other husbands, listening to conversation he forgot a moment later. For some reason he turned toward the house, saw the slow swing of her head as she looked out through the billowing smoke of a too-hot barbecue at their girls playing with the other children, laughing. From where he stood on the patio with a beer, he could hear the game on the TV inside, a quick news report of a few random, unexplained deaths. Her eyes on his were tender and a little sad. Her smile gentle. He couldn't do it anymore. He moved out that night.

* * * *

Two weeks after Hank moved in with Jack and Lacy, Lacy was dead. Then other people died. There was chaos, then quiet — still, almost abandoned streets. A feeling of watchfulness and suspicion.

Every day he called Beth. She didn't go to work. The girls didn't go to school.

"You have to stay inside," he told her. "Don't go out until this is over."

"This is never going to be over."

On the next call she told him that Ellen, one of their neighbors, came over and knocked on the door.

"You didn't—?"

"No. I wanted to, but I didn't. I just... I waited until she went away." Her voice broke.

"We have to think of the girls. You have to stay inside."

"I can't take this. God. I just want our life back."

On another day she said, "I let the girls out."

"Jesus Christ!"

"Just out back."

"I don't care."

"They have to go outside and play, Hank. They have to. You know that."

"I have to get you out of here."

"You're a good father, Hank. A good husband. I want you to know that."

"Don't talk like that."

She sighed heavily. "I wish we could do it again."

"Stop."

"You know I would do anything to save our girls."

"Stay inside."

The last time he called, he said, "I'm picking up some groceries. I'll see you in a bit."

"No, Hank."

And he knew from her voice then…raspy, whispery, lifeless.

"Beth—"

"Stay away."

"No."

"Please."

"Fuck that."

"Please, Hank. I won't let you in."

"The girls?"

"Hank… Hank…" Then nothing.

"*Fuck!*"

He gunned the car, tires squealing, dodging abandoned cars, racing through the blinking signal lights, block after block, a blur rushing by.

Supermarkets half emptied. Bars pouring out their last bottles. Silent movie theaters. Empty schools. His neighborhood. His house. He pounded on the door.

She came to the window, shook her head, and pointed to the back. Running back along the walkway, he hopped over the bikes nobody would bother to steal anymore. At the back door, he stopped against the slider, hands on the glass. She raised her palms to press against his.

"Stay out," she said.

Her voice was muffled and far away.

"I can break the door down."

Just saying that meant he wouldn't, though. He saw the flash of fear, the glitter in her eyes, the sorrow in her smile. She looked where their hands joined, then let hers fall.

"Wait here."

He pushed against the glass, straining to see into the dark family room, his family room—his family, his girls, red-eyed and sick, coming up to see him.

"Hi, Daddy."

"Hey, babies." He crouched down, knees on cement, fingers brushing where Annabelle's palm met the glass.

She put an arm around her sister and raised Matilda's palm to the glass, too.

"We have colds."

The pain in his chest made a choked sound come into his mouth. He let it out in a gusty sigh of commiseration. "That's no fun."

They snuffled, noses red, the red rimming their eyes growing a purplish color. A flash image of blood pouring out of their eyes came to him, and he lurched up and yanked at the door. Beth shuffled the girls away.

He tugged ferociously at the lock. Shadow moved behind the glass, and he raised an elbow, about to break it.

"Stop!" Her voice was clear and loud. Then her forehead came to rest on the glass and her breath floated across it. "Give me this."

"Give you what?"

He pressed his mouth near her face.

"You," she said. "Give me you... Knowing you lived." Her eyes came up. "You're my best friend, Hank. I'll always love you."

"*Jesus Christ!*"

"Please," she whispered, soundless. But he saw her lips move.

His head came to rest where she was. After a while, she straightened up and went back into the house, and he never saw her again.

* * * *

Present day

"I've never even told Jack this story," Hank said. "Not the details of it anyway. Not like I just told you."

Brey's face was stark and pale. He didn't speak or move at first. Then he got up and left the room. Hank was surprised, but then Brey came back again with Hank's bourbon a moment later. He poured Hank a glass then poured his own, set the bottle on the coffee table, sat back down and said, "Fuck, Hank. I'm sorry. Really sorry."

"Me too," Hank said, but he was thinking of Brey again. Insanely, dangerously certain that his family was alive. Hank was afraid for him. He took a swallow of his bourbon and said, "I told you my story. You tell me what's going on with you."

Brey's face closed. "Nothing."

"You're lying." Brey stared at him, and Hank saw a mix of hopefulness, anger, despair. He wanted that other look, the one that believed in him and sealed Brey forever into Hank's consciousness. "C'mon, Brey."

But the look wasn't there. Something bitter took its place, and Brey just shrugged. "I don't want to be here. That's all this is. I don't know what else you're looking for."

"You wanted a friend."

"Are you saying you aren't or you are?"

Considering him, Hank was silent for a moment. "I am, Brey. You can count on that."

A shadow of grief crossed Brey's eyes. Then he swallowed and went back to his book. "Thank you."

Chapter Nine

Talking to Hank made Brey happy and being even temporarily happy seemed to Brey like the kiss of death for any real happiness. So maybe he did it to himself, what happened at work one day. He was just glad nobody saw it. He thought he was dying, and he was pretty sure that wasn't a good look on him.

Lately, he was beginning to care again about the way he looked.

After his shower one morning, he stared at himself in the mirror. The shadows under his eyes had lightened to a pale lilac. His nightmares came, taunted him with escapes he never made. Men without faces chased him, but he didn't always wake up fighting. Sometimes he didn't even wake up Hank. He could see his ribs, his hips like sharp blades. The snake tattoo that inked its way up his flank, back and over the curve of his shoulder, jaws gaping over his nipple seemed bigger, menacing. Pale skin, freckled face and shoulders... He was beautiful. He knew that. He just needed a little more weight on him.

He worked, read, went downstairs to talk to Jack, made beer, tried not to think about the men he ran away from, running the wrong way, letting them catch him. There was a fear in his heart that he did let them—that a part of him just gave up, gave in to punishment. He tried not to think about escaping, of running this way instead of that. He enjoyed his lunches with Hank, talking about books with Issa, the feel of the sun reflecting off the sidewalks, bouncing off his broad-brimmed hat. The image of his parents' swimming pool surfaced in his heart, shimmering blue water, gray-splashed cement, chlorine, laughter, cold beer, gin and tonics.

Pleasure.

He wanted more of it. Conversation. Hank. The feel of Hank's skin under his fingers, Hank's lips against his. His cock grew lively again. In bed, he tried to pretend he wasn't aware of Hank there, tried not to rub his throbbing dick against the sheets.

His only dread was Josh. But he hadn't seen him in a while. He tried to relax.

One day Hank brought pasta salad and lemonade for lunch. After he left, Brey went outside with the rest of his lemonade. It was tart, and his salivary glands clenched in pain, but he drank it anyway. He thought of his parents' pool again and closed his eyes. Their voices floated in his memory—rising laughter, the splash of his brother's cannonballs. Will, his brother with strawberry blond hair, hazel eyes—a freckled face with their mother's dimples, serious, studious and randomly playful. He helped Brey with his math homework, and they played video games together. He brought home giddy girls, a woman he was going to marry. Brey never met her. She was dead now. Will too. Not his mother and father, though… Not his sister.

Opening his eyes again, he felt a sudden nervousness. Coolness like a cloud had covered the sun. The shade of the overhang above the door behind him spread across the pavement. He got up and stepped out into the sun. The old supply store was next door. He approached it, passing through the opening that was cut into the chain-link fence. In the cracks and crevices of the old asphalt parking lot, the weeds had turned brown and dry. He stared at a lifeless clump of crabgrass and suddenly couldn't breathe. His heart began to race, the sky darkened around him, distant buildings disappeared in a tunnel of darkness. Bands of tightness gripped his head and chest, and he started gasping. His pulse pounded and he swung his arms in a panic, trying to grab at something he could hold onto. His ears rang. He grabbed onto his shirt, trying to pull it away from his skin. His body felt hypersensitive. The ringing in his ears grew louder. His breath wheezed in his chest. He ran himself up against a post on the walkway outside the supply store, and he hugged it, pushing his cheek against it, gasping, *"Please, please, please stop."*

Sweat ran down his face. It dripped off his chin and jaw. His stomach clenched around the sour lemonade, and he struggled not to throw it up.

Then, very slowly, his heartbeat slowed, and his vision cleared. He stayed wrapped around the post, shaking in shock.

His breath came out in a raspy whine. "Jesus Christ."

Reaction set in, a tingling cold in the heat of the sun. He let himself sink down until he was sitting on the walkway. He began to talk to himself, his voice low, raw sounding. "Fuck. Fuck was that? Fuckin' crazy. Jesus Christ. You are a fuckin' basket case. Jesus Christ, Aubrey. You need to get it together. What's wrong with you? You can't even be outside by yourself? Is that it? Are you that fuckin' scared? Are you just gonna let this happen to you? Just wig the fuck out? Christ, what a pussy. You need to get it together. You need to get the fuck outta here, remember?"

His fingers came up to hook in the metal collar, and another thrill of fear sent his heart racing. He saw his happiness turning into complacency.

"You need to get away, Aubrey. You can't stay here." The sudden sorrow in his voice struck even him. "You aren't Hank's. You're on your own. You have to do this. Suck it up."

The aftermath of the panic attack left him cold and sick. He dragged himself up, hooking an arm around the post, looking sideways through the open door of the supply store. His stare fixed in the darkness through the doorway for a long time, then he pulled a hand down his face, taking a deep breath before he went into the room and began to look at Issa's collection again. On a table in back, a plot map was stretched out, corners taped down. It was a map of Waterfall—a small suburban sprawl spread out from the town's center. Farther out, farmhouses dotted the outer edges of the map. Some plots were circled in blue, some crossed out in red. He guessed the crosses meant that she'd visited those locations already.

A shadow filled the door, and Issa said, "I've been looking all over for you, mister."

"Just taking a break. What do the blue circles mean?"

She came up on the other side of the table, spreading her fingertips over the map, looking at it almost reverently.

"That's where people still live."

The tremors of the panic attack were still echoing inside him. He concentrated on Issa's face. He loved abandoned buildings. Their forgotten beauty was like starlight, intangible but real.

"I'll do it. I'll go out for you."

Issa's face came up, her expression eager, eyes sparkling. "Seriously?"

He nodded. "Yeah. I really want to."

Wondrousness filled him. Excitement.

He wanted to go out there where people lived — and everything ended.

He wanted to be brave again.

On those empty streets, the spirits of people he never knew could still be there, dreams like his still lingering. He would go back home too. He just needed to believe again.

Chapter Ten

No panic attacks. At least not for the last three days.

It was easier to avoid people the farther away from the town center he got. He was almost alone. Issa gave him a small version of her map that he carried folded up in a backpack with water, a sketchpad and a notebook. He didn't like taking things from people's homes, and he couldn't carry much anyway, so he sketched rooms and belongings, and let Issa decide if she wanted anything.

Issa offered him a bike, but he liked to walk and didn't want to go too far out right now anyway.

Empty streets crisscrossed in front of him. He walked down the middle of the pavement. A breeze stirred dust and dried weeds. The silence in this empty place was as profound as a sound. A held breath...waiting.

A feeling of wonder wound its way through him—a half belief that there was knowledge of things to come here. A hope like the hope he resented inside him. He warred with it, with the desire to run and reach his family, with the fear that escape was pointless. With the hope of love against Hank's cautious, distant stare.

Birds sang outside, but there were no people living in these houses. They didn't play their radios and stereos through half-open windows. There were no childish shrieks, cracks of balls against bats, laughter, barking dogs or lawn mowers. The lawns were all dead now and all Brey heard were the birds and the creaking of swing sets.

But he liked empty places and old buildings. There was a sad animation in the slow decay of walls and floors. He thought of ghosts in the echoes of crumbling plaster and falling ceiling tiles. Ghosts like Patric's — always haunting him.

At a crossroads, he took out his map, picked a house, and ventured up on the cracked sidewalk. Dark windows faced him. Doors with locks split when the people alive after Eve came looking for bodies. He could never say these homes were lifeless, but there were some places he wouldn't enter. Now he stood frozen on the walkway, not sure about the place he had just picked. All of the houses on this block had the same façades. The town was built in sections, and a few blocks over the houses had a slightly different look, all with heat-reflective paint and roofing, every nook and cranny sealed and high-density insulation in walls and attic spaces. The houses were cool and pleasant inside. In front of each house here a tree grew in the center of the lawn.

Brey wasn't sure what kind of tree he was staring at. Its bark was pale and bleached, the leaves tough and serrated, a dull, dark green. It absorbed the sun without reflecting it, spread out an illusory shadow of coolness.

Brey took his hat off, wiped the sweat from his forehead and went inside. He wore a coat to protect his skin, and he took that off too, relieved when the air touched his bare arms. He wore a tank top, jeans, and scuffed-up sneakers. Setting his pack down, he took out his sketchpad and went deeper into the house.

He knew the layout here. It was a repeat of about four different models. A short entrance beside a sunken living room. A dining room across from the living room. A combined kitchen family room and four bedrooms off a center hall on the other side of the house. He could look across the house from the front door through the dining room window into the backyard. Maybe somebody was looking back. He believed that because he felt a sudden prickle of nerves, the feeling he had all the time now that somebody was watching him.

He shivered in the warm, stuffy air.

The people who lived in this house liked neutral colors — grays and browns and creams. Nothing special reached out to him. There was a dusty flat-screen TV in the family room, a leather couch and recliner. Stainless in the kitchen. A bedroom made into a den with a heavy wooden desk, computer, and an overstuffed chair in a corner by a small table. Two boys' bedrooms, smaller TVs, desks, schoolbooks, unmade beds with bloodstains on the sheets of one.

A noise startled him... A noise in his own throat.

He thought about his cellmate, Carl, thrashing, blood flying. A boy died here, one of the bodies carted away.

Brey's eyes roamed, taking in the last sights the boy took with him. Posters of Jimi Hendrix and Bob Marley on the walls. Groups Brey had never heard of.

A guitar in a stand in the corner of the room. Brey picked it up, ran a thumb over the strings.

Off-key. A sweet sound, though, fading into quiet again.

Brey didn't know how to play. Sitting down with the guitar anyway, he ignored the bloody sheets, plucked at the strings, making sounds that weren't music. But he didn't mind. He pretended he was a fifteen-year-old boy again—talented, obsessed, almost crazed with focus. A young girl sat on that desk chair, uncomplaining, absorbed in her boyfriend.

Letting his fingers grow still, Brey felt that focus like a strange thing he could study but never feel. His escape, his journey home already faltering.

He swallowed almost painfully, thinking of Hank, feeling his cock swell and push against his jeans. He sucked in air and pushed the heel of his hand against his crotch, feeling almost sick at letting his thoughts go to his dick in the room of a dead boy.

Getting up, he gingerly set the guitar back on its stand. That was his trouble...that he continually wanted pleasure and fun, always in excessive amounts. It had made his father angry.

"You have an empty place in you, Brey, and you keep filling it up with everything except the things that might really make you happy," his father had said.

He hadn't been unhappy, though. He hadn't felt empty. His father had confused him. He'd had everything...except he hadn't.

Suddenly he needed to get out of that house and went quickly back down the hall, stooping to push his sketchpad back in his pack, wishing he'd picked some other house to explore.

There was something wrong here.

When he rose back up to pull on his coat, he saw the shadow of leaves on the living room window, elegant shapes casting more shadows on the walls. His thoughts went back in time. In his memory, the room grew bare, the windows larger, clear and full of light.

A huge canvas filled his vision. Leaves took shape on it, sunlit and golden. Nothing special, just leaves, but they seemed alive with movement. He could feel the breezes that once stirred them.

A long time ago, he'd taken a shortcut across campus through the school's art studio to his history class in the building next door. The leaf-covered canvas had caught his eye through an open door, and he'd gone inside and stood mesmerized.

The artist had heard him, had tilted a look back over his shoulder. Blue-eyed. Blond hair. A light-hearted, sweet smile.

Brey remembered his own rising smile, the stir of lust.

"Tell me your name."

"Patric."

A voice filled with good-nature, sweetness. Doomed.

* * * *

Six years ago

On the night Patric died, Brey waved at him from the stairs, propelled upward between the bodies of two men he didn't know. He didn't need to know them. His body craved them, cock throbbing, heart racing.

But he waved at Patric. "I love you."

He felt nothing but warmth and friendship for Patric. He enjoyed him. They fucked all the time. He liked waking up with Patric, and he didn't usually feel that way about anybody else. He counted on Patric — to be with him, to love him, to hold him loosely. He was pretty sure he'd fall in love with him one day. Pretty sure he'd marry him. Patric was his safe place to return to.

Upstairs, one of the men took his hand. There was a room in back for anyone who wanted to use it. A blue velvet drapery panel on a curtain rod hung over the door. A plain gray vinyl covered the floor. Inside, a man leaned against a wall, smiling, fingers gently tugging at the hair of a man noisily sucking him off. There were two leather benches against the other walls, a leather couch and an ottoman. Another couple lay on the couch, clothes askew.

Brey looked away. A pair of hands on his face pulled him close, lips against his — a tongue pushed in, wet and hot, roaming his mouth. He grabbed the front of the man's shirt in a fist and wrapped his other arm around the man's neck, rubbing his crotch against a hard hip. Then the stranger came up behind him, gripping his ass cheeks, squeezing.

Brey pulled his lips away, craning his head back to his mystery lover's mouth.

The first licked a trail up his neck, bit his jaw. "What's your name?"

A voice gravelly with lust. Brey tried to talk but the first man nipped his lips. He groaned, and a throaty laugh behind him vibrated against his throat, the man's mouth moving against his skin. "Okay. No names."

His heart raced in agreement.

Excitement tingled all through him.

They were both big, bigger than he was. His cock rubbed against a cock in front, a cock in back pressing against his ass. Fingers pulled his shirt loose, unbuttoning it.

The man in front had short, dark brown hair, a goatee, smoke-colored eyes. The man behind had hair like Brey's—light brown, wavy, but shorter—a bump on a once-broken nose, stubble, brown eyes.

"Sweet," the first man murmured. Goatee. His fingers traced the snake over Brey's ribs. His skin was electrified. He lunged forward and felt arms around his waist, pulling him back, fingers on his belt. Brown-Eyes. Brey licked his lips, stretching out for another kiss. He sighed into Goatee's mouth, opening up to the eager tongue. Fingers dug into his waist, the mouth moved away, and he groaned in protest. Goatee grinned over Brey's shoulder at Brown-Eyes.

"You know each other," he murmured.

A humming sound of agreement came from Goatee.

Brey smiled, feeling his pants coming down his hips, freeing his swollen cock. He gasped and leaned back, voice guttural. "You do this often?"

Brown-Eyes was plucking at his nipples, Goatee slipping to his knees where he swallowed Brey's cock into the wet, hot oven of his mouth.

He couldn't stop it. His hips bucked. "Oh, fuck!"

Hands grabbed him, holding him still. Brown-Eyes wrapped his arms around his chest, kissed and nibbled at the skin under his ear. Brey's head swam. Shadows skimmed his view, slipped out through the drapes. Goatee's tongue swirled around Brey's cock before he popped off to lick it up and down, nibbling gently at the head, sucking him down again. Brey gasped, toes curling in his shoes. Goatee lapped at his balls, pulled one into his mouth, sucking, rolling his tongue around the wrinkled sac. Brey let out a loud moan, then a whimper when Goatee sat back and cold air hit his heated flesh.

"C'mon," he moaned.

"Whadda ya want, sweetie?"

"Fuck me."

"That's me," Brown-Eyes whispered, gusting warm air into Brey's ear.

Goatee was gripping his ankle, lifting his leg, pulling his shoe off. He wanted naked so bad he could barely stand it. His knees turned to jelly. Goatee pulled off his pants then he was naked in front of them, his cock bobbing high, pre-cum dribbling down its length. Brown-Eyes stepped back.

Brey loved the exposure, shook with excitement, felt the blush in his cheeks.

The two men stared, eyes hooded with lust.

"Fuck, yeah," Brown-Eyes said.

At some point, Brown-Eyes had pulled one of the leather benches to the center of the room. Goatee dipped his chin at the floor. "On your knees."

Brey sank. The thin vinyl flooring was cold against his skin. His gaze rose as Goatee came closer, breath gusting between his lips. Brown-Eyes pulled his shirt off, and Goatee unzipped his pants, freeing a long, thick cock. Brey swayed. Goatee's cock was straining toward him, bobbing slightly, a dark, shiny red.

"Suck me."

Brey leaned in, clutching at Goatee's hips, lips closing over him. Salt and sour flooded his mouth. He swallowed, feeling Goatee slip in deeper. His dick was heavy on Brey's tongue, stretching his lips. Brey savored the feel of the satiny skin, swallowing again until the tip touched the back of his throat. Easing up a little, he licked and sucked, flicking the tip of his tongue at the notch under the head. Goatee's fingers clenched in his hair, pulling Brey closer as he thrust in. Another thrust, deeper, cutting off Brey's air. Brey jerked back.

A man across the room grunted loudly.

Goatee murmured, "C'mon, baby. Trust me."

Brey let himself be pulled in again. Goatee's cock moved in and out of his mouth, sliding across his tongue, bobbing against the back of his throat, fucking him.

"Yeah, baby. Good boy."

The fingers in his hair stroked him, kneaded his scalp. His own cock bobbed free, and he thrust desperately at the air. Fingers moved down his back, brushed at his crack.

"Fuckin' sweet," he heard as he lifted his ass. His hole fluttered, a finger stroking tantalizingly around the rim. "Fuckin' slut for it, too."

Straightening their clothes, the men from the couch walked by.

Brey moaned, his mouth full, and Goatee moaned too and suddenly backed up. "Not yet," he gasped then said, "I want 'im after you."

"Wanna see 'im suck my cock after I come inside 'im. Give 'im a taste of that sweet ass," Brown-Eyes said, and Brey shuddered at that and clutched the base of his dick, eyes scrunched shut.

"Shit!"

A wave of dizziness swept over him. Hands lifted him, dropped him onto the bench in the center of the room. He resisted grinding himself into the leather, afraid he'd come. Instead, he dropped his head down, feeling the coolness against his brow, ass in the air. Fingers pulled his cheeks apart then he felt something warm and wet against his hole, and he sucked a breath in, rocking back. A tongue fluttered around his rim, flicking at the muscle there, pushing in. He arched back, breathing out sigh after sigh, throwing his head up to watch Goatee slowly stroking himself, his glassy eyes on Brown-Eyes between Brey's ass cheeks. A sheen of sweat made his skin glow.

"C'mere," said Brey, pushing up on his elbows. "Lemme suck you."

A finger pushed lube into him, pulled out and pushed in again. The friction against his rim made him shiver. Another finger pushed in as Goatee straddled the bench, cock waving in front of Brey's face. Brey grinned up at him, felt the trickle of sweat on his ribs and a pulse of pleasure deep inside, rolling through him.

"Oh, God."

His mouth fell open and Goatee's cock slipped across his tongue.

Brown-Eyes rubbed a finger over Brey's sweet spot again, and Brey garbled out a groan, trying to concentrate on Goatee's prick. He worked his tongue on the hot flesh. He bobbed and squeezed, his fingers around the base of Goatee's dick, his other arm wrapped around Goatee's thigh for balance. Then Brown-Eyes pulled his fingers out of him and grabbed Brey by the hips. He pushed his cock in. Brey sucked in a breath and Goatee pulled back. Brown-Eyes stilled too, waiting for Brey to adjust. With another breath, Brey relaxed and pushed back, feeling Brown-Eyes slide in deeper, squeeze his hips, pull back and push in. Brey groaned and Goatee came back. The feel of the cocks thrusting into his throat and ass spun him out of control. Saliva poured out of his mouth. He gulped and rocked back, slamming his ass on Brown-Eyes' cock. Pleasure spiked, his balls ached, and he let go of Goatee's cock to grab his own, stroking himself into a frenzy. He was thrashing back and forth as fingers pulled at his hair and dug into his waist. The cock in his mouth swelled and pulsed, spurting cum into the back of this throat, almost choking him. He swallowed desperately, still jerking at himself. Goatee gave a sudden last pull on his hair, and the sharp pain sent him over. His body stiffened, ass and belly clenching as his dick swelled in his fingers, and he shot out ropes of creamy white cum. Behind him, the thrusting grew erratic, and Brown-Eyes pushed in roughly, spurting inside him, fingers clamping down like steel on Brey's hips.

Brey gasped, wobbling on his hands and knees, struggling to breathe. His chest heaved, and sweat burned his eyes. He shook his head, took another lungful of air and felt Brown-Eyes slip out of him.

The sudden emptiness felt cold, and he clenched his ass in loneliness.

A moment later he pushed himself up and sat down gingerly. They were alone in the room now. Goatee was sprawled on the other bench, leaning back against the wall, drawing in mouthfuls of air. He wasn't going to be ready to fuck Brey any time soon, and Brey didn't feel like waiting for him.

Brown-Eyes was smiling, rubbing his belly, but he didn't seem interested in anything else either. He picked up his pants and sat down by Goatee. Goatee looked at Brey and winked.

"Catch ya again, yeah?"

"Hell, yeah. Next week, maybe. I'm always here."

"Count on it."

Then Brey remembered Patric. He stayed in the room after Goatee and Brown-Eyes left, dressed again, and sat down with his elbows on his knees, trying to gather his wits about him. After a few more minutes he rubbed his face and started to rise, and that's when the curtain over the doorway swept back, and Patric was there, looking in at him.

Brey smiled ruefully. Patric knew him, he told himself. He didn't need to worry, but he was aware that he was worried anyway. They had an imperfect understanding because it was really only Brey's understanding. He knew that. He stayed up here because he didn't want to face Patric. Didn't want to let in feelings of guilt or shame for something that he didn't feel either one for. He just felt resentful because he couldn't explain any of this. Patric stared silently, and Brey hid his awkwardness with a grin.

"Wow. That was intense. I think I need a drink now."

"Christ, Brey."

"What?"

"You just fucked two guys you don't even know — with me here. You came here with me."

"You could've come up."

"You shit."

"What?"

"You promised. No more drugs. No more fucking around on me."

"I never promised that," he said uneasily. "I said I'd cut the drugs back, yeah, but not the other. Only that I wasn't going to fall in love with anybody but you."

Patric laughed. "Are you kidding me?"

"C'mon, Paddy. That was sex. You're my friend." He might have cringed at that, winced at the look of disbelief on Patric's face.

"Your friend?"

"I never said anything else," he said quietly, sobering, the high of the Ecstasy only a cold memory by then.

He got up to go downstairs for a drink, but Patric stayed in the doorway.

"You... Fucking... Liar."

"I love you. That's not in love. I can't do that yet. I can't feel that yet."

"Right," Patric said. "You just love me enough to invite me to your fuck-fests."

Brey blushed angrily. "That was bitchy."

"I feel bitchy, Brey. I feel totally fucked over by you."

Brey pushed past him, swaying slightly in the hallway. A woozy feeling swept over him. He was standing in a hall that led to a back passageway on one end and the staircase down to the club and bar on the other. He wanted a drink, numbness to dull the sudden pounding in his skull. But Patric grabbed him by the arm and swung him back. Brey was surprised.

"You can't do this to me anymore," Patric said.

"I haven't lied to you. I'm not a liar."

"Fuck that. You are a liar. You just want me to go along with it."

"With what?"

"You said you loved me."

"I didn't lie to you, Patric. I told you I can't be with just you right now. We're only twenty-four. We're supposed to be having fun. I love going out. I love fucking. I —"

"Yeah, yeah, yeah. You love me. You kind of love me. You sort of love me. You want to love me some day. You just don't love me now."

"Christ, Paddy."

A nickname only he used. Patric's eyes filled with pain.

"You're scared of being in love, Brey. You're scared of me."

Brey laughed, and, even to him, it was an ugly sound. "I'm not afraid of you, Patric. I just don't want you the way you want me to."

"You love me, Brey. I know that. You just can't deal with real life. You might get hurt. You might feel some pain—and not the spanking kind, the real kind. The kind you don't have the balls to take a chance on. You like having fun. Going out. You like being high or drunk. That's happiness to you. You don't struggle for anything. You have looks, money, good grades. You eat up love. You eat up feeling good. But the thought of losing the things you love scares you to death. You won't even take the chance. You'd rather do drugs than put your heart into anything you might fail at. You'd rather fuck than feel love. You think slutting around counts? That that's gonna fill you up?"

"Better 'n you do," he said and saw a stunned look come into Patric's eyes. His face burned with regret.

"You fuck," Patric whispered.

"Whatever," Brey said, yanking his arm free of Patric's grip, but Patric only grabbed on again, just as flushed, angry and hurt. "Let me go," Brey said.

"Make me."

Brey was angry, too, cracking apart inside with a different kind of hurt and betrayal. Panic.

"You aren't even a good fuck anymore, anyway. I hardly know you're there. You're such a pussy about it."

"You shit," Patric said, slamming Brey in the chest with his palms.

Brey staggered, grabbing onto the railing. His eyes swept dizzily over the floor below. His chest hurt, but it wasn't from Patric's blow. Something deep inside him ached. He pulled off the railing, a blurry veil across his eyes. He saw Patric's shape and went at it, slamming his hands against Patric's chest, sending him reeling backward down the hall. Patric went off the step, down into the passage to the other rooms in back—off balance, though. He swung his arms to catch himself. Brey reached out, but his feet were frozen. His breath caught, made an airless exhale— "Patric!"

Patric met his gaze. His knuckles scraped the wall as he fell backward onto his back, canted sideways, the back of his head bouncing off the mortared base at the bottom of the wall.

Brey found his voice. "Fuck!"

He scrabbled down the single step Patric had tumbled off and dropped down beside him, grabbing onto his shoulders. Patric was looking up, but he didn't blink, didn't move. Then Brey saw it, a dark pool of blood spreading out beneath Patric's head.

He moaned, "Oh, my God... Oh, my God," then started to yell, "Help! Help!" as he pulled off his shirt and pushed it under Patric's head, face close to Patric's, crooning at him.

"Please, Paddy. Please. I didn't mean anything. I love you. Please, baby. Please."

His voice was wet, but his eyes were dry. Colors and shapes swirled, people in motion all around him. He cupped Patric's cheek, and it was cold. Even the blood filling his hand was growing cool. The image of leaves clouded his vision, yellow green and sunlit. Patric's leaves. His heart split. The pain was horrific, so awful he opened his mouth to let it out, the burning pressure, but nothing came. It swelled inside him and rang in his ears. He was going to die. Time slowed, endless. Patric's blood froze in a motionless puddle. No, no, no. He looked up in a panic and saw a man looking down at him. A man with a slow frown. A cop with a distant stare. Calm and remote. Strong and safe.

Brey's breath came. A word. "Please..."

* * * *

Present day

That night in the present, the dream came back, the blow of the boot between his shoulder blades so real, knocking his breath out. He gasped out loud. Bits of gravel grated his knees and palms. Whimpering, he thrashed. Curled fingers bit into his arm, flung him onto his back. Blue sky. So free. So far away. A man knelt on his arms.

"No!"

Jolting upright he got onto his knees before Hank could grab him. Swinging away, he flung back an elbow and felt it jar. His nerves flared. Even like this, he could think. He'd hit the headboard, not Hank. He gasped in relief and grabbed the footboard, trying to pull away. The rest of his thoughts scattered. He just wanted to run, to turn in the right direction—the one where he got free, where they didn't follow. But an arm came around his waist, squeezed and pulled him back.

"Get the fuck off of me!"

The sound of his voice startled him, brought back some of his sanity. His arms were raised, hands fisted. Hank stared at him, a palm up.

"Okay, Brey."

Brey noticed his fists, pulled them down and shoved them under his arms. Panic started to race through him again. *I can't do this anymore. I can't... I can't.* Hank looked angry. Brey collapsed, lying on his side, pulling his hands up to cover his face, whispering a litany of *"Please don't... Please don't... Please don't..."*

The mattress shifted, sank. Hank was leaning over him. "Brey..."

"I'm sorry. I'm sorry. Please let me stay with you. Please don't make me go. Please don't. I didn't mean to fight you. I'm sorry. I'm sorry."

"Brey..."

"Please."

"Just let me touch you, okay? Just like this. Just a touch."

He could see through his fingers, felt a brush—a flutter of fingertips down his arm, back up. Gentle strokes. He shivered and pulled into a tighter ball. *You're not even a man now. You're nothing now.* The gentle fingers grew firmer. A palm rubbed his arm, warm and slightly rough.

"Please," he said again.

"Go to sleep, Brey. You can stay. I won't hurt you. I won't even touch you except like this. You can go to sleep. I'm right here."

Brey felt his heart squeeze, his insides hollow out, empty and cold. *Who are you now?* A crushing loneliness covered him up, weighing him down. He sank slowly into sleep where feelings of sadness awaited him.

Chapter Eleven

After that last nightmare, Brey wanted Hank with an incessant ache. The touch of those gentle fingers opened a floodgate in him. All he could think about was Hank, wanting him, fantasizing about the feel of his lips, the look of desire in his eyes, his cock. He wanted to run his hands all over Hank's body, to taste his skin and mouth, suck on his nipples, spread his legs and take Hank inside. Fear shook him, pain and memory, then lust boiled up again, then despair. Hank was a friend, gentle and kind to him, but nothing more. He didn't want Brey back, didn't even really like him.

Emptiness echoed inside him. His heart ached. His body hurt. His cock in his hand racked him with pain and pleasure.

Sleeplessly, he lay awake at night, listening to Hank's breathing, the heat from his skin making Brey sweat in the already warm room. So aware of him. So needy. So desperate. He scooted over, closer and closer, the touch of Hank's skin a breath away. His need confused him, mixed with the fantasies in his head. He felt hunted, kept seeing Josh's predatory eyes on him. He didn't want to be like Josh, do that to anybody else. He lay his arm over Hank in feigned sleep and shame washed over him. Lust was a feather fluttering over his sweaty skin. He waited for Hank to roll away.

The library wasn't safe anymore. Josh was back again, almost daily, sitting quietly in the main room — wary eyes on him skirting the room. Alert, like he was keeping watch.

Brey's confusion grew.

Out with Hank, he paid more attention to the people he saw. None of them young like Josh. He thought he could feel Josh's loneliness. He wondered about the boy's parents, brothers, sisters. Dead, he guessed. Or maybe he was an only child. Maybe his father or mother ran off before Eve. Maybe they were alive. Maybe Josh would find one of them one day. Brey felt sorry for him. He wanted to feel sorry for him. He was afraid of feeling hate, afraid of anger, of that one thoughtless moment that took Patric away. He was afraid, too, of the flutter in his belly that started up just by knowing that Josh wanted him, and he was glad that he was going out into the town every day.

Alone, Brey remembered his freedom, the luxury of choice, of being a man. He breathed deeply on empty streets and fear washed away. Out here, he seldom thought about the rape or his slavery. His uneasiness, the guilt as he intruded into other people's homes dissipated. Garden trolls, kitchens full of roosters, collections of beer steins and dolls, closets full of shoes and the occasional pink flamingo washed away his anger. He liked these people he never knew, wished he did know them.

On the other side of that, though, being alone also made him long for conversation, dancing, lights, even traffic slogging through rain, Goldy's soggy tennis balls.

The overwhelming feel of life still clamoring in empty rooms sometimes took his breath away.

He found a strip mall near the interstate. There was a Chinese restaurant, a Radio Shack, a hardware store with dead plants on a rack still on the walkway outside, a Hallmark store, a grocery, a CVS store and a hair salon. He stood in the parking lot and took imaginary snapshots. A dark window with an unlit *OPEN* sign. Glass shards in a broken door. A dark alley in the center of the mall. A garbage bin at the end of the alley with piles of scrap paper and leaves hitched against the back wall. Clusters of shopping carts in the almost empty parking lot.

He stepped over glass into the CVS store. A few of the ceiling panels had come loose, leaving dark, gaping holes. Racks lay on the floor, tipped over. The contents of most of the stores in Waterfall reappeared in new locations in the town center. Money didn't make much sense if everything was still free to take. Most stores were empty, the things that remained strange, or seemingly forgotten. Brey stepped over toys, cosmetics, flip-flops, sundials, garden balls. The pharmacy was bare, but neatly organized, all the shelves upright, baskets in a stack on the counter. Was that Jack? Or somebody like Jack? A doctor who came before him? Gone or dead now. The refrigerators and grocery shelves were empty, one shelf tipped over and lying precariously against another. There were pictures on the wall over the different sections of the store, torn and curling at the edges. A smiling, curly-haired girl. A dog with a lolling tongue. A bottle of wine and a pair of wine glasses. Pots of herbs and marigolds. A man in sunglasses, cropped dark hair, smiling lips.

Circling under the pictures, Brey came up on the photo section of the store. There was a row of monitors and photo printers on a counter against a wall and two large print developers with a chair in front of each one stood side by side. He eyed a few digital cameras in glass cases. Film hung on the wall, but there were only digital cameras in the cases. Issa took digital pictures in the early days before she ran out of ink for the printer.

Brey loved taking pictures.

Seeing a door behind the counter, he went in back.

One autumn, he and Patric had driven out of the city to take pictures, and Patric had painted an abstract of one of Brey's photos. For a moment, Brey felt a stab of hurt, not knowing where that beautiful painting had gone. Patric had hung it over the couch in his apartment because he wasn't ready to sell it.

The room in back was gray and gloomy. A single small window let in faint light. The room was part storage, part break room. There was still a microwave and coffeemaker on the counter beside a sink. One side of the room was a row of open shelving that looked like storage space for orders. A label with a letter of the alphabet printed on it had been taped to the flat edge of the shelving units at each section. Issa would have taken all the photos that were here for her collection. On top of a counter was a bundle that drew Brey over.

Three packages actually, taped together.

Photograph paper.

A sticky note stuck to the address label read: *Call for pickup. Add charge for Kodak Developer, $21.49.*

Brey's heart suddenly picked up speed. He pulled his map out of his backpack. The paper was expired but not by much, and Brey wasn't worried anyway. It was cool in the room with only the faintest light. He was worried that he was working himself up for no reason, that the Grant Marshall on the address label didn't really process his own pictures the way the paper and developer suggested. But Brey was eager to hope that he did, that he had all the chemicals, the film, the camera Brey wanted. He put the paper in his pack. The idea that he could take pictures again sent his heart racing.

Hurrying outside, he swung the pack onto his shoulder with a grunt and crossed the parking lot. The interstate passed by here, and he got onto its flat surface, catching sight of the orange post-line as he began to jog. Then he stopped for a moment and slipped his arm through the other strap on his pack. He tried to ignore his slave collar bouncing lightly on his collarbone. Soon he began to pant, sweat dripping from under the brim of his hat.

Grant Marshall lived about two miles away along the edge of town, bordering the wide-open stretch of nothingness that spread as far as Brey could see. There were no farms here, just scrubby bushes and sunburnt weeds. He tried not to picture a stream, the shadows of men looming over him. He thought about cameras, lenses, solutions and dark rooms. His heart beat fast with exertion and excitement.

Slowing his jog to a walk, he veered off the interstate, back onto the neighborhood streets.

Grant Marshall lived on Paintbrush Court.

Brey found the street that followed the slow curve to a cul-de-sac. The house he was looking for was right in the center. The backyard was a wedge, the side fences pushing out into dry weeds. There was no back fence, just open space beyond the remnants of a garden. The front yard was a glittery expanse of white rock. The house was white, the windows dark and reflective. A half-open bright blue door greeted him.

He brushed lightly at the broken lock plate in the doorjamb he stepped in. He moved almost hesitantly.

Mid-twentieth-century-modern furnishings were covered in dirt, but the lines were clean and crisp. There was a starburst clock on the wall in the living room. Photographs behind glass, black and white, nothing special — an empty playground with a melancholy swing set, storm clouds building behind the house. The products of a beloved hobby.

Brey looked in all the bedrooms, in the closets and cabinets. No children. Probably no wife. In the family room, he found the door to the garage, a silver SUV inside. Shelves covered in sundries. Crates of soda.

A feeling of disappointment started to come over him. Inside again, he pushed his tongue into his cheek. He eyed the backyard through the window. No shed, which was a good thing anyway. If Grant kept his photography supplies out there, the heat would have ruined everything. He moved his tongue into his other cheek, back and forth, then set his backpack down and approached the window. The same white rock covered the ground outside. In the center, a large tree spread out a dappled circle of shade. Colored glass in abstract shapes dangled from the tree's branches like wind chimes. The sun filtering through caught flashes of blue and red and orange. A path led through the center of the yard, split around the tree, then came together and split again a little farther out to curve back toward the house. Against the side fences were trellises where something viney had once grown. A few dried tendrils still clung to the slats. Almost out of sight where one of the fences disappeared around the side of the house was a dark gray protuberance. It was rectangular and angled slightly upward. Brey could see the handle then, and he went out through the back door and approached it curiously.

The structure was an entrance leading down into something like an old-fashioned root cellar or forgotten bomb shelter. Up close he saw the darkness of oxidized metal—a flat, rough surface. Grabbing the handle, he pulled, not really expecting it to open, but the door squealed and came up, releasing a gust of cool air. A deep, impenetrable darkness greeted him. On a shelf inside the door, just below a light switch, was a flashlight and a lantern with a box of matches on top. Neither the light switch nor the flashlight worked. Lighting the candle in the lantern, Brey stretched it out, illuminating a flight of stairs to a dark floor below. Strange smells rose up, dry and slightly sour. He put his other hand on the railing and slowly descended, goosebumps popping out on his skin.

The air was cool, and he felt giddy with excitement. This was fun. A feeling of euphoria washed over him. This was good. This he remembered—adventure, expectation. Once he got it from drugs, drink and sex, but this was good too. This was like dancing, meeting new people, taking pictures of autumn color, cannonballs in the family swimming pool—all the things cut off from him the day Patric had died.

The day Brey had killed him.

He felt his throat close. He swallowed a sudden rush of guilt and squeezed his eyes shut for a moment.

His brain yelled at him. *"Stop it! Stop it!"*

Logically, he knew he couldn't change anything, that he was still alive. And he was pretty sure this was wrong, not to cherish every second.

Opening his eyes again, he continued down, his heart just nervous now. Light from his lantern wobbled across the floor. No canned goods, no bottles of water. The walls looked like cinder block. Old. Maybe it was a bomb shelter once, before Grant Marshall turned it into a darkroom. Brey took a breath, held it, let it out in a rush of excitement. The lantern swayed, lighting up a table against a wall, a camera in its leather case and lenses beside it. He found film, developer, fixer, stop bath and paper, still sealed. The air was dry, the old shelter cold. Brey's fingers trembled. He knew this was all still good. He could take pictures again. Abruptly, he began to laugh, a happy burbling sound that echoed off the walls.

Setting the lantern at the base of the stairs, he looked around and found a small duffel bag under the table.

By the time he reemerged from the cellar, the sun was sinking, the air cooling. It was the end of summer already. Thin strips of clouds lit up with pinks and oranges.

Eager to see Hank, he started to run again.

* * * *

As shadows rose up the walls, Hank got up and looked outside the police station. The sky was a light gray. Up front, the door opened, heavy footsteps coming near then stopping. Jerry Rasmussen, one of his officers.

Hank went out. Jerry was leaning back in his chair as Hank crossed the floor for the door.

"You goin'?"

"Yeah," said Hank.

Jerry yawned loudly. "Okay."

Brey usually came right to the station after he'd finished for the day because he still didn't like to walk through town alone. But it was getting dark now, almost curfew.

Hank went down the block toward the library and got there in time to see Brian and Josh Garrison coming down the steps. His teeth gnashed. Josh glanced at him with that blank, almost calculating stare he had. It was hard to get into his head. Hank still didn't know if he liked him or disliked him. He wasn't neutral, that was for sure. Then he shifted his gaze to Brian. Brian he didn't like or trust. No uncertainty there. They crossed paths at Younger's once, and Brian didn't look very happy to see him. Brian's presence there surprised him. He'd never seen him there before. He didn't like seeing him there. Brian had given him a curt nod, and Hank had seen Josh too, sitting on the steps of the canteen with Pete Sawyer. Josh's stare then was just as bold as now. Brian attended all the Council meetings, argumentative but cordial enough to avoid problems. He supported slavery and fought against every one of Hank's changes. He was unabashedly Thom Donnell's friend and regularly met with Pete and others from Younger's group at the Water Spout. The bar was too far out for most Waterfall residents, but it had power and water and attracted Younger's people, especially for celebrations. There were rooms over the bar and hot water.

Slowing at the bottom of the library steps, Hank nodded at both Brian and Josh. A slow smile worked its way onto Brian's face.

"Evening, Hank."

"Nice one so far."

"Coolin' off a little."

"Feels like it," said Hank, looking up at the gray-blue sky as he went up the steps, and Brian and Josh moved on.

Issa was alone inside. "Hank. Hi."

"Hey, Issa. Is Brey here?"

She looked suddenly worried. "No."

He glanced at his watch. "Must've gone home. I'll check there. Any trouble with Brian?"

She scowled. "Trouble, no. Irritation, yes. It's water again. I'm tired of talking about this at every Council meeting. We need to conserve and I, for one, don't see any reason to make it a slave issue."

"Isn't it always?"

"I'm quoting," said Issa. "'Only slaves should have to conserve.'"

"All sixteen of 'em?"

"And Younger's."

"Really?"

"An' besides," said Issa. "I'm quoting again—'Evaporation becomes condensation, an' condensation becomes rain.'"

"What rain?"

"Yes, well, common sense aside, I don't think that's really why he was here. I have a bad feeling," she added, surprising Hank away from another glance at his watch. "I think Brian was here because of Josh."

Hank was confused. "Josh?"

"Yes. I'm pretty sure Josh has a crush on Brey, which is fine. There's no harm in that. But if Brian's gotten into the mix..." She trailed off. "Anyway, I'm worried. An' Brey doesn't talk much about things."

Hank frowned, aware of the growing dark outside. He remembered Brian, and his stomach clenched. This was everything he hated about Waterfall, and maybe the reason he stayed.

Hank spoke quietly, this time out of clenched teeth. "Brey is my property. *My* property," he reiterated. He saw Issa wince but knew she wouldn't think he was talking about ownership. She knew him. "Brian's best friend is Thom Donnell."

"I know."

"I have to go look for Brey anyway. I thought he might be here."

"No." She spoke sharply now, her face pale.

The sky out the windows was a shade of dark blue close to purple. It was almost curfew. Hank frowned, then forced a smile.

"I better go."

On the street, he quickened his steps back to the station and went into the communications room. Jerry followed. Another officer, Anderson Cole, sat in front of the radar, staring at it disinterestedly.

"Anybody far out?" Hank asked.

Anderson looked up. "Couple. Farm workers. One on the other side of town. Started back in about an hour ago."

"Thanks. I'm gonna go meet 'im."

"Yours?"

"Yeah."

"You comin' back in after?"

"Hell, no."

Jerry and Anderson laughed behind him, and Hank heard a chair squeak as Jerry got comfortable in the front office again.

Back outside, Hank turned away from the town center and headed for the residential section. The air was warm, pink and orange clouds on the horizon. A dry sky, dry earth. He laughed at the thought of rain, the sound of his laugh sounding distant to him. Longed for rain—fat, pummeling drops. Perspiration gathered on his forehead then he saw Brey. A dark shape, but he knew the shape, the walk. Sex on a stick. *Christ.* He was bent a little to the side, as if carrying something heavy. Then he was moving more quickly, trotting, wearing those gray trousers he seemed to love. At least he wore them more often than he did his jeans. Baggy, low on his hips, always dragging them up as he walked. No reason they should look so good on him, and maybe they didn't. Maybe it was just Hank who could picture his body moving underneath the fabric—lean. Slim, sinewy muscle.

Closer, he could hear Brey's heavy footsteps. Besides his backpack, there was a canvas duffel bag hanging off his shoulder. He tilted as he came to a stop, letting the bag slip to the sidewalk, hiking up those pants.

Fuck.

"God damn it, Brey. Where the hell have you been?"

Brey gaped at him, mouth open, breath coming out in heavy gusts. Then his face flushed a darker red, and a glare shot out from under the brim of his hat.

"What the fuck, Hank?"

"Curfew, Brey. Remember that?"

"Yeah. I fuckin' remember that. Like I can fucking forget. Thanks for the fuckin' reminder, by the way."

"You have a filthy fucking mouth."

Brey stared at him for a moment then began to laugh. "Well, excuse the hell outta me. I was in a good fucking mood too. Teach me. Piece a shit life," he added, his laughter suddenly dead again, yanking up his backpack and bag with a glare.

Hank reached out. "Give me one."

"Fuck you."

"Nice."

"Beat me, why don't you?"

"Good idea."

Brey shot him another glare, but this time there was a look in it that sent a bolt of heat straight to Hank's cock. *Shit.* He swallowed and moved off, glancing back to see Brey try to juggle the bags and hitch his pants up at the same time. *Damn pants.* Brey smelled hot and sweaty too. His skin radiated.

"C'mon," said Hank. "Gimme a bag."

Glaring at him, Brey let the backpack slide off his shoulder. Hank took it, looked at the canvas bag, sighed internally then asked, "What've you got there?"

Waited for Brey to bite his head off.

The scowl on Brey's face told Hank that he was considering it. Brey didn't speak, shifted the bag up then abruptly set it down, stopping Hank on the sidewalk with a sudden, dazzling grin.

Hank blinked dizzily. *Okay. Back to the good mood.*

"Look at this!"

Chapter Twelve

His first picture was an apple fritter.

"Seriously?" asked Hank.

The pastry sat on a blue plate on the cabinet under the living room window. Bright, indirect light filled the room. The cabinet was a dark walnut, the plate a glazed sky blue, the pastry a caramel brown.

Brey looked awestruck. "It's a work of art," he whispered.

The camera made Brey happy. The light outside slowly changed, bright with autumn. He took a picture of the same swing set in Grant Marshall's framed photograph to compare the two.

After a couple of rolls of random pictures he decided to save his film. He went back to his sketchpad. One sunny, cold day he sat in a grimy lawn chair in someone's backyard and sketched a dollhouse on the far side of an empty pool. Empty flowerpots lined the front of the little house, and there were empty window boxes under the plastic windows. He wondered what flowers the little girl grew. He wondered how old she was. Paint was peeling off the walls, and the door had a splintered look around its edges.

The little girl grew up, Brey decided. Grew up and moved away. Became a microbiologist and lived in a government installation underground where she was married and had her own little girl now.

His gaze roamed the cracked pool, aqua tiles.

He ate a chunk of cheese he had brought with him, then packed his sketchpad away and went back out through the house. He hitched his bag up and pulled open the front door.

Froze.

At least on the outside. On the inside his heart pounded and his lungs squeezed.

Josh was staring at him, a taller, bigger man behind him, a stranger. The bigger man nudged Josh aside and came forward, backing Brey up.

Brey pulled in a breath, let it out in a stammering rush. "Wha-whadda you want? I have to go."

"You have time."

"We-we-were you waiting for me? I don't understand."

"I think you do."

Brey backed up again, his bag in front of him. His mind raced now, calculating the time it would take to get to the back door if he whirled and ran. *Stupid.* One would just follow through the house, the other go around back. They had waited for him—let him feel secure. He watched Josh shut the door, look near him, but not quite at him. A cold shiver ran through him, and his vision began to tunnel. He couldn't do this again. He focused on the man, cold-eyed but good-looking, like Josh would look one day. Slowly, he let his bag drop from in front of him, held it by its strap, met the man's eyes.

"Who are you?"

Amusement cross the man's face. "Brian."

"What do you want?" he asked again.

"You."

"I don't understand," he said again.

"You understand. I finally figured out what was so fucking fascinating about the library. My kid here likes you."

"So fucking what?" His anger surprised him. He could feel his blood reddening his face.

"So you're going to reciprocate."

"Reciprocate? Are you fucking nuts?"

The hand that suddenly slammed across his face knocked him sideways, almost into Josh, and stole his anger. He clapped his own hand to his face, squinting in pain.

"Dad!"

"Fuck," Brey muttered.

"Fuck is right," Brian growled, grabbing Brey by the collar. "Don't act like a fucking virgin."

Shaking him, Brian pushed Brey back into a wall. He skittered away. He was in the hall now where light slanted out of bedroom doorways. Brian came at him. He backed into a room—a bright and cheery room with sunny walls.

"You can't do this. I don't belong to you."

"You're a whore."

"No, I'm not." The minute he heard it come out of his mouth, he couldn't believe that he'd said it—that he was defending himself. "You stupid fuck."

That just got him another slap in the face. He tried to bolt, pushing Brian away, running back for the door. Brian staggered sideways, but Josh rushed him and pinned his arms to his sides. He felt Josh's lips touch his ear. "He'll hurt you. Stop."

"You already plan on hurting me."

But he grew still, and Josh let him go. "Don't hit him anymore," Josh said.

Brian ignored him, focused on Brey. "Get undressed."

Brey whispered, not wanting to, knowing its uselessness, but the fear was welling up again, choking him. "Please don't do this."

"Get undressed, an' be nice to my kid. Then you get to go home. Are we clear?"

Brey swallowed. He couldn't speak.

"Are we clear?"

"Y-y-yes," he whispered and started to take his shirt off.

He shook, his fingers numb on the buttons.

"Okay?" Brian asked Josh.

"Yeah, yeah. I'm fine. But you aren't... You aren't stayin', are you?"

"You sure you wanna be alone with 'im."

"Yeah. I'm sure. You'll be right outside. What's 'e gonna do?"

Brey didn't look up. He worked on his buttons, fumbling, gasping at the fingers suddenly yanking his head back. Brian put his face close.

"Behave yourself or I swear to God..."

He didn't finish, and Brey tried to nod against the grip on his hair. Brian released him with a push and strode past Josh, slamming the door behind him.

Brey's breath was a sob. He took off his shirt, his shoes, pulling his T-shirt up, stopping at the feel of a hand gently tugging his arm back down. Josh's fingers came up to his lips. Confused, Brey wadded the hem of his T-shirt in his fists. Then Josh sat down on the side of the bed and pulled Brey down beside him.

His voice was low. "I won't do this. Don't worry."

Cold and hot needles seemed to prickle Brey all over. "Really?"

Josh nodded and looked at Brey with a speculative, curious stare. Josh wanted him, Brey could tell. Could see him think about it—the wanting, not the doing. His eyes never grew soft, but they were friendly. He bounced a little on the bed. It creaked and thumped against the wall. He spoke again, quietly. "I'm not like him."

Brey clenched his jaw, feeling the tears he'd been holding back begin to fill his eyes. "Thank you."

"Don't cry."

He shook his head with a smile. "I won't."

Josh bounced again. "You are pretty, though."

"Thank you."

"My grandpa took my dad to a prostitute—a girl. My dad likes to talk about that. Like him an' his dad were special or somethin'. Or—I dunno exactly—just not like my dad's mom. Better. My mom would freak right now. My parents got divorced when I was five. I hardly knew my dad before Eve. Now I don't have anybody else."

"I get it."

"It's my birthday today. I'm eighteen."

"I thought you already were."

"No. Today."

"Happy birthday."

"Thanks."

"I was your present?"

"Yeah."

"That's fucked up," Brey said.

Josh gave him a wry smile. They made the bed bounce against the wall again. Then Brey began to smile too. He was unsure of himself around Josh, though. Brey could tell that Josh knew things—things

Brey didn't know at almost twice Josh's age. Things about people and motives and excuses. Josh didn't make any excuses. He just liked Brey. Wanted him. Was honest about that.

Brey chewed on his lip, then he surprised himself and said, "I can...you know." His eyes dropped to the crotch of Josh's jeans. "I can do that."

Josh frowned. He looked bewildered. Then he shook his head almost dizzily and took a deep breath. The skin of his neck began to flush then he looked back at Brey, but he didn't look scared or embarrassed. He didn't look easy to scare.

"You don't have to."

"I want to."

In fact, the prospect was arousing him. It had been a long time since he'd willingly sucked anybody's cock, and Josh had a doubtful look on his face, clearly wanting it, but not quite believing Brey did. His face was solid and strong, like Hank's, his eyes without malice or aggression. He had all the control and took none of it. With a father like Brian that was an amazing thing. Brey admired him suddenly.

"Really," he said. "I want to."

Josh looked frozen. He just stared, and Brey reached out cautiously. His fingers brushed over Josh's crotch and Josh shuddered. Then Brey gripped Josh's stiff dick through his jeans and squeezed gently. Josh thrust up. Sliding off the bed, Brey got on his knees between the boy's legs and unbuttoned his pants, carefully unzipping him. Josh watched him, breathing through his mouth, pupils growing larger. Then Brey was tugging on his jeans.

"Lift your hips," he said.

Hooking his fingers in the waistband of Josh's boxers, Brey pulled his jeans and underwear down at the same time. Josh's cock, red and thick, bounced free. Brey drew a breath in and grinned suddenly. "Lovely. Really lovely."

Josh blushed and his hot, velvety flesh slid against Brey's palm. Groaning, Josh bucked up again, thrusting into Brey's fingers.

"Has anybody ever done this for you before?" Brey asked.

The boy groaned again. "No."

Squeezing gently, Brey leaned in, inhaling deeply. "Then I get to be the first."

Starting at the root, Brey licked up Josh's length with the flat of his tongue, lapping greedily at the leaking tip. His own groan joined Josh's. He loved this. He let his lips slide over Josh's cock, tongue swirling and flicking, sucking, bobbing up and down. Josh fell back, lying flat on the bed, fists bunching up the pink and yellow bedspread, muttering, "You... Oh... Wow..."

Brey kept his eyes closed, reveling in the feel of a dick in his mouth again. He was drowning in sensation—the heavy, musky scent, the feel of hot skin on his tongue, the sounds of Josh's low groans, his own starved-sounding ones. Keeping one hand wrapped around the base of Josh's cock while he sucked and bobbed, he worked his own zipper open, wriggling, pushing at his jeans to pull himself free. He jerked his dick.

Arousal swamped him.

Josh's body writhed against his. He could feel every nerve, electric, tingling. Slowing his movements, he almost pulled away, almost let Josh fuck him. His belly fluttered with desire, and he pictured himself with Hank—Hank's cock in his mouth, Hank's cock in his ass.

A groan rose in his throat, and his eyes watered. He sucked and bobbed, wanting Hank. Wanting him to know that Brey was a monogamous type. That he was Hank's, even though Hank pushed him away. This was just Josh's prick in his mouth. Gratitude and friendship. His love, his surrender, that was Hank's — a man who didn't want him. A man too honorable to walk away.

Sliding his lips up, he popped off and buried his nose in Josh's balls, nuzzling the soft, furry skin. The deep, ripe odor invaded his nostrils, and he lapped at the soft skin, stroking himself faster and faster.

"I can't..." Josh's voice grated, tense. "I can't... Fuck!"

Brey rose up again. "Yeah. Close, huh?"

"Yeah... Yeah."

"I'm gonna swallow every fuckin' drop of you," Brey said and went back down on Josh's cock, sucking him into the back of his throat.

The instant he swallowed, Josh screeched and bucked up, shooting ribbons of hot spunk deep into Brey's mouth. "Fuck! Fuck! Oh, shit, shit, shit."

Shudders racked Josh's body, and he pushed at Brey's head. Brey let him go and sat back up, rubbing his chin on Josh's bare leg.

"Okay?" he asked.

There was a delay. He watched Josh blink and swallow, then roll his head until he could see Brey still kneeling there. Josh's smile was bright, mischievous. "Best fucking birthday present *ever*."

Brey laughed, a low chuckle. His own cock still throbbed, and he sat back, leaning on one arm, fingers stroking until Josh sat up and stared at him. "Let me."

"No," said Brey. "You don't have to." His hand flew.

"Stop. I want to. I might never get another chance."

Shocked, Brey clamped down on the root of his cock and squeezed his eyes shut for a moment. Then he breathed and looked back at Josh. He caught a fleeting glimpse of sorrow in Josh's eyes. At Josh's age, Brey had all the sex he wanted — boys his own age or older. He got hit on from the time he was fourteen. It was a merry-go-round that never stopped. He saw a sudden blur of faces, all the people he cared about, at least at the time — people he couldn't even remember now. He never felt used or ashamed, not even with Josh. Everything was changed now, and he realized it was possible that Josh would never fall in love. Likely that the man Brey loved would never love him back.

"You want me sitting or standing?"

"Standing."

Josh slid to his knees on the dusty yellow carpet, resting his hands on Brey's hips. He looked up, nervousness suddenly in his eyes, but he smiled affectionately and Brey stroked his hair and smiled back.

"Just don't bite me an' nothing you do will be wrong."

"You smell fucking amazing," said Josh before leaning in to kiss the tip of Brey's dick.

Then Brey closed his eyes and smiled up at the ceiling. The warm, wet feel of Josh's mouth drew a sudden gasp from him, and he let his head drop back down again and watched Josh's lips slide down his length. Saliva was collecting at the corners of Josh's mouth. He sucked and slurped, and his eyes widened with a look of surprise.

"Yeah, like that," Brey whispered.

The feel of Josh's tongue swirling and flicking at him made his head swim. He wasn't going to last. The kindness and sweetness in the eyes looking up at him made his balls tighten and ache. Pleasure washed through him and washed away a little of the pain. Gentleness and love lapped against the darkness. He was being cleansed in Josh's goodness. Dimly, he felt Josh's fingers digging into his hips. Then Josh was pulling back, sucking just at the tip, and Brey grabbed handfuls of Josh's hair, trying not to thrust.

"Jesus Christ. You're gonna… I'm gonna…"

Josh sucked him all the way back in again, nose pressed against the curly hairs at the base of Brey's cock. Electricity shot down his spine, vision whiting out as he came in mind-numbing spurts into Josh's mouth. His knees buckled, wobbly as water, and he fought to keep on his feet. His fingers dug into Josh's shoulders, and his heart raced, his breath coming in stunned gasps. Then his vision slowly cleared, bringing Josh into focus again. Brey watched him rub his lips with his fingers, a slightly surprised look on his face.

"You swallowed?"

Josh nodded.

"You okay?"

Josh stood up and kissed him, then crouched down again and helped Brey pull his pants up. "You really gave me something special. I won't ever forget this."

Brey's throat tightened and his eyes stung. He waited until Josh had his own pants back on, then pulled him against him, kissing him again, slowly this time, opening his mouth to Josh's tongue, sliding his own in, teeth clicking, lips swollen and sore by the time he pulled away.

"You could have hurt me," Brey whispered.

Josh shook his head. "That isn't me."

Brey stared, smiled a slow smile. He was ashamed. He picked up his shirt. Josh zipped up his jeans.

He'd never be like Josh. He didn't just fumble through life. He didn't even look at it. He thought of all the smiles Patric gave him that he never really saw. Patric could see that Brey wasn't a real person, but Brey couldn't.

He picked up his bag.

"Thanks, Josh."

Josh gave him a peck on the cheek. "Like I said. Best birthday present ever." His eyes were filled with affection, and Brey gave into it.

Gratefully.

Josh liked him. That counted. Maybe he counted.

"See you?"

"Yeah. We're friends," said Josh.

Only cool sun met him outside, and he walked away without looking back.

After a while the sky grew almost colorless and cold gray shadows covered sidewalks and open spaces. Almost home again, Brey shifted his bag on his shoulder and tugged the strap from his neck where it was biting into his skin. His fingers brushed his slave collar, and he dropped his hand back down to his side as he came up on the back of the library. The sun slanted across the corner of the sidewalk, thin and watery. It gave him an uneasy feeling that he couldn't place. Familiarity. An image from a distant memory — or nothing. That's what Jack would tell him later. The mind plays tricks. He lived his whole life in the same house. His first bike was a birthday present, and he learned to ride it on a long circular driveway. He never rode on suburban sidewalks. No reason to picture a boy like himself yanking his bike into low jumps off the curb on a summer twilight.

His fingers slid up to his collar again, and he walked past the library, half-trotting down a shady sidewalk, the dappled park on the other side of the street.

Then he saw it again. A boy on a bike on a quiet, suburban street. Neighbors who knew each other. Children who played together, but that wasn't his neighborhood. Josh's maybe.

His shoe hit a curb, and he tripped over it, his bag slipping off his arm. Catching the strap in the crook of his elbow, he swung the bag back up. Then, bizarrely, his shoulder hit the wall of a building, and he went sideways off the curb again. Air stuck in his lungs. He tried to breathe in and couldn't. *No! Fuck!* This was stupid. A fucking panic attack? *Why?* Josh didn't scare him. He wasn't afraid. Nothing bad happened. He wasn't hurt. Wasn't forced. He participated. He made the choice. He got his own pleasure. But his ears rang, and the world swam around him—gray pavement, buildings. *Please!* His heart was slamming inside his chest. His fingers locked in his collar. His knees went loose.

Hands grabbed him under the arms, pulled him up. He thrashed. "No!"

Yanking himself free, he ran. He was zigzagging. On the curb. Off. On. "Wait!" But he didn't want to wait. He wanted to get home. He wanted his mother and father. He wanted Hank.

"Wait! Wait!"

Hands again. People slowing him.

"Lemme go!" Shame flooded him. This wasn't who he was. Nobody would recognize him now. He could be shattered by an eighteen-year-old boy on his birthday. "God," he moaned.

Then he heard a voice he knew. Jack's voice. Close to his ear. An arm went around him, shook him gently.

"C'mon now. Settle down." The shaking got stronger, rocking him. "You've been through this before. You can do this. Nothing new."

"I... I can't... I can't breathe."

"You can breathe. You aren't dying. Just feels like it. You're gonna be okay." They kept walking, closer and closer to home. "Gonna get you inside. Settle you down. Get you a nice, strong drink."

He made a noise of assent. "Yeah... Yeah."

His hair stuck to him. His legs were jelly, but his breathing began to slow. The gray at the edges of his vision began to fade. He didn't want to cry. He didn't want to be who he had become. He knew he looked pitiful to Hank. Weak. A burden.

"Your face is bruised."

Caution entered his thoughts. He wheezed in a couple of shallow breaths. Gasped. "I fell."

"Yeah?"

"Tried... Tried to catch..." He patted at his bag with his camera inside. "Couldn't put my hands out."

He couldn't see Jack's expression. Cooler air was coming through an open door, making him shiver.

"Next time save your face."

A sound warbled out of him that might have been a laugh. He wanted to laugh. Missed the old Brey who could laugh at anything. Celebrate anything. Enjoy every day. That was a man he liked. Not Patric's Brey, though. That was a scared man. Mean. At least he wasn't mean anymore, but he didn't like the man shaking under Jack's arm either. And he believed he was getting stronger again. It couldn't be Josh. Brian maybe. He had the face of a man who could hurt him and not think twice. Wouldn't worry about somebody who didn't really matter anymore.

He heaved a sigh, air finally rushing into his lungs.

"C'mere," said Jack, pushing him down onto one of the cots in the clinic. "Be right back." His hat tipped off the back of the head, and he pushed it away and covered his face with his arms. "C'mon. Sit up an' lean back."

Pillows sank underneath him, and a cool, damp towel covered his head.

"Oh. That's nice," he muttered.

Jack began to pat his face with another towel, smoothing it over his forehead, rubbing his neck.

"Your skin's hot."

"I wore my hat."

"You haven't had a panic attack in a while."

"I don't know what caused it," he said again quickly, opening his eyes. Jack stared at him speculatively, put the cloth in his hand and sat back in his chair. "I was just walking," said Brey. "Then I pictured a boy on a bike, taking jumps off the curb, not exactly my experience. I have no idea where it came from."

"The mind can play tricks. Might not have been that anyway. Your panic attacks probably have a very specific cause, Brey. You were hurt. We really weren't made to be hurt. We were made to take care of each other."

Brey's gaze settled on Jack's. The sentiment surprised him. Jack had always seemed imperturbable, grudgingly adjusted to his new world.

"I don't like it here," said Brey, fingers rubbing the smooth metal segments of his collar. "This isn't right."

"Nope," Jack agreed. "It's not. Hang tight a minute. I'll get you that drink I promised."

Brey took the towel off his head and laid it on his chest. His heart was still pounding but beginning to slow. Closing his eyes, he took a deep breath, let the vision of the sunny sidewalk—the birthday bike—

float through his consciousness. When he opened his eyes again, Jack was back, and he looked at the bottle in his hand and said, "Fuck me."

Jack grinned. "Hank's private stock. I pilfer."

"Why am I only drinking moonshine?"

"Cuz Hank's greedy."

Jack gave Brey a glass and poured a generous amount of Jack Daniel's into it. Then he poured his own glass and tapped it against the edge of Brey's.

"To better days."

"No shit," said Brey, downing half his glass in a single swallow. It burned his throat and reddened his face, but it made him happy, and he knew Jack's grin was mirrored in his.

Chapter Thirteen

Hank yawned at the wall across from him. He was lying on his side, morning light stretching across the plaster.

Brey muttered, "Oh fuck," and Hank rolled over.

Brey was squinting, a look of distress on his face. His bleary eyes moved to the window, then he whispered, "Shit," and clamped an arm over his face.

"Teach you," said Hank. "That was my bourbon you stole."

"Jack stole it. Pilfered it."

"Pilfered? You should know that Jack is notoriously euphemistic about his own shortcomings."

"Well, I'm innocent."

"Not even on the day you were born."

Brey peeked up at him from under his arm. "That was mean."

Hank got up, heading into the bathroom. "You're tough."

He heard Brey sigh. A heavy, affected sigh, but Hank knew Brey was grateful that he wasn't talking about the panic attack. Talking only seemed to make him worse. Ignoring it brought on random, happy smiles, that strange look in his eyes—a look that unnerved Hank but in a good way. He woke up the other morning to Brey wrapped around him, a dreamy glow in his sleepy eyes before he yawned groggily and let his arms and legs fall away. His fingers lingered, trailing across Hank's skin.

"Sorry," he murmured.

Hank's skin felt scored in fire.

Now it tingled under the spray of the shower. He soaped up, smelling the scent that Brey sweated out in his sleep. His fingers slipped to his cock, stroking. He bit his lip. Imagined the feel of Brey's tongue and suddenly flipped the water temperature to cold. With a gasp, he finished washing and rinsed off.

Out in the hall, he smelled chico and followed the aroma into the kitchen. Brey was up, sipping a cup, looking less squinty-eyed at him now. By the time Brey was showered and dressed, Hank had the oatmeal ready. Other days Hank made the chico, and Brey made the oatmeal. Synchronized. It made Hank sigh.

"You going out today?" he asked.

"No." Brey was quick to answer. Hank looked up at him. He didn't know why he was bothered. But Brey didn't look at him, twirled a spoon in his oatmeal. "Will you come have lunch with me?"

"I can't," Hank said. "I'm going up to Younger's."

"Oh."

Hank saw the bruise then. It was barely more than a shadow. Jack didn't think Brey fell. *No abrasions,* he said. The things Brey hid guarded his sense of vulnerability. He lived without any real power but as though he had it. Hank knew Brey didn't want reminders of all the dangers around him. He wanted his old life. All his old pleasures. His family. His freedom. His prison now was in pretending he was free. But Hank understood that. He understood pretending, but he wouldn't pretend that Brey wasn't really in danger. He'd been hit. Scared enough to bring on another panic attack. Upset enough to drink it away. Resilient enough to pretend it never happened. He didn't want to be where he wasn't wanted. Brey wanted happiness. But the power of that desire was like a fault line through his well-being. Everything rode on it.

"Why don't you come with me? You can take pictures."

Brey's eyes flashed eagerly, then dimmed a little. His fingers went to his collar. "What about this?"

"That doesn't matter."

Brey's eagerness didn't spring back, though, surprising Hank. "You don't *have* to come with me."

"No. I want to."

Hank looked into his eyes. Honest enough. Brey's fingers still brushed his collar. Of course he dreamed of escape—that dreamy look. *Just let him go.* Hank had thought of that. Remembered the pictures he saw of Brey before Patric's death. That impossible happiness. Uncontainable. Fervent.

Like a prayer. Like a hallelujah.

"C'mon. We'll stop an' let Issa know."

With a quick nod, Brey disappeared, came back with his coat on, backpack slung over his shoulder, hat crushed under his arm. "Okay. I'm ready."

Smiling again, he beat Hank out of the door. Hank didn't hurry. He watched Brey walk ahead of him, his ass swinging slightly in his low-slung pants.

Hank smiled in the cold sun.

* * * *

Brey remembered the garage and everything that had happened in it. He even remembered Hank there, not that he'd known him, just that there was somebody there who'd let him go and taken him away. All the rest was foggy, a vague memory of water and his name — *"Aubrey!"* — being called out in a way he hadn't heard in a long time. He couldn't recall the trip away from the garage or where that garage was.

As they rode, the cold of the air intensified, and Brey squinted into pale brown distances, at the hills and rising pine-covered mountains.

He shivered, then Hank's voice came to him. "We're taking a longer route than I usually go. Prettier."

Brey's horse, Walden, rolled under him, and he shifted uncomfortably. He used to ride, but, of course, he had the best saddles in those days. Now his ass hurt and not in a good way either.

"Picture pretty?" he asked.

"Just scenic. If you like that for your pictures..."

There was something indulgent in the way that sounded. It irritated Brey a little.

"Leaves," he said.

Hank's head cocked to the side, sliding a curious glance over to him. "Leaves?"

"Yeah. Patric painted pictures of leaves. I told you that, didn't I? I could see him being famous for that. Just the way it hit your eye... Abstract, but obviously leaves. One leaf was like a world, a second in time just frozen there." Brey closed his eyes against the sun and smiled. "I liked that, though. The fantasy of just hanging out forever in one perfect moment."

"An' miss all the others?"

"You know, Hank, you have absolutely no sense of romance."

Hank didn't reply right away, just reached out to snag the hat Brey was carrying and plunk it on his head. "Nope," he said. "I'm practical. Sun's fierce."

Hank rode up ahead then, and Brey's stomach rolled at that slightly protective gesture. *God, you're easy.* He couldn't tell if Hank liked that about him or not. Brey knew he was obedient by nature. His rebelliousness all those years ago wasn't defiance. He was just full of energy. Until he was taken away, his father still grounded him. He only defied Patric and only because Patric let him. But this, the way he gave in now wasn't the same as before. It was fearful, and he didn't like it. He didn't think it was him, but maybe the old him was lost like so many other people were.

He was quiet as they rode, not thinking of hills or leaves. Thinking of garages instead, of places where people hurt him. He glanced at Hank, looking comfortable in just his jeans and sweatshirt. He envied him his calm, his stoicism, his principles and certitude. He wondered if he could sneak in under his arm and absorb it like body heat—a big strong arm, round with muscle. He inhaled, imagining spice, something woodsy. Hank's head swiveled back, a smile curving his lips. His hair was getting longer, ruffled in the breeze. A day's worth of scruff darkened his jaw.

Brey's thoughts of Hank drifted lazily to other lovers, floating from dimples to lust-filled eyes, blue, brown, freckled skin or sun-kissed, broad shoulders, slim waists, the taste of cigarettes, mints, coffee, strong hands, safe, warm, gentle, back to Hank's jaw. A faint sensation of roughness against his lips startled him. The realness of it. Sinking back into his fantasy, he ran his lips across that jaw, pecked small quick kisses, flicked the tip of his tongue at the corner of firm lips, licking and nipping gently.

He suddenly squirmed, cock stiffening, rocked in the saddle and bit back a moan. *Stupid idiot.*

Taking a deep breath, Brey looked away from Hank, smelling dust and pine.

They were higher in the hills now, moving up into the mountains, the bright sun turning into a pale disk, the air crisp and cool. The smell of sap was sharp and sweet, the sky deep and blue. Brey thought about the quiet now, no planes, just space and color, the way it was a long time ago. He breathed in the pine-scented air as they rode into the shade.

Hank glanced back. "I want you to stick pretty close to me. Don't go off too far to take your pictures."

Brey swallowed his irritation. It wasn't really Hank that irritated him. It was the idea that he needed protection — couldn't take care of himself, that he was helpless. He wasn't. He wanted Hank's protection for other reasons. Wanted his care, just not in the way he was giving it. He wanted his possessiveness, his absorption — his heart.

He made his voice sound light. "I'll try an' manage."

Hank looked back again, but the shade shrouded his expression, and Brey couldn't read his thoughts. Hank didn't say anything in response, though.

The cool air here became cold, the sweetness a damp mustiness. The pines thickened then began to thin. Brey could feel Hank's watchfulness and felt the hairs on the back of his neck prickle. There were people nearby, hiding, observing. With a press of his heels, Brey urged Walden forward, keeping close behind Hank. Then the path leveled out and buildings appeared. Open space. The stumps of felled trees. The place was bigger than Brey imagined.

Hank looked back again.

"This was a resort for hunters an' fishermen. The reservoir's on the other side."

They passed smaller, cabin-like buildings and skirted a split rail fence that circled a roundabout of asphalt. A road led through the center of the resort, disappearing in the distance. At one of the cabins, two men sat on the front porch, watching them without expression. Closer to the center of the resort, laughter bellowed out of one of the buildings.

"How many people live here?"

"About thirty, plus about five slaves for cleaning and handiwork. They survive by hunting and renting the other slaves to Waterfall for a share of the crops."

Hank was sliding off Trixie in front of another larger building, wrapping the reins around the porch railing.

"This is the lodge," he said. "General gathering area, meeting hall, that kind of thing. That building," he added and pointed to the one where the laughter still came rolling out, "is the canteen." He pointed again. "General store, hardware, barber shop, doctor's office. Jack comes up about once a month."

Then he started up the steps of the lodge, and Brey followed him. Any inclination he had to explore died at the sound of that laughter. It crept under his skin — no single laugh, none separate from another, none recognizable, just a mob-like roar. He shivered but inside pushed the unease away and pulled his camera out of his backpack.

He was standing in a great room, rough-hewn wood walls, polished wood floor covered in Navajo-style rugs, a fireplace set in a wall of river rock, leather couches and chairs throughout, a long wooden table opposite the fireplace where several men sat. They nodded at Hank, but Brey felt their eyes sliding over, settling on him. He couldn't help it. His fingers rose, curled inside his collar. A flush of heat told him that his blood was rising. He looked away, looked at the paintings on the walls — pine-covered mountains, rivers, a still, inky black lake, books piled on top of coffee tables in front of the couches. He went over to look.

A man's voice followed him, talking to Hank. A low voice, hardly above a whisper, but it carried. It had weight. Brey knew people followed it.

"Heard about that," the man said. "You didn't mention it. Not really like you, buyin' a slave."

"We live in a gray world, don't we?"

The man laughed softly. "We always did, Hank."

Brey chafed at the familiarity in his voice, the fact that the man knew Hank, could call him on his morals.

He shot him looks out of the corner of his eye.

Longish hair, dirty blond. Gray-blue eyes. Things hidden inside. A little younger than Hank, a little older than Brey. With a sudden flick of his gaze, the man met one of Brey's surreptitious looks and smiled in mockery.

Brey made himself hold back. The look wasn't actually unkind, just knowing.

Hank was sitting at a table now. There were plans of some sort laid out on the surface of the table. The man — Brey knew he must be Younger — looked at the other men at the table with a long, thoughtful stare then said, "You wanna lay out your ideas?"

Hank looked startled, angry.

"Ideas? As opposed to the ones we agreed to last time?"

"I'm still in agreement," said Younger.

One of the other men almost bristled. "We are too. You're the one pushin' contracts for people who are fuckin' slaves." The man's eyes sidled to Brey in open offense. "That's not part of this."

Hank shook his head. "We offer contracts. That's the deal."

"You can't decide that for the rest of us."

"I didn't," said Hank. "You did. We agreed."

"We didn't sign on it."

"The project won't go forward without contracts of release, Pete. I can guarantee the votes on that, unless you want to take the project on yourselves."

"We can do that."

"No worries then. You remember, though, the dam and aqueduct belong to Waterfall."

"The reservoir's ours."

"That's right," said Hank.

"Which you can just drain," added one of the other men, giving Hank a watchful stare.

Hank smiled. "You know better than that, Bill. We don't have to."

"Yeah, yeah," said the man with a roll of his eyes. "Global warming, right?"

"You doubt it? Did you forget your grade school science on evaporation? You got an easy A on that one, didn't you?"

"That's what rain's for."

"You sound like Brian."

Younger was smiling mildly, head tipped sideways, resting on his fingertips, elbow on the table. "Why don't you boys go talk to the others," he advised. "We need a decision on this."

The others rose, Pete spinning away angrily, pushing his chair back. His gaze swept over Brey again, burning with sudden malice.

"Outta my way, pretty boy."

Brey wasn't anywhere near him, but he backed up anyway. Then he met Hank's gaze, smiled and nodded when Hank mouthed, "Okay?"

He lifted his camera and tipped his head to the door. Hank looked at Younger.

"Okay if Brey takes some pictures?"

"Matters not to me," said Younger, with that same mocking smile.

Brey went outside. The air was dusk-like under the pines. It smelled good up here. The slight damp was like a soft caress. He could almost like this place — spare and simple. A quiet life... Not primitive. Not atavistic. Not the way the laughter in the canteen made it sound. Not cold. Not cruel. Not heartless. A place he'd go with his family to swim in a dark mountain lake where the stars were ablaze at night.

These people didn't want lights or electricity. He knew that. Felt it. They wanted slaves, the thrill of bending a neck. Wanted to cause fear and force obedience.

Brey adjusted the settings on his camera and snapped a picture of the canteen with its wide-open door. Under the cold, sweet scent of the air was the smell of onions and herbs and meat. The sky was blue. Out from under the pines, the sun was still shining. He imagined the sounds of children playing but didn't hear that, just another burst of laughter.

Then he saw her.

A woman, hurrying away from the canteen. She was barefoot, wearing a peasant blouse and a long skirt. Her hair was long and loose. He knew without seeing it that she wove thin braids throughout her hair. She disappeared into a small building across the bare lot beside the canteen. The smell of smoke and meat intensified when she opened the door—a smoke house. She swung away again, and he saw the basket she was carrying then he was running across the road to the side of the canteen.

"Molly!"

Silence greeted him. Nobody there. He crept slowly under a row of dark windows. A back door was open. He jumped quietly up the steps and went inside.

Gray, quiet light drifted through the kitchen. The room was long and white with counters and cupboards on three sides of the room. A pot was bubbling on a big industrial-sized stove. Brey went over curiously. *Propane?* There was meat on the counter. Smoked. It smelled good, and his mouth watered. Voices swelled suddenly, settled again into laughter.

A door directly across from him opened onto a hallway. He inched tentatively across the room then there was a shadow on the wall, and she appeared. In the seconds it took for the plates she was carrying to drop and shatter on the floor, all of his memories of her flashed through his mind. The kitchen he grew up with, black and white tiled floor, all light and airy space. Sitting at the table with the fruit and tomato juice cocktail she used to make him. Sweet and vitamin rich to soothe his hangovers. Her quiet laughter.

"You sure you shouldn't be living on a commune somewhere?" he'd asked her once. "Meditating? Living in spiritual communion with nature?"

"Food is spiritual." She'd rub his throbbing temples sometimes, letting him rest his head back against her stomach. "You should give a commune a try. You might find your bliss."

He'd cranked open achy eyes. "Sex is my bliss."

"Slut," she'd said. Sweetly. Conversationally. She had worked for his family for almost a year before he'd gone away.

Off work, she'd worn her hair loose with tiny braids. Working, her hair had been wound up in a knot on top of her head. She'd been close to his age but seemed years older. He'd looked up to her. She'd had a core of certainty he admired, doubted he'd ever have. She'd been almost frivolously happy in the way that he'd been, but bravely, fully, without that strange desperation he'd known was in him, that fear that there just wasn't enough, or that he wasn't enough.

The face that stared at him in shock now was older, tougher, and strong—a survivor's face. The plates crashed and shattered, and he saw her eyes light on his collar.

"Run," she said.

But he didn't. Froze instead, staring at her—a face too close to his family. Confusion swamped him. The strange confluence of Hank and Molly here in this place was a wonder he couldn't quite grasp. *Could hearts gravitate?* He felt his own swell, and he surged over to her, almost stumbling.

"Molly."

She wasn't wearing a collar, but her eyes darted sideways in panic. "Run, Brey."

Then she stooped, collecting the shards of crockery, looking down the hall. "I just dropped these," she said to somebody in the hallway.

But Brey was standing too close now, his shadow visible. A man with red hair and a smashed nose came forward, others behind him, peering in curiously. Pete and Bill were there now too. Molly rose.

"You okay, hon?"

"I'm fine, Frank."

"Who's that?" A voice in the hallway.

"Don't know," said Frank.

"Hank's," said Pete.

"Yeah." A grimace of distaste appeared on Bill's face. "Fuckin' nerve bitchin' at us about slaves." He pushed into the doorway. "Step back, Molly."

"You step back. I have to clean this up. You too, Frank."

The man named Frank scowled at her. "I'm not goin' anywhere. I don't know this guy."

The room pulled in. It was just Brey in a circle, and he couldn't run. He felt hot. The walls were close, no space between him and the others. Pete pushed by Frank and Molly, and Molly pushed by Pete and said, "I think I can get somebody a glass of water without any help from you, Pete."

Frank pulled Molly back, thick fingers wrapped around her elbow.

Pete's head cocked, almost pleasantly. "That right? You thirsty, boy?"

"I might be. What the fuck do you care?"

"Whoo. Listen to him. Smart mouth."

"Hank spoils 'im." The others pushed in and backed up behind Pete.

Pete was grinning. "That right, pretty boy?"

"Ow!"

Molly darted up, Frank rubbing at his side. Pete flung out an arm, almost knocking her back. She pushed him away. "You fucker."

"You got a mouth on you, woman."

Frank was pulling on her again. "C'mon, honey."

She was looking at Pete. She was electric. Brey's father used to call her a spitfire. He almost smiled.

"You leave Brey alone, Pete."

Frank scowled over her head. "Brey?"

Pete laughed. "You like this guy, sweetheart? No worries, Molly. We're gonna like 'im too." He looked back at Brey. "We're gonna like 'im a lot."

Brey couldn't see Molly anymore. He could only see Pete, a blur of faces, the back door, smudged gray in the shadows. Shadows circled his vision. Not real shadows. Just him, he guessed, blanking everything out. A gray room, growing lighter, blocking out the laughing faces.

He could smell the violence. It mixed up with the smell of meat and the soup on the stove, and his stomach rolled. He almost closed his eyes, just for a moment to catch his breath, but he knew what he'd see in the quick dark—bushes and a clear blue stream, the dirty garage, the cracked cement floor, cum-spattered and stained with oil.

Then he heard that laugh—thin and reedy—and the air left his lungs. Whirling, he ran for the door, jerking free of Pete's snatching fingers. Outside, he bolted halfway down the stairs before he saw men down there too, already coming up to block him in.

Dizzily, he ran back inside and crammed himself into a corner the counters made behind the butcher block. Pete approached on one side of the butcher block, Bill the other.

Molly yelled again, "You fuckers," and Pete looked at Frank.

"You might wanna take Molly home, Frank. These guys are gonna get riled up in a minute. No countin' on their control."

Then Brey heard a wheeze, realized distantly it was him. The room zoomed out, lost detail in the rim of shadow. He felt a strange absence of fear. Absence of everything really. He was going to die—one way or the other—and he almost didn't care anymore. The men advanced, dark, dim shapes.

He almost didn't care.

* * * *

Getting up, Hank looked outside. Behind him, Younger didn't move. He was facing away and when he spoke, it was as if he wasn't really talking to Hank. "I'd like to think people change... I'd like a lot of things. A hot shower. A good sport's bar."

Hank smiled, but he was only half listening, eyes skating up and down the street. No Brey.

"You know where the showers are. You have the Water Spout." A place Hank never went to. But it was a bar. It had electricity. A kitchen. Rooms upstairs.

"And a clientele that reminds me people never change."

Hank was beginning to frown now. Worried. Nothing to worry about. "Are you trying to tell me something?" he asked.

"Just another cliché. History always repeats itself."

"Meaning we should prepare?"

"I never let a Boy Scout get one up on me."

Hank barked out a laugh. "That leaves me out. I always had my hands too full to worry about being a Boy Scout."

"Preparation's not a bad thing."

"Neither is the canal."

"That's a necessary thing. I'm with you on that."

"I'm not with you on the slave issue."

"I'm not with you or against you on that. I can go either way. You might have to back down on the contracts, though."

"I can't."

"Here's another cliché for you, Hank. Nothing's certain even if nothing changes."

"Why the riddles?"

"Clichés."

It was at that moment that Hank saw the woman. He'd seen her before. Frank's wife. No children. Hardly any women and mostly barren. Maybe humans would just die out soon. The biggest cliché of all.

Frank and another man were leading her across the road. She jerked loose and spun back around toward the canteen. The men darted in front of her, pushing her back. She shoved Frank in the chest, and Hank could hear her shout, "You heartless fucker!"

They grabbed her again and dragged her off.

Yanking open the door, Hank ran outside. He could hear Younger rising behind him, but he didn't slow. He dashed across the dusty road and barreled inside the canteen. The main room was empty, but there was laughter and the sound of scuffling in back.

"Yeah, baby, I like 'um feisty."

Somebody hooted. "You ain't scared, are ya? Get 'im."

"Shut up."

The hall was crowded. Hank yanked at a shoulder that just yanked back. He grabbed at his revolver, half pulling it out of his holster before he let it go again, gritting his teeth angrily. *Fuck!* They'd probably kill Brey at the first shot. Spinning away, he ran back outside. Younger was already rounding the back corner of the building. He waved at hand at Hank.

"C'mon. Hurry up."

There were other men on the back porch, but not as many as inside. Younger waded through them easily, Hank following.

After he'd stepped inside and his eyes adjusted to the dim light, Hank stared in shock. The men in the kitchen were keeping their distance from Brey in his corner. But they were joking, jostling each other.

"C'mon, Pete. You're scared a that?"

Bill had his hands up, palms out. Pete was red-faced, sweaty. "Fuck you."

A man in back let out a high-pitched laugh, and Hank saw Brey cringe and push deeper into his corner.

"You get 'im, an' we'll help paddle that pretty ass."

Pete inched closer, face split in a grin. "You like that idea, boy?"

Hank edged in but not too far. Close enough to the back door that nobody inside could get behind him. Pete took another step, everybody else backing up now, mainly because Brey was clutching a large butcher knife in his hands, holding it out in front of him. But his eyes were dazed, unfocused.

Not noticing Hank yet, Pete looked back at his companions. "Get me a blanket an' some leather gloves."

"Cut right through 'um."

"I got a plan."

"I don't think so," said Hank.

His voice didn't register with Brey, but Pete glared at him. "You got a mouthy slave, Hank. We put a stop to that real quick up here."

"That's a shame," said Hank. "I like mouthy slaves."

Pete flipped an arm up, and Brey flinched, but Pete was only poking a finger in the air, swinging his arm around the room in a flourish. "Up here, we call the shots. An' your damn slave's got a lesson comin' to 'im."

The blood in Hank's head made it feel like it was going to explode. His fingers were aching because he refused to clench them. His vision was pushing through a haze of rage. He wanted to hurt Pete, to pound and smash him through the floorboards and beyond, but he couldn't. He couldn't break his ties to Younger's group.

"Settle down, Pete. Brey isn't the type to cause trouble."

"That little punk swore at me. Mouthed off. I have rights, Hank."

"Not to Brey."

"You let 'im loose. You got 'im in trouble."

"I'll take care of it."

"I want to. I have that right, an' you know it."

"You have a right to go to the Council. You can complain about your treatment at an official meeting. I have no problem with testifying to the fact that twenty of you were tormenting my slave. You are not abiding by the law right now, Pete, an' I will be fucking honest about that. *Brey!*"

His shout startled even Pete, but Brey just gave a small jerk, unfocused gaze still fixed on a spot on the floor.

"Brey. Look at me. Now."

With a shudder, Brey seemed to come to himself. His eyes rose slowly. His lips moved. Hank thought he saw his name on them, and something swelled inside his chest. Something painful, terrifying, humbling.

"Come over here."

Pete glared at Brey's shuffling step. "You better not let him get away with this."

"With what?"

"With that!"

He pointed at Brey's knife, and Brey's eyes dropped down to it and widened in visible shock. Then a look of horror followed and he let out a low sound, something like a moan, and flung the knife away. It almost hit Pete, and Brey froze. Then the knife bounced and skittered, and Pete lunged.

Crack!

A gun went off. Hank's. Pete dropped to a crouch on the floor, staring at Hank in disbelief. Plaster dust drifted.

"Jesus Christ."

Hank was pointing the gun at him now. "You touch my slave, an' I will blow your kneecaps off."

Pete swallowed. "You can't do this, Hank."

"I told you I'd take care of it."

"You're gonna punish him?"

"I said I would. Now come here, Brey."

Brey had his hands over his ears. Moving slowly, he let them drop, then his eyes drifted to the knife with the same sick fascination rubberneckers gave traffic accidents. As he came closer, Younger reached out past Hank, took Brey's elbow and pulled him outside, past the men still congregated there. Hank followed, Pete close behind.

"I'm keepin' you to your word."

"You just keep away from Brey. An' don't insult me with reminders."

Younger was already leading Brey back across the road. Shadows were drifting out of the pines. Brey leaned away from Younger, and Younger let him go, looking back at Hank.

"You'd better stay tonight," he said quietly.

Hank nodded, knowing it wasn't a good idea to be out in the dark now. He heard the footsteps of men following him. In the lodge, he took Brey's arm and led him across the room. Brey looked woozy, desperately tired. The blood was still hot in Hank's head, even though he was cold everywhere else. He resisted the shivers he felt under his skin.

"I want you to kneel in the corner," he said quietly.

Brey looked confused, stared, frowning, trying to understand. He licked his lips. "What?"

"We can't go home right now," he said. "We have to wait."

"Okay," Brey said.

"I have to do this, Brey."

Brey was silent for a moment. He was struggling to grasp this. Then his confusion faded. "I don't... I don't want to."

"I know."

Brey was about to beg. Hank could see that and his heart broke. Those wondrous eyes looked at him, but they weren't looking for help anymore. The lids lowered slowly, and he sank wordlessly into the corner.

"That's all?" said Pete.

"Shut the fuck up," said Younger.

* * * *

They took a room upstairs — bare, dusty and quiet. Brey sat on the window seat, leaning up against the pane of cold, dark glass. Trees crowded close, blocking out the sky, but there was a gleam in the distance that made him picture the reservoir. A feeling of wistfulness almost made him dizzy. He imagined standing in the dark by starlit water, watching the shine and glitter of windswept waves. He inhaled, smelling loam and damp and pine and breathed out a cloud against the glass. His eyes closed, and he wished fervently that he could open them underwater and sink to someplace peaceful and painless.

"Who was she? That woman?"

Or swim. Swim strong and fast, climb out running. He'd run in the right direction with his heart pounding but no footsteps behind him — unless...

Unless he didn't have to be alone.

"Molly was our cook. I couldn't talk to her, though."

"I shouldn't have brought you."

"I'm sorry for the trouble." But he wasn't sorry. His voice was bitter, sarcastic — at least to him.

Hank's voice was soft, as if he heard something else from Brey. "I didn't think. My fault."

"You could solve your problems, you know? Just fucking let me go."

Hank didn't look at him. They had a candle, but he wouldn't be able to see the calculation in Hank's eyes anyway, which was a good thing because that calculation crushed him. Brey wasn't exactly a pawn, but he knew his freedom stood in Hank's way. In the way of whatever he was doing with Younger.

"I can't."

"You won't. I'm not the idiot you think I am. I see —"

"I don't think that."

"The way things are. I just don't have great plans. I never did. Everything's black an' white to you, Hank. Right or wrong. I never looked at that. I didn't care. I don't care. I want to be happy. I want my family. You look at the big picture. You save the world. I don't give a fuck about it anymore."

"I can't save anybody's world, Brey."

Now the wistfulness was Hank's, and he sounded almost jealous of Brey. But Brey had nothing about him to merit jealousy, and he laughed, a laugh he couldn't control. It spread out a gossamer snowflake of condensation on the glass, so beautiful. His laugh faltered, and he choked on the silence.

"Brey…"

He didn't respond, didn't look over.

"I'd never hurt you."

"But you did," he whispered.

He heard Hank sigh, clothes rustle as he lay down on a bedroll in the near dark. Candlelight warped the wood walls.

"Get some sleep."

"In a minute."

He stayed where he was, closing his eyes on the darkness outside.

* * * *

The sun glowed on the horizon, spread out across the flat land in a wave of gold. Coming out of the pines, Brey stopped to watch. It was like a living thing hastening across the landscape, chasing after the fleeing dark. The sight brought goose bumps to his skin, and he shivered. It was cold, though, too, the light hard and clear.

Hank swiveled, looking back.

"You okay?"

Brey made Walden move up again, but he didn't answer. It felt like too much effort. The spark of life the sun brought puffed out in the cold and fatigue. He was worn out and now on his horse's rolling back, he dozed. His fatigue grew, as soft and heavy as a warm blanket, drawing him under. The cold shrank back. He dreamed he was pulling weeds in Molly's herb garden at home. The house was empty, dead leaves rattling across the floors in the breezes through the open doors. The pool was empty and cracked, but Molly's garden was lush and fragrant. He knelt in the cool soil, smelling the sweet earth, looking up in surprise as a shadow spread over him, and Hank was there, reaching for him.

"Brey..."

He startled, pulling away from the hand Hank put out to steady him.

"Almost home."

He saw the first buildings and nodded, yawning. The look of relief on Hank's face worried him. He wasn't sure why Hank wanted to get back so badly. Maybe Waterfall was home now, an anchor, except he didn't think that was it. Didn't think it was Fuck — A — Friend Ken either. Thought it might be about him. Brey knew Hank didn't want him the way Brey wanted him to, and the poetic justice of that made him hurt inside. This was Patric's pain inside him. He believed Hank wanted him only because he was a part of Hank's old life — a part he could keep at a distance, but also a part he could wrap up in good intentions. Brey wasn't exactly without morals, but he told the truth. He didn't look at the big picture. He wanted Hank, and he was never going to have him. He couldn't measure up to Hank's duty. He was the memory of another time and a burden already. He felt his life flowing away like the racing sun. The sun that made the shadow of Hank loom over him, smiling at him maybe, until his dream Hank disappeared in the cold light.

It was time to go, and it didn't really matter anymore the way that he went.

Chapter Fourteen

Brey remembered his first day in Waterfall when he stood at the open window of Hank's bedroom and played with the idea of jumping off the terrace. He didn't think he could — afraid of heights. And he'd still been half hopeful then that he could get away somehow. He wasn't hopeful anymore. He wasn't going to get away. He wasn't strong enough. The man who ran out of his prison cell three years ago was braver. He could do things — get a car, a bike, get home, act on his resolve. He liked that man a little. He liked the man he had been before Patric especially. That man was likeable, happy, generous and eager to please.

Eager to be pleased too. Eager to be loved.

Now he was broken.

He knew it was still in him — wanting to make people happy — Hank, Issa, Jack, but it felt like a weight now, a physical thing like a cannonball inside him or a solid, impenetrable shell around the better parts of him that he wasn't strong enough to carry or crack anymore. He could only detect it in despair, the evidence of everything he'd lost and would never have again now, and he couldn't live that way.

But he couldn't jump either. An oily tendril of fear slithered through him at the thought.

He had a list—jump, cut his wrists, eat or drink poison, hang, put a gun in his mouth.

He examined each option, imagined the process, tried to guess his emotional response to each one. He didn't want to be afraid or hurt.

Considering all this gave him something to do, occupied him. He didn't think he looked depressed. He made sure to talk and smile.

Walking with Hank to the library one day, he slowed a little, falling back to look up at the roof of their building. *Their* building. That hurt. A stab of grief right in the heart. There was no *their*. He was alone. His eyes blurred on the ledge above him. *Fuck. Get a grip.* He blinked furiously. He pictured himself on the ledge. He wouldn't even lose consciousness. There wouldn't be enough time. He could dive head first, but, *fuck, that's too damn scary.* He saw the pavement racing up, scrunched his eyes shut.

"What are you doing?"

"Got somethin' in my eye."

He caught up to Hank. He could just let himself fall. Lean out. No resistance. He pictured that—a slow, languorous descent then a jolt at the idea of the actual impact. He might not die.

Four stories? Not foolproof. Everything would just be worse. *An' I am a fuck-up.*

He remembered a girl from school who had cut her wrists. It surprised him. There was nothing particularly fragile about her. She'd always seemed fairly practical. She'd worn black a lot, but that really wasn't much of a clue. Her roommate had found her.

According to the rumors, she'd been sitting in a pool of blood in the bathroom, but she still hadn't died. She'd ruined the tendons in one of her wrists and hadn't been able to cut deep enough into her other wrist.

Brey knew enough to cut up his wrists, not across. He'd have to wait for Hank to go to see Fuck-A-Friend Ken. He'd be gone for a couple of hours – or Brey could stay home sick, although there wasn't a lot to get sick with anymore. A headache? He'd sit in the tub. The thought of Hank finding him made him queasy – all that blood, assuming he did it right. Assuming Jack didn't show up with a cup of willow bark tea or Issa didn't come by with a stack of books. They checked up on him a lot. They liked him, and he was going to leave a bloody body or a broken one, smashed on the pavement or hanging.

Poison?

No. He'd just puke it up probably. Concoct it all wrong. Or Jack would catch him stealing his medicines or the hardware store clerk would tell Hank that his slave was buying some interesting chemicals.

A gun.

Hank's gun.

That was the way. He'd wait for him to go out. He wouldn't need a lot of time because he wouldn't even need to pull the trigger. Probably couldn't. But he could take the gun, go out past the post-line, wait for the patrol and point the gun. *Suicide by cop.* The image brought a lurch of guilt, but he smashed it down. This wasn't his fault. *They* made him a slave. And this was the only way. The people he loved wouldn't really be a part of it.

The people he loved.

He didn't think there could be any more pain. Twisting him up. Flaying him alive. He couldn't do it anymore. Couldn't be alone like this without hope. He was never meant to be alone. He knew that as sure as he knew anything.

Without love, he was nothing.

* * * *

Jesus...

Hank screwed his eyes shut, ran his fingers through the shaggy hair on the head bobbing on his lap. With a pop, he suddenly came free, and his eyes snapped open. Ken's strong fingers gripped him, stroking, hot, wet tongue licking in long swipes from root to tip, flicking under the ridge, sucking him in again.

Fuck.

His fingers knotted in Ken's hair. As good as it felt, though, a sick feeling fought with the pleasure in his belly. It wasn't Brey — Brey's lips. Brey's pale blue eyes looking up at him, playful, lust-filled, loving. He stared down into a gaze that wasn't pain-filled and desperate, that didn't hide behind the flutter of nervous lashes. A gaze that didn't beseech him, beg him...

Grabbing Ken's shoulders, he pulled him up and pushed him onto the carpet. With a grunt of surprise, Ken looked up at him — warm and friendly, not in love. *Thank fuck.* Ken's T-shirt was hitched up, cock lying rigid and rosy on his belly. Lying down on him, Hank kissed him frantically, nipping at him, plunging his tongue inside, grabbing their cocks, thumb smearing pre-cum — stroking. Ken grabbed his shoulders, fucking into his hand, his hot dick sliding against Hank's, making sparks burst behind Hank's eyes. The friction almost hurt. He squeezed and thrust and Ken groaned, throwing his head back against the carpet. His neck and belly tensed and suddenly his cock pulsed, spurting out hot gobs of cum. Hank gasped at the smell, electricity racing down his spine, filling his balls with fire, shooting out of his throbbing dick. His fingers clenched spasmodically, squeezing the last creamy dribbles out of their cocks.

Ken looked stuporous.

Lying back, Hank closed his eyes and panted up at the ceiling. A moment later he felt Ken come up onto his elbows beside him.

"What the fuck was that?"

Usually he was companionable. Leisurely. Not frantic.

"Sorry."

"Don't be sorry. I didn't mind, but what's wrong?"

Hank didn't say anything for a moment, letting his heartbeat come back to normal. Considered silence or a lie. A change of subject. Then he just took a deep breath and said, "How do you know if somebody's thinking about committing suicide?"

"Are we talking about your slave?"

"Brey."

Ken nodded, got up, and grabbed his jeans off the floor. "Want a drink?"

"Yeah. Please," said Hank, getting up too.

Ken disappeared and Hank went into the bathroom to clean up. Dressed again, he sat back down, and Ken reappeared with two glasses of bourbon and ice. Giving a glass to Hank before he took a swallow out of his, he sat down on the couch with a sigh and said, "Back to Brey. I think you already know. You're asking the question. You wouldn't ask without suspecting it."

"He's depressed."

"Most depressed people don't even come close to killing themselves, at least not outright."

"He's hiding it."

Ken took another drink. "Could be other reasons for that."

"I don't think so."

"Like I said, you're answering your own question, Hank. You're worried for a reason."

Hank told him about the trip to Younger's. "Christ. I saw him in that canteen with that knife an' that look on his face, an' I made him kneel in a corner like a fuckin' kid."

"Blaming yourself isn't helpful."

Hank glared. "Thank you, Dr. Osborn."

"Is his mood worse? The same?"

"The same I'd say, just flat. Smiles, jokes, but it's all on the surface."

Ken took another swallow of his drink, rattling the ice around. "He still won't talk to me?"

"No."

"You're gonna have to go with your gut on this, Hank. Wait a minute," he added, holding up his palm at another glare from Hank. "You want me to tell you that this thing or that is a clear-cut sign. I can't do that. You can assume that he's at least depressed. That's not a good thing."

"Jack's making him some tea made out of St. John's Wort."

"Might help. In time."

"That's what I'm worried about."

"You need to talk to him, Hank. You know him. You're worried for a reason. Good for you. You paid attention. You can't back off now. Talk to 'im. Could be he wants you to stop him. Without medication, this is a tough situation. Even with medication, you don't always win."

"The hell I won't."

Ken sighed, half smiled. "I don't want to lie to you, Hank. You aren't rational about Brey. You couldn't be." Hank looked sideways, and Ken shrugged. "You're in love with 'im."

Hank choked. "Love?"

"That's all right. I know we aren't—in love, I mean." Ken got up, came back a moment later with a Mason jar of whiskey. He filled Hank's glass, then said, "You're sleeping with him, aren't you?"

"No! Of course not!"

Ken rolled his eyes. "For fuck's sake, Hank. You love him. I've seen the way he looks at you. The worst thing you can do is make him think he's alone. Talk to him. Pester him. Spy on him. Screw 'im. It's not fucking rocket science."

Hank gaped. He was shocked. He imagined Brey's eyes filled with nothing but love. He shuddered suddenly.

Ken looked surprised. "That thought disgusts you?"

"No," he said.

He swallowed a mouthful of whiskey. He remembered the liquor cabinet he and Beth bought. It looked more like a book cabinet, deep shelves, under-mounted lights. They kept the liquor for parties there. He kept his Jack Daniel's in a cupboard and drank only occasionally. He was scared to death of becoming his parents. He wasn't anything like them, except that they loved each other without ever knowing it.

He loved Beth too, though, and he couldn't just stop that, even now.

"I'll make sure he's okay."

Ken nodded. "Sure, Hank. You do that."

* * * *

A block away from the library, Hank stopped to watch as Brey came outside and sat down on the steps. Hank stood still, not moving. Brey stared at the sidewalk for a moment before he leaned back on his elbows, legs sprawled, and tipped his face up to the last splash of cool sun. He closed his eyes, and his face was peaceful. He didn't look unhappy. Hank breathed out slowly.

Yesterday, when he'd come to pick Brey up from work, he'd smelled lemon. Through the door he'd seen a wide swath of marble. The library floor had glowed with a glossy light—waxed and buffed.

He'd heard Issa quip, "You missed your calling as a school custodian, young man," and Brey had laughed, an easy, happy laugh.

But a tingle of unease had filled Hank anyway.

Brey's face had had a sheen of sweat on it. He'd smiled with pleasure at the floor. "Looks good."

"Beautiful," Issa had said. "The trick now is to make sure nobody walks on it."

But Brey had just shrugged. "I've been meaning to get to it." And that's when Hank had felt his stomach clench.

Then he'd chided himself. *It's just a floor. It's not a fucking loose string he needs to tie up before he caps himself.*

He wouldn't do that. At least the happy, effervescent boy he once was wouldn't. But the man he had become was gutted and hollow, no longer a fountain of life that once glittered across the paparazzi's horizons—a sparkling star.

All night Hank had lain awake, puzzling over that floor—a chore, a task, a job? Not Issa's. She hadn't asked and had seemed surprised. The air had smelled of lemons, and there was a sparkle and glitter everywhere else. The power of a reverent act. The way a small devotion could awake a revolution. Any of Brey's last acts would be heartfelt.

In the morning, Hank had said, "I have something to talk to you about tonight," and saw Brey's eyes shutter.

"I told Jack I'd help him bottle."

Jack and his beer. He'd tried to find something in Brey's eyes to reveal that he'd miss that and saw nothing. "Okay. Tomorrow night."

Brey's lips had flickered in a smile. "You're going to the concert."

Fuck... Then Brey's words had registered and Hank had said, "Me? Aren't you?"

"Yeah. Sure. I'm going."

"We can talk after that."

"Okay."

Now, seeing Brey on the library steps enjoying the sun, Hank felt a lift of hope. Brey smiled as he saw him approach, squinting at him, and there was nothing dark in his eyes.

Hank grinned at him. "Hey, you."

"Hey."

"You polished the floor yesterday. What about today? Paint a mural on the ceiling?"

Brey guffawed. "Yeah, that's me. The Michelangelo of the new world."

"Why not?"

His smile didn't falter but his tone was almost flinty. "I have no talent, Hank." Then he got up with his backpack and his camera and they walked home.

Brey was drunk when he came upstairs from Jack's and fell face first into bed. In the morning Hank shook him awake, and Brey groaned and buried his face in the sheets. "Sick."

"On beer?"

"Jack."

"Jack what?"

Brey groaned again, dismally. "Your Jack."

"Bourbon?"

Brey's head moved, a nod. "Snuck it."

"Snuck?"

"I feel sick."

Hank's hand rose, absent of any intention on his part, and he stopped it just before he touched Brey's sweaty head, fingers aching to brush through the loose waves, to stroke and soothe. But instead he clenched his fist and swallowed his own sickness.

"I'll tell Issa."

"'Kay." Brey's eyes were shut, and he grew still again. Hank ran a hand down his face, didn't move for a moment. "'M okay," Brey whispered. "You can go."

Then Hank swallowed again and leaned down. "Are you, Brey? Okay, I mean?"

He felt Brey stiffen warily, saw his squinty eyes slit open again. "Whadda you mean?"

Hank choked. Nothing came out. He couldn't do any good. He couldn't break up his parents' fights. He couldn't love Beth enough. He couldn't break down his own back door and save his girls. He could follow the law but couldn't comfort the ones it never saved. He saw the big picture and even the little parts. It took Brey to show him that the parts meant more. But he didn't know what to do with that, even though he could hear Ken's voice again—*It's not fucking rocket science!* But it was to him. He loved Brey. That was true. He rescued him, but he couldn't save him. Brey had to know that about him now, that Hank wasn't that man, the man Brey once thought he saw. The one that could save him.

"Hank?"

"This isn't forever, Brey. The way things are."

Brey's eyes opened all the way, but he didn't move otherwise. "I know that, Hank. You don't have to worry about me."

"I want to let you go."

"Do you?"

The sheets muffled his voice, dulled it. *It was just the sheets.* "Just give me some time to think of a way."

A small smile curled Brey's lips, one side of his mouth showing in Hank's vision. "Okay, Hank."

"Promise me, Brey."

"I have to wait, Hank. I don't need to promise." He sounded confused, tired, eyes closing again.

"Promise me anyway."

Brey sighed heavily, pushing his face into the mattress. "Okay, Hank. I promise."

Hank's fingers made another move toward Brey's head before he pulled away and got up. Maybe he should follow those fingers, trust the manifestation of all the choked feelings inside him. He wasn't certain he wouldn't burst open, though.

* * * *

Jack was surprised at Brey's condition. "On a glass of beer?"

"Bourbon."

Jack shook his head. "Wasn't enough for that."

They were at Starbucks where Hank found Jack sitting at a table by the door. Now Hank was drinking his chico, an apple fritter in a container in front of him. He pinched the bridge of his nose, gazing at the plastic container. Pain expanded in his chest, a hollow place made to accommodate it. Nothing messy or cluttered or crowded in there. No heart. Antiseptic. Black and white. Clear. *Just follow the rules.* He made those rules his life. Gave his life, and it made no sense to him that a pretty, spoiled boy with pale blue eyes could look at him and believe he'd rescue him from the chaos that that boy had welcomed inside him. Hank wanted nothing to do with chaos. He'd come from it, run from it. And all of a sudden, there it was again, inside Brey. Drunken and drug-addled. Sluttish and passionate. A monogamous type with too much time and too much money—too much hope. That abiding faith in his family's survival was irritatingly illogical.

Unreasonable.

But it was Brey.

Fuck the life you don't want. Believe in the one you do until you can't anymore.

"I have to go."

He almost forgot the apple fritter. Snatched up the plastic box at the last moment.

At the close of the door, Brey rolled over and stared blankly at the gray expanse of ceiling above him. The morning light shed a dull pallor in the room. Slowly, he rolled again, sat up, looked down the long hall to the closed door and felt a stab of panic. He almost ran to the window, wanting to see Hank below, follow his stride out of sight, but he knew he was too late for that. His breath came quickly, and he scrubbed at this face. He felt the collar move as he swallowed, touched it with his fingers.

He thought of Josh, who'd come to the library the other day, sat a table, and watched him wax the floors.

The machine buzzed and hummed, pads spinning. "Why are you doing that?"

"I like seeing the finished product."

"You won't for long, not with everybody walking all over it. Your pictures are better for that."

"Pictures don't do anything." He'd actually felt a flush of pride he didn't want to feel.

"Yeah, they do. They tell the truth."

Brey smiled at the floor.

Getting up now, he pulled his pajamas off on the way to the bathroom and got into the shower. He wasn't hungover, but he was tired and he felt numb and strange—weirdly mixed up. He almost believed that it was Hank and Issa and Jack who'd left the world and not him about to.

Washing, he stared at the shower wall and tried not to think, tried not to picture the faces of his friends. He scrubbed and rinsed, concentrating on the smell of the herbs in the soap, the rasp of the towel against his skin. He brushed his teeth and ran his fingers over his scruffy jaw. His face was dazed-looking. Swallowing, he put on a pair of jeans and sat down on the side of the bed, looking at the gun safe on the shelf of Hank's beside table. Hank had his service revolver with him. The gun that was in the safe was smaller, a pistol. He didn't know what kind, but he knew it could kill, otherwise Hank wouldn't have it.

A few water drops fell off the ends of his hair and trickled down his back, distracting him. He squirmed, bending his arm back to swipe at the dampness. The smell of herbs filled the air. Rosemary. Lavender. He shivered in the coolness of the room. A shadow moved. Another distraction. Another delay.

A voice in his head... *You can't!*

Another... *Stop! Stop thinking!*

Except thinking wasn't a problem. It was the feeling. The sense awareness of scent and temperature. He almost laughed when his belly gurgled. *Fucking traitor.* Awareness of emotion, of affections. His plan, his thought-out plan growing gray and distant. Anger surged in him and he grabbed the safe and set it on his knees. Hank took his weapons out in front of him all the time. Never hid the combination. Pain stabbed his jaw as he gritted his teeth. But he opened the safe. He took out the gun. He pulled out the magazine the way Hank did and stared at it. His knees felt wobbly even sitting. He put the magazine on the tabletop and took a deep breath. His heart beat fast. He looked for that epiphany he felt when he realized he could do this. The idea of killing himself was like a lightening flash of sudden sanity. It made sense and the relief that washed over him was dizzying. He could go with good memories, fill his last moments with the images of his family, the bike he used to ride in circles on the driveway, his school, brick and ivy, blue skies, carpets of orange and yellow leaves, rolling in piles of leaves with Patric, giggling goofily at each other. Goldy, plumed tail, lolling tongue. Clubs, lights, dancing.

Suddenly, the gun felt lighter in his hand.

But his visions shifted. He saw Issa, white blonde ponytail, cheerful eyes, the bomb shelter where he found his camera, jugs of Jack's loamy beer, the touch of Josh's fingers on his cheek, his promise — *I won't hurt you* — and Hank, always gentle, mysteriously hurt, strong and worried, forgiving and stern.

And suddenly he was assailed with the scent of apple fritters, sweet and sticky, and his eyes popped open.

Fuck.

He didn't want to die. He didn't.

When the front door shot open, he wasn't even surprised. He just watched Hank toss his jacket and a plastic box into the living room and Brey sat frozen with the gun, staring as Hank steadily approached him, closer and closer, a giant filling his vision. The door seemed to swell with his shape.

And there he stopped, just staring at first. Then a look of pain came onto his face.

"Brey," he said softly.

Brey wanted to deny what Hank saw, but nothing came out. A swallow was the only movement he could make. Then Hank stirred, glanced at the magazine on the table, came closer and looked down, cupping Brey's cheek with his palm. Brey leaned into it, his lips moving against Hanks warm skin, his gaze rising up.

His voice was only a whisper, but all his heart came out on that soft rasp.

"I don't want to die."

The feel of Brey's breath against his palm tingled up Hank's arm. He moved his thumb against Brey's jaw, tipping his head up. Sparks raced up his spine — Brey's skin against his, a whiskery cheek, his breath warm, soft, regular. All of that, though — desired and dreamed of — was nothing to those eyes, open again with expectation, unimaginable, undeserved faith.

Hank moved away, fingers slipping off Brey's chin.

"I won't let you die."

Brey swallowed — or tried to. His Adam's apple rose — stuck. A shudder shook him then he swallowed again and said, "I don't... I wasn't..."

Hank waited for a moment. Then he motioned to the safe, the gun still in Brey's shaky hands. "I'm going to take that, okay? I'm just going to put it away."

He moved slowly, Brey's eyes following his, fingers spasming as Hank's touched his, pulled the gun away. He heaved a sigh and met Hank's glance with an uncertain smile. Hank put the gun and magazine in the safe, put the safe away, then sat down slowly on the side of the bed next to Brey.

"Didn't you know I'd come back?"

Brey blinked at him, and Hank watched him think — confusion, surprise, relief — sliding across his eyes.

"I don't... I didn't know."

"You scare me."

Brey shook his head, smiled back, embarrassed and chagrined. "I'm sorry. I didn't mean to scare you. I really wasn't going to. I just had to work it through."

"I care about you. I care a lot."

Brey's smile faltered. "I love you."

Hank heard his voice, hoarse, incredulous, amazed, grateful. "Fuck, Brey."

He couldn't remember the moment that Brey came into his arms, just that he was there — hot, delectable skin, lips crushed together. He pushed Brey backward and felt Brey's fingers digging into his back. The lips beneath his were warm and pliant, opening to heat, slippery wet — a heady, earthy taste. Hank devoured him, plunged his tongue in, Brey's pushing back, fingers clutching at him, hips humping up. Heat and steel beneath his jeans. Brey twisted his mouth away, then lunged back with tiny, nipping kisses, breath coming in shallow pants, legs wrapping around Hank's hips.

Unease pushed at Hank's lust. Dread. Worry.

He pushed up on his elbows, and Brey wrapped his arms around Hank's neck, pulling him back down. "Please," he murmured, laying gentle kisses across Hank's jaw, electric tingles following the featherlight flutters. Kisses down his neck. *Christ.* Sparks lit up behind his eyes. A roar in his ears drowning out every sound but Brey's soft exhalations. He grabbed a handful of Brey's hair, still cool from his shower, silky soft, tangling in his fingers. He sucked at the skin under Brey's chin, the rasp of whiskers like licks of fire across his lips, slid down to suckle at his Adam's apple. Brey thrashed and bucked underneath him, pushing his stiff cock up against the bulge trapped in Hank's pants. He ached, and the pain was a space for the worry to return. He slid his lips back up Brey's throat, kissing his jaw, the soft skin under his ears.

"Aubrey," he whispered.

"Yes, Hank, please."

Brey was pulling at Hank's shirt, trying to reach his buttons, his lips chasing after Hank's as Hank pushed up, head swimming, trying to blink sanity back into his brain. Brey stared up at him with desperate, amorous eyes. He hauled in a deep breath and pulled at Hank's buttons again, yanking at his shirt, fingers finally skating across Hank's skin, heat following in fiery trails of delight.

Brey was beautiful. Color rose in his face, pupils giant in his pale eyes, swollen lips.

But he wasn't only beautiful.

Hank saw his joy and excitement. The dazzling beauty of the pictures he took, never realizing the wonder, the sorrow, the anguish he could capture. The memory of people's happiness were in those pictures, their day-to-day boredom, the sweetness of a future never lived. He saw all of this — Brey's loyalty, his faith, the bravery of his irrational, illogical hope. All of those things, battered and beaten, fluttering for life in him like the pulse in his throat.

Hank pushed up, breathing in, arms trembling underneath him. The image of Brey in the garage assailed him, and this time there was no arousal. He felt his cock shrinking at the same time Brey was squeezing his legs around his waist, his palms on Hank's cheeks.

"Hank…"

He remembered the tremble of Brey's legs. The whip marks and bruises. His raw, weepy asshole.

Fuck!

"Hank."

He was a brute. Wanting. Taking. About to take. He wanted to give Brey nothing but happiness. To only love him. To care for him and protect him always, because he knew Brey was a better man.

"Aubrey."

He couldn't take this from him even though this was the only way Brey knew how to give and take love. There was a psychologist at Brey's trial who said that sex was Brey's currency, but she was wrong. Sex wasn't his currency. It was everyone else's. A pretty face, a willing body, but he was worth sacrifice. Worth loyalty. Worth the gift of love without a price.

"You don't have to do this."

Brey looked panicked. "Fuck, Hank. Please don't make this about that. I love you. I want to know what fucking somebody I love feels like. Patric. That wasn't Patric yet. Please don't leave me, Hank. Please."

"I won't leave you, Brey."

He let his eyes roam Brey's face—pale again, angry scared and bitter. Brey shook his head violently.

"You already are. I can see it. Fuck, Hank. Please. Give in to me. I love you. I want you. You keep putting up this fucking wall, an' I'm too tired to climb it anymore. I'm gonna fall. I'm gonna break, Hank.

Please." Without waiting, Brey lunged up, arms like iron chains, pulling Hank down again, kissing him harshly, his breath hot, skin feverish. "I won't let you go."

Every kiss scalded. Brey's fingers were back, pulling at his shirt, and Hank reared up suddenly, yanking it off. Brey grinned, eyes alight, and threw his arms over his head, wriggling on the sheets. "Fuck me, yeah?"

Hank was quiet for a moment, pulling his fingers slowly down Brey's ribs, watching the shivers race through him. He was lean and lovely.

"You are my dream come true, Brey. I don't want to hurt you."

"You won't."

"I love you too."

Brey smiled again, sweetly, everything about him gone docile and gentle again. "I know."

Unzipping Brey's jeans, Hank tugged gently on the waistband, and Brey's hips rose up. He was almost flaccid now, his pink penis lying placidly against his thigh. He let his lean legs fall open, inviting Hank back in. Hank could feel his own smile stretching his lips, pulse picking up again.

"You are amazing," Hank whispered.

The flesh between Brey's legs began to swell again, and Hank got out of his pants quickly and bent down, sucking Brey's soft cock into his mouth, jerking with the lurch in Brey's hips, his cock growing instantly, filling Hank's mouth with steely, satiny heat. His flesh was hot and heavy, and Hank moaned around it, feeling Brey's fingers in his hair, clutching gently, not pushing or pulling. Hank lifted up, burying his face in Brey's balls, inhaling the scents of herbs in his soap, hearing him hiss in breath after breath. Pulling a testicle into his mouth, he rolled it around on his tongue and felt Brey's legs open wider. The smell of him was rich and exotic. He sucked him down again, tang and salt filling his mouth. All of his dreams evaporated. This was Brey, real, lean muscle under hot skin, soft raspy hair on his rigid thighs. A shadow of hair across his chest—sour and sweet, sweaty and steamy.

Brey's legs began to quiver.

"Close... Close," he whispered.

Rising up, Hank bit one of Brey's nipples, eyes twinkling as Brey's eyes shot open. He licked at him, reveling in the feel of the nubby flesh against his tongue.

His own hot breath blew back at him. His heart pounded. Sensation consumed him. He buried his face in Brey's armpit, licking and nipping, sweaty hair tickling his nose. Brey arched, and Hank could see the strain of the muscles in the arms over his head. Brey grabbed onto the sheets, pulling and clutching at them.

"Fuck, Hank. Fuck me, okay? Yeah?"

His hips bucked.

Hank licked at the sweat-beaded skin on the snake tattoo sliding over Brey's ribs before biting the nipple under the open fangs.

"You have a dirty mouth," he whispered.

"Jesus, Hank. C'mon."

Brey's hands came down, his fingers digging into Hank's shoulders. Hank lifted his head, smiled almost languorously at him. "I need a kiss."

The half-crazed look in Brey's eyes receded, and he smiled and rose up, elbow underneath him, seeking Hank's lips. Hank sighed against his mouth, licked at his bitten, puffy lips, pushed against his hot, slippery tongue, sealing their mouths. His hand cupped the back of Brey's head and he kissed him gently, pulling at his lips with his own, burying his tongue in Brey's warm mouth, absorbing every sensation while Brey's hand found his cock, pulling and stroking, rubbing across the slit with his thumb, laughing into Hank's mouth as Hank's hips jerked involuntarily.

With a gasp, Hank pulled away, and Brey put his thumb into his mouth, sucking on it with glassy eyes.

"Fuck," Hank muttered. Then he got up and said, "Wait a minute." Behind him Brey flopped back onto the sheets with a blustery groan of frustration.

By the time Hank got back, Brey was lying with his knees up and wide open, rosy red cock straining against his belly. He looked at Hank and let out a gasp.

"Lube?"

Hank shrugged. "I guess you could say I collect things."

Brey laughed. "Yeah, baby. Jack Daniel's an' lube. Awesome priorities."

With a smile, Hank got between Brey's legs and Brey cupped his palms under his knees and lifted, exposing his hole to Hank's eyes.

Blood sizzled through Hank's veins, overheating him. He felt woozy. His head swam. He swallowed and rubbed a slick thumb over Brey's hole, feeling it flutter in eagerness. Brey's eyes almost rolled. He was panting, his chest and face flushed red. Hank pushed with his thumb and felt Brey's opening begin to relax. Brey hissed, lower lip between his teeth. His face was a mask of concentration.

"Relax," Hank murmured.

"Hm." Brey nodded.

"Aubrey... Look at me."

Brey opened soft eyes, gave him a soft smile. "I like you saying my name."

"Are you afraid?"

"No."

"Tell me if I hurt you."

"I will."

"I love you, Aubrey."

"I love you too."

Hank pulled out his thumb, slid a finger in, eyes on Brey's face. Brey's body clutched at his finger, pulling it into his heated interior. Hank pulled it out, added another finger, saw the tightening around Brey's eyes, stilled until he felt him relax again, saw his smile. He moved his fingers, relishing the heat, the intimacy of Brey's body, the vulnerability of this place, this act.

The power Brey gave him only made him feel humble, awestruck.

After a moment Hank got up onto his knees and slathered more lube on his cock, eyes never leaving Brey's. Brey pulled his knees up higher, letting his legs fall wide. Hank leaned down to kiss the inside of one thigh, then the other before he set the head of his cock against Brey's hole and gently pushed in.

The expression on Brey's face was only of pleasure, warm waves of it washing across his features. His expression was beatific, his head rolling slightly side to side as Hank pushed in deeper. Brey's insides gripped him, pulled, relaxed. He opened with a sigh, and Hank slid in until he could go no farther. His body was electrified, pleasure sparking on every nerve ending. He slid in and out, slowly, teasing, thrust in quick bursts, watching the smile on Brey's face again. Brey was breathing through open lips, Hank thrusting quick and shallow, slow and deep. He leaned in, cupping Brey's thighs with his palms, seeing a blissful daze come onto his face—eyes in slits, lungs pumping out shallow sighs. Hank rocked him gently. His vision was a haze of gray light and blurry outlines. He tipped his head back, pleasure like pain in his balls, filling his cock with fire. The feel of Brey's skin, the smell of his body, the wonder of his pale eyes, the tension of his muscles transported him. He was filled with ecstasy.

He sizzled, vision tunneling, eyes on a white light softly glowing in the room.

Brey's whispers came to him slowly—barely whispers, almost soundless. A litany spoken almost silently.

Swallowing air, Hank blinked sweat out of his eyes and looked down. Brey was clutching at his collar, fingers curling inside it, jacking himself furiously with his other hand, softly, almost soundlessly whispering, "So long... So long..."

Hank's hips stuttered, and he bit down on his lip, tasting blood, pain pushing back the pleasure. He thrust faster, pushing Brey's legs up higher.

"Come, sweetheart. I wanna feel you come around me."

Brey's pants sped up, and he rolled his head back, fingers flying over his dick. Hank bit his lip again, feeling Brey's body suddenly clench around him, stiffening and jerking as his cum burst out of him, shooting with every jerk and shudder. His neck strained, arched back, tendons popping. His fingers squeezed, tiny shudders racking him. The smell of Brey's cum, the clamp of his body pushed Hank barreling after him. Gripping Brey's thighs, he pulled him closer, pushing in deep, pumping cum with every pulse of his cock into Brey's body. He gritted his teeth, muscles spasming, pleasure shooting through him like fire, emptying him of all sensation.

A boneless shell.

He fell wearily next to Brey's body, reaching out to cup Brey's face and pull him over, resting his cheek against Brey's forehead before everything slipped away.

* * * *

Sugar pooled in Brey's mouth, and he swallowed flaky bits of crust, tiny nubs of apple. He found the fritter in a plastic container with the coat Hank threw into the living room when he'd come in.

In pajama bottoms now, Brey leaned in the bedroom doorway and stuffed his mouth with the pastry. A groan of pleasure rose in his throat.

"You never made any noises like that with me."

Smiling, Brey let his eyes roll back down, sucked noisily at his sticky fingers. Hank sat up with a grunt, pulled his boxers back on and yawned sleepily.

"You're a cliché," said Brey.

"I don't always go to sleep right after," Hank answered.

There was a seriousness to his face that Brey didn't like. "I knocked you out."

"Yeah, pretty much."

"In a good way?"

"Are you fishing?"

Brey shrugged, got on the bed and pushed back against the pillows. "I like compliments."

Hank leaned over, kissed him gently, smiling against his lips. "Sugar. I like that."

"Beet sugar."

"You're qualifying your sugars?"

"Just being accurate."

Brey watched Hank's eyes move over his face, the seriousness back.

"We need to talk, Brey."

"We are."

"You know what I mean."

"Hank, I wasn't going to."

"You weren't hungover."

Brey put his head back, scrubbing at his face for a moment before he dropped his hands and said, "Can we fuck again?"

"Brey."

"Okay…" He sighed. "I wasn't going to. I was… I was upset. I wanted out. I was scared an' pissed off – at you, at me. Every time I came up with a good way to off myself, though, I'd come up with a good reason not to. All the ways it might not work. I was never gonna shoot myself. I was gonna go past the post-line an' make your guys do it. I didn't want you to come home an' see me like that – you or Jack or Issa or Josh." Brey saw the flicker of surprise on Hank's face and gave a tiny smile. "I guess I have friends. Fuckin' pain in the ass to realize. An' I don't have it in me anyway. I mean, I was sitting here without any bullets. I can't do it. I really loved being alive once."

"I know, Brey."

"At Younger's" – he stopped and stared up at the gray white surface above him – "a man laughed. High-pitched. I heard it before."

"At Thom's."

"Yeah." Brey felt a hand take his, Hank's warm breath as he kissed the backs of his fingers. "You put me in that corner, an' all I knew was I couldn't do anything. I have no rights. No power. I almost couldn't breathe. I feel that way here too, like the breath is getting sucked out of me. I have to see my family, Hank. I have to go."

"Brey, you're pinning everything on your family being alive."

"They *are* alive. I know they are. I know they're waiting for me because my father told me. He wanted to come back for me but knew he might not be able to. We planned it. They're alive, Hank. You have to believe me."

He put all the force of his being into those words. He knew it. He projected it. It was about faith and belief and the will to resist doubt.

"You have to believe me," he implored him.

Hank was staring at him, focused and intent then he leaned forward slowly and let his forehead rest against Brey's. His eyes were open and Brey's filled with green-flecked amber. Autumn leaves. He felt safe, a strange, irrational safety that always came to him from Hank. "I will get you out, Brey. I promise I will get you out."

Chapter Fifteen

Orange flames glowed in the dark and wood smoke floated in the air. People sat around scattered fire bowls in the park, spreading out from the gazebo.

Gaze skimming over the crowd, Hank found Jack and Issa sitting on a red blanket beside a fire bowl, drinking Jack's beer out of brown bottles. He took Brey's hand, glancing at him just as Brey smiled.

His heart jumped. *Amazing.*

Amazing to be here.

To be anywhere with Brey.

Even in the dark, he could see the twinkle in Brey's eyes.

His happiness spread inside him. Once, during the intermission, he caught Ken's glance, his wry smile. Brey was drinking Jack's beer, laughing loudly. Then Ken gave Hank a wink and looked away. Hank let his eyes drift over the crowd again, looking for Josh. Issa told him about Josh's feelings for Brey, not about Brey's for Josh. Brey's reference to him as his friend came as a surprise. He felt nothing but unease around Brian and could never separate Josh from his father in his feelings. Watching Brey, he wondered about Josh. He felt no jealousy, only wonder, meeting the smile that Brey flashed over his shoulder at him, scowling at Jack's grin.

Over the weeks, he and Brey fell into an easy habit with each other. Hank didn't forget his promise. It lived behind every thought and smile he gave, the kisses he lay over Brey's pale body — the happiness he saw in those pale blue eyes.

* * * *

On the morning of the next trip to Younger's, he woke in the dark, Brey's warm back pressed to his chest, ass resting against his lap. He ran his palm over Brey's belly, then gripped his half-hard cock and stroked him erect. Quiet whimpers fell from Brey's lips, sounds he never made awake. He fucked into Hank's grip, still asleep as Hank kissed his shoulder, the curve of his neck. As Brey's movements quickened, Hank scooted back, pulling him over, covering Brey's cock with his mouth.

"Oh, fuck."

Awake now.

Hank took him all the way in, nose in his crotch. He smelled wonderful. Strong. Musky. Hank swallowed and Brey hissed, fingers in Hank's hair. Gentle tugs. Fingertips ruffling. Resting his weight on his elbow, Hank pushed between Brey's legs, humming in approval as Brey opened wide. He brushed at the soft hair between Brey's ass cheeks, pushed a fingertip against his hole and rose up as Brey bucked. He wriggled his finger, sucking at the silken steel in his mouth. His eyes stayed closed and he sank into the sensations of that hot flesh moving on his tongue,

Brey's pucker gripping and releasing his fingertip, the tension of the body underneath him, thighs vibrating, the sound of his pants, the cock in his mouth pulsing with Brey's thunderous heart. The roar of the blood in his own ears. Then the clutching of Brey's fingers, the bucking of his hips before his body went rigid and cum spurted into the back of Hank's mouth. He drank it with the same humming sound he sucked him with, milking him until Brey's tremors and shudders slowly eased, and he lay panting, radiating heat.

Covering Brey with the blankets, Hank kissed his cheek and rolled away.

A feeling of unease began to fill him.

Younger. The dark. The space between him and Brey. A promise he didn't want to keep. Worry. He didn't like to leave Brey alone, but he couldn't take him — not again.

Coming back into the room from his shower, he saw Brey's eyes open in the near dark.

"Owe you a blow job," he murmured. His voice was sleepy, but it had Hank's worry in it too.

"What are you doing today?" asked Hank.

"Pictures. The farmhouses."

There was a pair of farmhouses on the outskirts of Waterfall. Old. There before the town had been built. Hank knew Brey hadn't been there yet. They bordered the post-line near one of the pumping stations.

"Long way."

"I have a bike."

Hank went to the dresser and pulled clothes on in the gray room, just the light from the bathroom stretching out. Brey was asleep again, breathing slow, easy breaths. Hank fluttered a kiss over his forehead, switched off the light and made his way down the dark hall.

He closed the door without a sound but swore that it echoed.

* * * *

Ice lay on the ground, thin and friable. The sky was gray and Brey's breath came out in puffs. His lungs struggled in the moist air. Panting, he slid off his bike and let it drop to the side of the road.

Walking was easier.

His shoes crushed the ice, too thin to be slippery.

He cursed the cold, the dismal gray. His memories of winter went to orange crackling fires, bare woods with spindly tree limbs that took the place of Patric's leaves, pumpkins and chestnuts and Christmas lights. He loved decorations and glowing store windows and shopping for presents. Wrapping paper. Ice rinks. Parties and hot toddies.

But those were other winters.

He was here for now. For a while. He couldn't run away in a cold like this. No rain. Just the sting and bite of the chill air.

The sun was a hazy white circle in the sky.

Breathing into his hands, Brey walked quickly, occasionally reaching up to resettle the pack on his shoulder. His thoughts kept wandering off to Hank. Younger's. He didn't want to be there, but he didn't want to be away either. Hank's secrets were a danger zone he skimmed without straying too close to. He didn't doubt Hank's integrity—nobody could, not even Younger. He pictured Younger with his amused and watchful eyes—his calm, the languid way he sprawled in his chair, moved without hurry. The strong and gentle fingers he wrapped around Brey's elbow as he led him from the canteen. Younger wouldn't doubt Hank's character. He was like Hank but wasn't like him. No idealism. His world view was a tired one.

Worn out, like Brey.

Brey was better—because of Hank's promise. And because optimism was Brey's nature and like an energy he craved. But Brey wasn't made for this world. He was ashamed here. In the old world it didn't matter if he wanted a man to take care of him, because it wasn't about giving him anything he didn't really already have. It was for show, a proof of love. He wanted safety. But it was a hidden thing because he wasn't in danger. A man who cosseted him was a man who loved him. Here safety was real and away from Hank, he wasn't safe. He wasn't strong or brave.

He wanted strong arms and faithfulness, pleasure and joy, but he was becoming ashamed of those things now.

Even Josh was stronger.

Abruptly he stopped and forgot his thoughts. A thinning of the clouds let the sun gleam through, and the light sparkled like diamonds on the frosty skeleton of a bare tree near one of the farmhouses. He got out his camera and got the shot just before the clouds swallowed the light again. A smile grew on his face. The tree was stark and lovely. As he got closer he saw the flutter of little birds shifting to higher branches. The sight lightened his mood. Those little birds reminded him of intangible things like Patric's leaves, stilled in perpetual motion. This moment in time. This world.

A fixed reality for him.

But maybe just for now, maybe not always.

The old world was still here. A flutter of wings. A beam of winter sun.

In the farmhouse he took pictures of a kitchen with apple-covered wallpaper and a windowsill lined with milk glass bottles.

Sometimes he imagined he was taking pictures for some weird apocalyptic interior design magazine. His eye kept looking for that special something... But there never was anything really. Just empty houses.

The inside of this one was musty, dusty and sad. Brey guessed it was always pretty sad-looking, an almost charming mix of very old with very cheap. Early American meets tourist-trap kitsch.

His steps stirred up dust, even in the cold, heavy air. A window was broken and a cold draft blew down the hallway. Curtains stirred.

A bedroom in back surprised him, completely out of harmony with everything else. Blue-gray wallpaper, still with a hint of shine. A crystal chandelier. Gilt framed mirrors. Hollywood Regency. Brey ventured in slowly, walked on the plush, once-white carpet, now gray-brown and dingy. He didn't take any pictures. It would simply be a room, one out-of-place room. Any clues to the specialness of this space to the people who lived here vanished with them.

Outside, the bare tree was empty, the little birds gone.

Walking quickly now he followed the road as it curved toward the canal and the post-line. A mist was filling the air, still and hazy. The cold hurt his nose, and he swore at himself for forgetting his gloves. As the other farmhouse came into view, he could see the orange posts and his heart quickened. A short chain-link fence bordered the canal. In places, the chain-link curled away from its supports. Brey could see a building in the distance alongside the canal where it angled toward Waterfall—windowless, black painted cinderblock.

Blowing into his hands, he stomped his feet before going into the house, knocking off dirt nobody would care about anymore.

His nose itched. Mold. Cold. Damp. A squishy feel to the floor—creaky, uneven boards. The house was over a century old, half-empty. No couch in the living room, just a rocker, a recliner and a TV. Half the cupboards in the kitchen were empty. The refrigerator was white, old-fashioned, with rounded edges—neo-retro. A century-old style. Avocado green stove top. Almond-colored oven.

He went back into the living room and halfway through a board sank underneath him. He staggered back, stumbling.

"Fuck!"

Without his weight, the board popped back up. Now the floor looked flat and even again. He tapped a foot out. The floor held, but he backed up anyway, took a picture, then curled his arm up to settle the camera strap back over his head and caught a flash of color out of the corner of his eye. It came through the living room window. He stared, lowering his arm slowly, making no other movement. At first, everything was still and silent. No wind. No trees to creak. No fluttering birds. Just the haze of mist and the orange of the distant posts.

Then a man appeared, stepping away from the cinderblock building to approach the canal. His clothes were gray, almost the color of the mist, but he wore a black, blue-trimmed ski cap. Brey lifted his camera again, trying to focus through the window. The dirty glass created a blur. Quietly, he went outside onto the porch, setting his bag down, hiding behind a strip of trellis that trimmed the steps on either side. His breath plumed, and he whispered, "Shit," waiting for the man to turn back. After a moment, he did, tugging the cap down low, chin tucked, face almost invisible. Brey felt a spurt of panic, afraid the man had seen him, but the man didn't look up, didn't run. Brey snapped a picture. Then the man stuffed his hands into his pockets, looked quickly around him, circling away then stilled for a moment as he looked into the distance. Brey started to raise the camera again just as the man whirled and ran at him.

Shocked, Brey froze. Then he back-pedaled, spun, barreled through the door, skidded to a stop, and dashed back out again for his bag and the rest of the film. He snatched at the strap just as the man thudded up the steps and slammed into him. Brey flew over the threshold. A second later the man grabbed Brey's hair and wrenched his head back. His mind went blank. Fear consumed him. He smelled the dryness of leaves and heard the babble of that little stream again under the rasp of air and the thunder of his heart. He struggled, trying to wrench himself free as the man pulled him away from the house. He was mindless with terror. Noises tumbled out of his mouth. Then the man grabbed him by the back of his jacket and flung him away. He fell flat on his face. His lungs emptied and he couldn't breathe. He got a knee underneath him then the man dragged him back up and slammed him down again. Pain exploded in his head. He collapsed, clawing weakly at the ground.

Then his name floated in the air, a dim, faraway sound. *"Brey... Brey..."*

Then another voice. "C'mon, fucker. Get up."

He got his knees under him, sprawling backwards. The man was dragging him over to the canal. The orange posts wavered in his view. He slid past one and a panicked gasp burst out of him.

"Stop! Fuck!" He wasn't running. He didn't want Hank to think that. "You asshole!" Wrenching sideways, Brey got up onto his knees and staggered away.

"Brey..."

Closer now, that voice. He looked back and the man's fist plowed into the side of his face. This time he grabbed the man's arm and held on. The man was trying to run now. He yanked out of Brey's grip then lunged back to snag Brey's jacket and suddenly Brey was flying, arms pinwheeling. His feet hit a cement apron in front of the canal, and he went tumbling through a gap in the chain-link, throwing his arms out blindly. One of his hands hit metal, and he clutched at it. His skin froze. The sensation confused him — cold or pain, he wasn't sure. Then it was pain, a red-hot burn as his skin started to peel away from the frozen pole. The momentum of his fall spun him in a circle. Gray sky, the light gray of the sides of the canal, black fields, the black water beneath him. It was just a split second then he flung his other arm around the pole, catching it in his elbow.

Gasping, he hung on, his stuck palm growing numb again. His feet scrabbled at the wall, slipped free.

Sirens whooped with the blood in his ears. His eyes focused on the orange posts. The man was running, jumping over furrows in the icy, fallow ground. Brey resisted resting his face against the pole. He tried to kick a leg up. He swung and pain seared his palm.

He was panting. There was sweat on him.

Fuck. Not good.

Then the sirens stopped and there was a ringing silence, broken a moment later by slamming doors. A man's hands reached down, grabbing onto the back of his jacket.

Somebody yelled—"No! Don't! Wait!"

A bolt of red-hot pain shot from his hand to his elbow.

"Stop!"

Another pair of arms came down, this pair wrapping around his head and back, holding him still. "You're okay. You're okay."

"Josh?"

"Yeah. Hang on."

He closed his eyes to get rid of the dizziness. He didn't understand. His stomach churned, his arms ached. He kicked at the wall, but the toes of his shoes just slipped. Shadows came near, the two men in the vehicle again.

"You idiots!" Josh snapped. "You just let that guy go."

"This is our runner. Our job isn't some guy who didn't break the law."

"Hank's. Your runner is Hank's." There was a moment of silence, then Josh's voice again. "Go get me some water."

Brey almost didn't recognize Josh's voice. Looking up, he saw a face blanched with cold, eyes dark with anger. No uncertainty. No innocence.

Brey squeezed his elbow around the pole, trying to hitch up.

Josh leaned down. "Brey, I'm gonna pour some water over the pole, okay? Wiggle your fingers a little bit."

The water was tepid, warmer than the pole. He felt it seep between the metal and his palm, and he pulled his hand away.

"Shit," said Josh.

Pieces of Brey's skin stuck to the pole. An icy numbness gripped him. The cops were grabbing onto him again, pulling him up. Confusion made him struggle. He wanted away. He wanted to go home. Hank's two cops were wrestling for his wrists, and Josh was pushing in the middle.

"Knock it off! Let 'im go!"

"You have no business in this, Josh."

"I have all the business I wanna have."

The two cops stared at Josh. They didn't have name tags, but Brey knew the big one was named Vince Kelly and the other one was Anderson. Anderson smiled at him on occasion, but Vince pointedly ignored him. But Vince wasn't ignoring Josh. Brian was Vince's friend. Brey panted, unpleasantly aware of the fire in his palm. He squeezed his wrist, looking at the cops, the calculation in Vince's eyes. He wasn't afraid of Josh, not really, but there was a measure of respect in his expression. Plus, there was Brian to consider. Josh was giving him a blank, cold look that Brey had never seen — or maybe just a little of it, that first time in the library. Josh had power. Brian's power. His own.

Vince shrugged. "You can come in with us. We'll have some paperwork for you."

"After we see the doc."

Brey squeezed his wrist again, forcing the pain away. It wasn't bleeding. Too cold maybe.

Josh took his elbow. "C'mon."

"My bag," said Brey suddenly, whirling around, grasping at his neck for the camera that wasn't there. He used his hurt hand, and it stung. His camera, the pack with his film. He hurried back to the house, Josh following him. His camera lay on the walkway. He scooped it up with his good hand, cradling it with his other arm.

"Is it okay?"

"I—I think so."

He looked it over while Josh retrieved his pack. The cops followed halfway, stopped. The pain level in Brey's hand inched up. The sun was sinking, and the cold grew harsher. Brey was shivering, the earlier sweat dried on his skin. Maybe it was the aftermath of adrenaline, but he was angry, angry in a way that made him itch—a way he didn't like. With a restlessness because he didn't understand anything.

"Why are you even here?" he asked. He could hear the bitter tone in his voice.

"I was following you."

"Yeah? Why? I mean... That's... That's a little scary."

Josh sighed. "Hank asked me to."

Brey laughed, a sound he didn't even come close to recognizing out of himself. He didn't even want to contemplate the two of them together in Hank's thoughts. They were friends. That's all. That's all Hank knew.

"I need a babysitter?"

Josh's eyes took on that look of dark anger again. "This is a screwed up place, Brey. You were my fucking birthday present, remember?"

Brey looked up at the sky. Cloudy. Thin gray clouds. Mist. Dark enough for stars, but there were none. The day had disappeared. He tried to focus on the little birds from earlier. Tiny, cold bodies huddled together.

I keep sayin' it an' nobody really hears me.

"Fuck, I hate this."

"Me too, Brey."

Josh sounded sad, and Brey remembered back to his own eighteenth birthday, the black Porsche waiting for him on the driveway, his first year of college, friends and parties, the future he blissfully lived for and never doubted.

"I wanna go home."

"Okay. We can pick up our bikes on the way."

He'd forgotten about his bike. Wondered why Josh had run here if he had a bike. "Where's yours?"

"Stuck."

"Oh."

But it didn't really matter. They didn't need those bikes. There were lots of other bikes — more bikes than people now.

* * * *

The door locked shut, blocking out the light. Brey leaned back, feeling the buzzing of his temper in his ears. He could sense the presence of Hank outside the door, and it grated on every nerve. He could almost feel the jangle of Hank's anger.

Well, fuck 'im.

He thought of the look on Hank's face when Hank came to pick him up at Jack's. Definitely not the look Brey expected, that was for sure. He wanted relief, support, comfort. Instead, he got anger. Anger at him, which made Brey angry too. Then when Hank said, "Are you looking for trouble, Brey? Is that it?" Brey gaped at him in shock.

"Me?"

"You see an obvious outsider, clearly up to no good, an' you try to take a picture?"

"I believed I could help."

"You almost got killed! Whipped, at the very fucking least!"

That was it, he knew. Brey had scared him. Hank was here to help, to save him, to rescue him.

"I don't need you to take care of me," he said bitterly, with a sinking feeling inside because that wasn't true, at all, and he didn't even want it to be. He just didn't want it to be a burden. That hurt. And he covered his hurt with his own fury. "And I don't need a fuckin' babysitter!"

They were still downstairs, and the whole time Jack kept discreetly quiet, but there was a vague look of amusement on his face and Brey found himself wondering which one of them Jack thought was the biggest idiot. He grabbed his bag and pushed past Hank into the hallway. It was early morning and he was tired, way too tired to sleep. Hank kept behind him on the stairs.

"We need to talk, Brey."

"I need to get the fuck outta here."

"That bad?"

He spun and Hank stopped. Tired. Strained. Purple skin under his eyes. His face was flushed with cold. Brey's eyes took on his angles, the sharpness of jaw and cheek, the softness at the curves of his mouth. *Christ.* He was melting just at the look of him. The love of his life. Unlikely. Random. Lost and found.

"Yeah," he said, hitching up the strap of his bag on his shoulder. "That fucking bad."

Now he let his bag slip down to the floor and fumbled for a chain above his head. He gave it a sharp tug and light flooded the little room.

His darkroom. A supply closet between Jack's and Hank's places. When he was angry, he never thought of upstairs as his place. His anger grew as the silence grew outside. A sick sense of familiarity washed over him. His anger at Patric, at being misunderstood — at being a coward for misunderstanding himself. He was furious at Patric, furious at him for seeing into him. Mocking him with words — like his father's.

"You'd rather do drugs than put your heart into anything you might fail at. You'd rather fuck than feel love."

He imagined a breath stirring his hair, warmth against the back of his shoulders, the heat from Hank's palm through the door.

Run!

Go away!

"Open the door, Brey."

"No."

"Aubrey!"

"Fuck you, Hank!"

"Open up, Brey. I mean it."

"Is that an order?"

"Do you want it to be? Is that what you need?"

"I need you to go away."

"Open the door or I'll kick it in."

"Asshole," he muttered.

But he opened the door. And the step he was about to take backward suddenly took him forward instead until he was crashing into Hank's chest and Hank was pulling him in close, crushing the air out of him. He planted his face into the curve of Hank's neck and shoulder and breathed. A deep inhale that was all Hank and warmth and home.

"Fuck," he muttered.

Hank's fingers were in his hair, pulling his head up. He felt the hardness of lips and teeth, a painful kiss. Then Hank pulled away, and his eyes were still angry.

"This isn't only about you, Brey. You can be so fucking selfish."

"I got attacked." The plaintiveness was false because Hank was right and he knew it.

"I love you. That makes you a part of me. I have a right to be fucking scared."

"You mean pissed. You're swearing at me."

"I'm not swearing at you. I'm not even mad at you. I'm mad that I wasn't with you."

Brey dropped his head on Hank's shoulder and took a deep breath. "I wanted to get a picture. I wanted to help."

"You did help. You set that guy an' his pals back in their plans. We know for certain that they're up to something."

"What? What are they up to?"

"I don't know yet. I just know we have enemies who are prepared to act."

Brey raised his head to look at him, and he was sure that Hank wasn't telling him the truth about what he knew. There was a sinking feeling in him, that recognition of being a burden.

"I'm going to develop my film. Maybe I caught something."

"Come to bed. Aren't you tired?"

"God, no. I'm fucking wired. You go on. You can buy me a fritter later."

"I'll bring it home," Hank whispered. "You can eat it naked."

Brey grinned. "I like that idea."

"Me too," said Hank then he kissed him again, a little painful still. He wasn't quite forgiven.

"I love you, Hank."

That got him a gentler kiss. "I love you too, sweetheart."

Brey closed the door after Hank left and leaned back against it again, letting his unease sweep over him as if it might leave a clue in its wake. There was nothing, though, just the unease, so he picked up his bag and got to work.

* * * *

Snow came. A thin blanket that melted into sludge and froze into ice. A persistent haze clung to the ground.

Hank gave Jack Brey's photo, and Jack nodded and gave it back.

"Yeah. That's Sean."

"You know anything about 'im?"

"Just medical. Can't share."

Jack was decorating. Christmas decorations. He wasn't the only one. Brey was almost giddy when he saw the boxes of garlands and ornaments in the hallway outside Jack's clinic that morning.

"Fuck me! Are you serious? Christmas?"

Hank smiled a stiff smile and caught Jack's look. Then Jack was smiling at Brey, though he shot Hank another look, commiserating, but with that lack of false sympathy that was all Jack. "Got an extra Christmas tree if you want it."

Brey pulled in a quick breath, tugging on his gloves at the same time. "Hell yeah."

Hank was waiting for him at the door, gritting his teeth, willing Jack to look back over. Jack was nudging the boxes up against the wall, out of the way.

"Come back tonight an' pick any ornaments you want."

Brey bounced on his toes, knocking against Hank's shoulder on his way out. Hank waited for Jack to look at him. Jack gave him an unsmiling, unrepentant stare.

"You have happiness starin' you right in face, Hank."

"I don't need your help."

"Hell you don't."

Both of Hank's girls were born in December, and Jack had known that. Hank realized that Jack could guess at how torn he was. The love Hank had now wouldn't be possible if his wife and daughters were still alive. Brey was the secret desire that only found a place in the vacuum made by Eve. In real life, Brey would have been a bittersweet memory of a life he didn't pursue, but Jack knew how often Hank went to Brey's trial, that Brey wasn't entirely relegated to the life Hank didn't choose. In his heart, Hank sought a way to him. But then Brey was in prison, and Hank had a wife and two daughters, Jack's sister and nieces. In this dark and frozen month, he was stricken with grief and regret. Every look at Brey knocked at the foundation of his life.

Wasn't this what he'd always dreamed of?

He wanted his girls back, but he didn't want to give up Brey. And every time he thought that, he could picture Jack's unsympathetic smile.

"You don't have to choose, Hank. You can't. Accept it."

Except Hank hated the color gray. And this was gray — the greedy selfishness of love.

He let Brey pick out the ornaments. A birthday came, and Jack brought up one of Hank's pilfered bottles of Jack Daniel's. Hank didn't tell Brey about the girls' birthdays. Maybe Jack told him, Hank wasn't sure, but Brey was painfully aware of him. Almost ghostlike, he slipped away on the first birthday, and Hank and Jack drank a toast to Matilda. They celebrated all the birthdays this way — Beth's in

January, his girls in December, Lacy's in April. Easter slipped by easily. Thanksgiving in Waterfall was a giant potluck—game birds, stuffing, gravy and sauces... Brussels sprouts, kale, parsnips and pumpkin pie. Brey ate until he almost popped, and Hank liked Thanksgiving this year.

Christmas was always a gunshot to the chest—an ache that wouldn't ease until the ground grew sloppy and the sun grew warm.

Heat gave substance to the end-of-the-world scenario he was living.

Everything took on a blasted, whited-out look.

Winter froze and dripped and froze again. And the merry, festive colors and celebrations mocked the truth. But Jack decorated anyway, and they drank to their memories.

On Annabelle's birthday, Jack came over, and Brey went off by himself again—sensing it, Hank guessed. Patient, not prying. Later, Hank found him in bed, reading. Brey was quiet, sent a flicker of a smile over the top of his book, then set it down and turned off the light as Hank got into bed. Hank was grateful for the dark, even grateful for Brey's warmth when Brey rolled up against him.

"Can I help?"

Hank reached over to touch his face, ran a finger over his bristly cheek.

"Today was Annabelle's birthday."

"Fuck, Hank."

"Tilda's was the sixth."

Brey was quiet for a moment, then said, "You an' Jack..."

"This is how we remember."

He moved an arm so that Brey could settle against his chest.

"You don't do Christmas, do you?"

"This year I do."

"I'm sorry."

"I'm not. We're still here, an' Jack has no patience for self-pity."

"Jack is amazing," Brey muttered against his chest. "I like that I can't live up to him. I don't have to bother trying."

Hank laughed. He laughed out loud, and it shook him. Then Brey laughed too and Hank brought him up close and kissed his cheek.

"You are a wonder."

Cold Christmas birthdays. Splashes of bourbon and grim memory.

Brey's soft mouth. The hardness of muscles working underneath him. The smell of spit and cum.

They'd gone to see the Nutcracker on Matilda's birthday. She'd wanted Nathan's hot dogs for dinner. At home they'd had cake and ice cream.

Memories hit like sledgehammers in Hank's brain. He squeezed Brey's thighs and slipped out of him. Mesmerized by that loose, red hole.

"When's your birthday?"

Brey looked surprised. Hank watched him try to catch his breath. "June. An' yours?"

"July."

"I was here. I missed it."

Hank nodded, raised Brey's leg to kiss a knee. "I know. I missed yours too, but I won't this time."

Panic skittered across Brey's eyes, and Hank felt him try to close his legs. He didn't let him, squeezed a knee, staring into his eyes. Brey licked his lips. "Will you come with me?" he asked.

"Will you stay?"

"Hank..." The sound of anger and betrayal. "You promised."

Hank nodded. "I didn't promise to make it easy."

* * * *

Hank took Brey's picture of Sean to Younger. Younger confirmed it too. "Yeah, that's Sean."

Even though there was little face to see, just the blue trim on the ski cap. The lock on the pumping station's door was broken, but there was nothing else out of the ordinary. Hank suspected Sean returned after the patrol left with Brey and Josh and cleared out whatever had been in there. Vince and Anderson didn't think to look inside. It didn't really matter.

Younger pushed the picture back at him. "Sean's a bit player. Never strays far from Pete or Brian," he added quietly.

Hank didn't even blink. Of course, Brian. That made him wonder about Josh again. Nobody got to be young anymore. Josh was tough and watchful like Brian, and most of the time Hank saw Josh, Brian was nearby. Josh was raised by him, fed by him. Until Brey, he was Brian's shadow — a part of Brian's world. Now Brey's friend. A boy with a crush? Or a boy with convictions? Hank wasn't sure that Josh could walk away from Brian, and he needed to be sure for Brey's sake.

Because he made a promise.

A promise he didn't want to keep.

Twinkling lights drew him home in the dark, the Christmas tree in the park. Blurry globes of cheerful color in the icy night.

Chapter Sixteen

"C'mere."

It was Christmas Day. Brey was in the park with almost everybody else in Waterfall. The big tree, a blue spruce—the only tree even remotely green in the park—was lit up, twinkling foggy color in the wintry gloom. There were seven children, from five to eleven years old. A man dressed like Santa. Somebody had raided the party store in town. It amazed Brey how many things remained intact here while there were entire cities stripped bare. Waterfall was home. People didn't leave here. Christmas carols warbled and hissed on the staticky public address system. It was cold, and Brey would rather burrow in bed with Hank.

But then a voice murmured, "C'mere," and Josh took him by the elbow and pulled him away.

He went quietly.

He knew he should resist Josh's bossiness, but it was his nature to comply. Besides, he liked Josh's smile, wanted to see it, smiled back at him. "Merry Christmas to you too."

Josh looked around him and a flash of irritation swept through his eyes. Brey looked around too, slowing up a little, settling his gaze on Brian, all the way across the park. He was tall, his stare passing over the tops of everyone else's heads to bore into Brey's eyes. Dismissive. Amused. Because Brey wasn't anything. Josh's crush, except it wasn't exactly a crush. There was nothing boyish about it anymore. Amused. Brian was laughing with a man beside him. Not a high-pitched laugh. Brey couldn't hear it, but he knew the sound of it. Rough. Cold. Like ice on gravel. He'd heard it in Thom's garage. Not as memorable as that other laugh, but he remembered it now. Remembered the painful slap of Brian's palm across his ass. *Fuck. Of all the fucking times to remember. On Christmas.*

"Hey, Brey? You okay?"

He blinked. Tried to focus on Josh. "Yeah. Sure."

"You look sick."

He shook his head, forced a smile. "No. I'm fine."

Fuck that bastard.

This was Brey's life. Christmas. Christmas with Hank and Jack and Issa. Brian was taking that away. No. He wasn't taking anything away. Brey wasn't going to let him. He took a deep breath. "I said Merry Christmas. You didn't say it back."

Josh grinned at him. He angled himself so his back was to Brian, blocking him from Brey's view.

"You know you're a bit of a stalker," Brey said, and Josh laughed.

Brey let Josh protect him just because there was nothing lighthearted about it, nothing lighthearted about Josh. There was a glitter like the hardest metal in his eyes.

"Merry Christmas, Brey."

Then he reached into an inside pocket of his jacket and pulled out a box. Brey looked aghast, and Josh said, "I'm not giving you this as a Christmas gift. It's not a gift. I just... I want you to have it. You can remember me by it."

"Remember...?" Brey's voice faltered.

Josh squinted painfully at him. "Take it. You can think of it as a birthday gift if you want. I owe ya one," he added.

Heat scorched Brey's cheeks, and Josh grinned at him again. He pulled the lid off the box, and the contents gave him a stab of—shock, fear, gratitude, hope?

"Fuck, Josh."

Josh took the compass out of the box and stood with it for a moment. Then he tilted his head to the side, away from the park, past the Centre Park building, Brey's home almost, to the hidden interstate that stretched out past the post-line. "California," Josh said gently. "That way."

"Hank told you?"

"I knew where you were going. I know where you want to go. I wish I was you, Brey. I wish I had something to go to."

Brey was shocked and a little scared. Scared that Josh knew, because the knowing made it all the more real. Made it hard to pretend that it wasn't real. Pretend on those days when the idea of leaving Hank drove the air out of his lungs.

"You keep surprising me," Brey said.

Josh shrugged. "I dunno. I'm pretty normal."

Brey thought back to that day in the library, the feel of Josh's fingers on his cheek, scared to death of him—of everybody. Fearless, brave Josh. Now Brey was halfway smitten. With a quirk of his lips that made

Josh smile back at him, he leaned in and gave him a quick kiss.

"I like my birthday present. I liked yours too."

Josh rolled his eyes, blushing this time. "I better get goin'."

Giving Brey his compass back, Josh turned and walked off through a crowd that instinctively gave way for him.

* * * *

At home there were other presents. Brey had put garlands over every door and set the Christmas tree in a corner of the living room. The lights glowed off the glass door to the balcony. Issa gave away hand-knitted sweaters. Brey gave Issa scarves and a set of bangles he found in the old drugstore in town. Hank gave her a silver hand mirror etched with tiny tarnished roses. There were bottles of beer and bourbon, apple fritters. A floppy canvas hat that Jack gave to Brey.

Hank's present to Brey and Brey's to Hank stayed under the tree. Brey's was wrapped in a square of old blanket, Hank's to Brey in a box.

"You peek an' I'll beat your butt," Hank said after he set it out.

Brey was sitting on the couch, reading one of his library books. He peered over the top with a lascivious gleam in his eyes.

"Maybe that can be my present."

"Be a good boy, an' it might be."

Brey grinned at him. "That's a happy thought."

Now he drank Jack's beer, and they ate roasted grouse, cornbread and a butternut squash casserole for dinner. Afterward they drank champagne and ate little cakes sweetened with bits of dried fruit and fennel seeds. Brey was sleepy and almost drunk by the time Jack and Issa left. The living room was warm from the stove, whistling orange flames crackling behind the grate. Hank switched out the light and shadows jumped on the walls. The light in the hall was on and they could see each other.

"Oh Tannebaum, Oh Tannenbaum..."

The sound came from the park, carols still playing on the public address system, flames glowing in the fire bowls, almost ghostly snatches of laughter.

Brey smiled up at Hank's approach. A box came down to rest on his knees. It was heavy, and there was a soft slide and thump from inside.

"You didn't look?"

"I didn't look."

"Good boy."

Brey's smile broadened into a grin. Sitting up, he set down his beer and opened the box. He drew in a breath, whispered, "Oh, God," and pulled out the books inside. "These are mine? To keep?"

"Yes."

"How? All the books are in the library."

"There's a community college about thirty-five miles away. On one of the days I said I was going to Younger's, I didn't. I took one of the Jeeps instead."

"Hank."

Hank shrugged. "So sue me."

"God," Brey whispered again. There were books on the Civil War, twentieth century inventions, dictators, Russia, the Renaissance, Irish Americans and the mysteries and detective novels Brey loved. All paperbacks. Portable. Easy to carry. He could take the ones he wanted with him. "I haven't owned a book in over six years."

"That matters to you?"

He nodded. "I love everything from before but not just from before," he added, making the pensive look on Hank's face fade.

Hank gave him a slight smile. "I know you're a little partial to apple fritters."

"And to you."

"I'm from before."

Brey felt surprise, but, of course, that was true. "Yeah, I guess so."

He liked that without really knowing why. He remembered vaguely about cycles, time loops, circles. But he was a little drunk and couldn't quite keep the logic of that thought process, just the pleasantness of it.

"Open yours."

Hank retrieved it, then came back to sit on the coffee table. Brey gave him a framed black and white photograph of the picture he took of the tree by the farmhouse. The little birds were just smudges, but the tree glittered like a bejeweled sculpture.

"Brey, this… This is amazing."

He shrugged, uncomfortable and pleased. He knew it was a good picture, and it surprised him that he could really produce anything of value instead of just being the cheerful, amenable, willing man that he was. This was from him but outside of him, too.

"I'm glad you like it."

"Like it? You're fucking talented, Brey."

"I got lucky."

Hank ran a hand over the glass, then raised his hand to Brey's face. Brey leaned into it, smiling almost wistfully. Hank's smile was broader, surer.

"No, sweetheart. I got lucky."

* * * *

The lights in the spruce were unlit, soggy garlands drooping from the eaves of the gazebo. The air grew drizzly, but the clouds stayed a pale gray, blew quickly across the sky. People stayed inside. Cold seeped out of everything stone or paved.

Occasionally, the clouds parted and a bitter white sun shone through.

Brey waxed the library floors again. The pale light flowed like water on the marble.

Brey was happy and unhappy. Time passing brought him closer to home, closer to goodbye. Issa's twinkling smiles swamped him with guilt.

Fuck.

He wouldn't stay. Couldn't. Even though he could make a life here. Survive. Be happy. Staying was giving up, giving in to his tiredness, to his desire to stop fighting, to his belief that they all would rise away from this—that this wasn't the end of the world they had made.

He ran his fingers across a shelf of books, glossy paper covers, rough fabric against his skin. The smell of dust, decay, abandonment. No, he couldn't give in. He had to struggle, had to fight his way back to the way the world was. Everything here was unraveling, people clinging to pale traditions.

Like New Year's Eve.

The lights on the Christmas tree would go back on. Music. Drinking and celebration.

This was Brey's New Year too. His new life.

* * * *

They didn't go out to celebrate. The lights on the Christmas tree filled the living room window with color. Outside, the gray mist pressed against the glass. Inside, the fire popped, and the air was hot and dry.

The clock on the credenza was ticking, easing toward midnight.

Brey giggled into his champagne glass. They had real coffee at breakfast and champagne now, and Brey was drunk already, sweating in the hot room.

"Dom fucking Perignon. I can't believe it."

"I stocked it away for a special occasion."

"I love your priorities."

Hank shook his head with a slight smile. He was sitting on the edge of the couch, opening up another bottle. At the pop of the cork, Brey toasted the air.

"Yeah, baby."

He was shirtless. Breathless. Hank's look of admiration stirred him. He dipped his head to give him a smile from beneath his lashes then stretched out his glass. Hank refilled it, and he took a sip, letting his palm stroke down his belly, watching Hank's eyes follow him.

"I wanna dance," Brey said.

Hank just grunted and leaned back against the couch.

Brey took another sip, watching him. His head was buzzing slightly. "You don't want to?"

"You dance. Dance for me."

Brey looked Hank over, barefoot, jeans, T-shirt, slouched comfortably, one arm across the top of the couch. He licked his lips, thought about being naked in front of him and felt his cock start to fatten. His pants hung low on his hips, just below the line of his pubic hair. Hank's eyes dropped, focusing there. He rubbed himself through his pants, pushing his dick against his palm.

"I can dance."

"Do that for me," Hank said softly.

Brey swallowed the champagne and let Hank fill his glass again. Then he went over to the credenza, put a CD into the player and turned up the volume. A sudden thrumming heat filled him. It pounded inside his chest and head, and he let it work inside him, begin to stir his muscles. He stood with his back to Hank. He knew he was moving and he closed his eyes, let his memory go backward to the feel of other bodies bumping his, to the sight of lights strobing all around him, flashing shades of blue, the air wavering, scented with sweat and liquor and sex.

Brey circled the floor, swinging back around to face Hank, his hips liquid, carrying him in a fog of longing. His heart pounded to the drumming beat. His arms swayed over his head, pelvis undulating, heat in his belly. He slowed and swallowed his champagne, fingers popping the button on his pants, tugging down his zipper. Hank's arm slid off the back of the couch, and he scooted up, hooded eyes on Brey's. Brey smiled at him, swayed and sashayed away. His pants slipped as he went, twisting and bumping his hips from side to side. The waistband scraped the middle of his ass. His feet moved, small sideways steps, up, back, pirouetting with a jerk of his hips, a bump and thrust, his fingers pushing at his pants. His cock popped free, and he moaned out loud and caught Hank's gasp over the pounding strains of the music.

"You like that?" he asked, panting at the heat scorching through him.

"You know I do. I want your noises."

"Like a porn star?"

"Yeah," Hank agreed, and his face was almost blank, eyes fixed.

With a flick of his hips, Brey's pants slid to the floor and he kicked them away. The air licked at his skin like tiny flames. His cock swelled and bobbed in front of him. He drank with one hand and stroked his dick with the other, groaning as his hips swayed and his feet carried him in a slow circle. His ears rang, his chest thrummed, the lights of the Christmas tree swirling against the glass. Strobe lights, flashing faces, the feel of a hand on his hip, one on his belly.

Hank's hands.

Groaning again, he leaned back, felt Hank's palm skim his torso, pull and twist at his nipples. Hank's breath was a hot blast against his ear.

"Aubrey..."

The world came back — this world — Christmas lights, no swirling disco balls, no sea of orgasmic faces. Hank's rough fingertips. His tender passion.

"I'm so fucking in love with you, Aubrey."

Brey swung around, smashing his dick against Hank's jeans, sloshing champagne as he flung his arms around Hank's neck. His hips bucked and his head fell back, his groans bubbling out of his throat. Hank grabbed him by the hair, yanked his face back in and he gasped against Hank's lips, opened his mouth, devouring the tongue that pressed inside, feeling the room slowly spin. His arms locked tighter around Hank's neck, fingers clutching at his empty champagne glass.

Hank pulled back, bit him, smothered him with his mouth, sucking up Brey's air. Brey tried to gasp, lungs swelling, beginning to struggle. He was swamped with sensation — wet, hot tongue, the music a pounding heartbeat, lights glowing on glass and walls, Hank's hard cock pushing against his, denim scraping his skin, sending shocks of pleasure through him. His mouth fell free and he sucked in desperate lungfuls of air. Hank's palms played across his back, dug into the flesh of his ass. His hips bucked, cock rubbing rough fabric.

Electric pulses of pleasure shot through him. He didn't know where the words came from. He was stunned, embarrassed, insane with desire. *"Breed me..."*

Shock and lust crossed Hank's face too. Then, with a nod, he pulled off his T-shirt, and Brey swayed, grabbing onto him, nails scraping skin. He caught Hank's forearm, and Hank yanked at the buttons of his jeans one-handed. Sliding to his knees, Brey gave Hank the champagne glass, pulled at his jeans, freeing his dick, revealing the long, strong stretch of his legs. Brey groaned again, running his hands up warm flesh, swallowing Hank's leaky cock, burying his face in pubic hair and musky skin.

"Fuck!"

He winced at the fingers knotting in his hair and pulled off a little. He curled his tongue, flicked at the tip, sucked and hummed and swallowed. His mouth filled with saliva and the taste of Hank.

Then the room fell abruptly silent, the CD at an end.

He could hear his slurping noises, a pop as he released Hank's cock, fingers curled around the base, lapping up and down the sides, nibbling and sucking at the tip again.

"Aubrey... Sweetheart. I don't wanna come."

Brey moaned, a strangely loud sound in the quiet room, and Hank's hands took him under the arms and pulled him up. A faint cloud of confusion passed over him when Hank thrust the bottle of champagne at him and said, "Wait for me."

Brey was dizzy with desire, cock throbbing. He took a swig of cold champagne, shivering as it chilled his overheated belly. His toes and fingertips tingled. He was happy, crazy happy with champagne and Hank. He loved him. His stoic courage and stalwart heart. His body, strong, fragrant, sweet and spicy. He loved to sleep in Hank's arms with Hank's hairy chest beneath his cheek. He loved him... Loved him with the desperation he loved his family with before the prison doors shut him away. The champagne sizzled inside him, cold and fizzy. He let the bottle slip, thunk onto the coffee table then Hank grabbed him and picked him up. Brey's legs went around Hank's waist, and Hank smiled at him.

From outside came whistling and popping sounds, laughter and cheers. People ran by the building then the sounds faded.

Brey ground his crotch into Hank and opened his mouth on a moan. Hank bit him in the neck, and he whimpered and writhed.

"Yeah," groaned Hank against his skin. "Like that. I love those noises."

With an arm under his ass, Hank carried him over to the credenza across the room but didn't let him down right away. Brey's legs hitched higher on his waist and Hank gestured to the bottle of lube he brought out with him.

"Slick me up."

Grinning, Brey pumped out several squirts and took the hot flesh pinned between their bodies. Hank hissed, eyes fixed on Brey's. Brey stroked, his lips twitching mischievously.

"You too, sweet boy."

Then Brey bit his lip and stretched his arm back, dipping and twisting his fingers in his hole. He sighed deeply. "I'm your porn star tonight, Hank. Your whore. Cheap an' dirty."

"Take my cock, sweetheart."

"Yeah," Brey whispered.

Then Hank set his ass on the edge of the credenza. His legs squeezed Hank's hips and he leaned his shoulders back against the cool wall. The Christmas tree glowed with light, and the room was dark and soft with color at the same time. He gasped as Hank's pushed his cock in, panting at the burn, little cries escaping at the pain. He rocked his head against the wall, opening, splitting. Then his breath blew out on a stab of pleasure. Hank pulled out and pushed back in, and Brey met him, rolling his hips, biting back his cries, squirming, whimpering.

"Oh fuck... Oh yeah... Yeah... Yeah..." Every thrust pushed his breath out, a groan, a whimper. "Fuck my ass... Oh yeah... Like that... Just like that..."

A wheeze and a cry came out of his throat, and he wasn't playing anymore.

"Oh God. Hank... Oh God."

His shoulders knocked against the wall, his head thwacking it. He pulled his legs up and let his knees fall to the side. Hank's fingers dug into his hips. He was split open, exposed, bare. The noises he made floated up from the hidden places of memory, of the way he used to be, loud and raucous and joyful—the way he couldn't be in prison. His father's money bought him protection. He was never hurt. He wasn't alone either. A few of the guards wanted him. He was quiet, drawn in, restrained, fucked in utter silence, quick and furtive. Afterwards pushed away. A secret. An infraction. A crime. A risk. An ass, wide open and anonymous.

"I need... I need to...to hear...you love..."

"You, Aubrey. I love you. You. Only you."

Hank was pushing in and out, plunging in deep, his belly rubbing Brey's rigid cock. Brey's balls were on fire. The lights on the Christmas tree swam in his eyes.

Cries burst out, escaped the loosening in his chest. All his body was alive with pleasure, throbbing bursts at every thrust. Hank's cock moved in him, slid and pulsed and split him wider. He was free. Like ghosts escaping into the daylight, his fear floated away, his grief and despair. He was his father's and mother's boy. That carefree, happy boy. The one of faith. The one who believed and loved and shouted hallelujahs.

He yelled, "I love you! I fuckin' love you, Hank!" All the while knowing he was going to leave him. But he was free this night, this New Year's. "Come in me!"

Hank's growl startled him. "You're mine, Aubrey. You'll always be mine."

Brey's vision went white and his body spasmed, the contraction of his belly jerking him down on Hank's pulsing cock. In the whiteness that surrounded him, he felt perfect peace and perfect happiness. Hank's arms stayed strong around him, one hand cupping his ass, rocking him as his body went slack and everything faded away.

* * * *

It was colder than cold. Plus, he wasn't wearing gloves. Neither was Brey, who was puffing into his hands as they walked across the street for chico and fritters. The Starbucks was crowded, and they stood up against the wall in the corner. Hank saw Ken and nodded, saw Brey trail his eyes behind him as they passed. A muscle twitched in Brey's cheek, and Hank hid his smile in his cup. Steam warmed his face as he drank. The feel of Brey's shoulder pressing his surprised him. Brey's moods were strange, up and down, his temper quick. His expressions were mobile, played across his face without artifice, showed a conflict he wasn't talking about. Hank wanted to believe that Brey wanted to stay with him, but he didn't dare. He promised. It wasn't right.

Wanted him forever, though.

He drank the rest of his chico with the weight of Brey pleasant against him. Eyed his pink, cold cheeks, his unruly waves and curls.

Brey's pale, clear gaze met his.

"You ready?" he asked.

Brey nodded.

They took their cups back up front, hunched against the cold outside. Clouds billowed on the horizon, dark as bruises. The wind picked up, biting and damp.

"Think it's gonna rain?" Brey asked.

"I hope so."

Brey grinned. "I wanna play in it."

Hank laughed, liking that image.

They parted at the library, but Hank continued past the police station. On the other side of the park, he followed a street that began to meander in a sinuous curve, out of keeping with the grid-like design of the rest of Waterfall, but Hank liked it, thought of older towns, homes with porches, shade covered sidewalks that cracked and sloped over surfacing tree roots.

He moved cautiously here, careful of ice.

Wind gusted, and the clouds loomed, blotting out the sun. A false twilight spread shadow across the ground.

He passed empty, boarded-up shops, clothing stores, a bookstore, hair salon, a card and gift boutique. The windows were dark, sadness behind the glass.

At the end of the block, a parking lot opened up, a pair of cars on flat tires still there, near a church, white-painted and square, heavy, black doors in front.

Crossing the lot, he went around to the back where an outdoor walkway separated the church and the community center where the Council met once a month. The doors there were open, and he smelled more chico inside, two canisters on a table with cups set out.

There was another long table up front, a podium beside it, several rows of folding chairs in front. Nate Vallero, Paul Zimmerman and Ken were already at the table, Younger and Pete standing at a window, looking outside, Brian at a chico canister, eyeing Hank as he came over. Josh was sitting on one of the folding chairs, forearms draped over his knees, staring at the floor. He yawned once then sat back in his chair and crossed his arms over his chest. Yawned again.

Hank poured a cup of chico, nodded at Brian.

Brian nodded back. "Hank." It wasn't quite a smirk. Was barely there.

A desire born deep inside rose in Hank—a desire to pound Brian's face into a pulp. He smiled at him, tipped his cup, glanced at Josh as he moved on.

"How you doin', Josh?"

"I'm okay." Sleepy voice.

Hank walked over to Younger, leaned against the wall. "Think it's gonna rain?"

A smile twitched on Younger's face, a silent laugh in his quiet voice. "Till kingdom come, according to Brian."

Hank nodded. "The monsoon theory."

The truth was that once it started, the rain would continue for days. But days weren't enough. Even as the ground was saturated and water ran through the gutters, the water table barely rose. The reservoir continued to shrink, but it poured with the illusion of forever.

"How's your boy?" Younger asked.

"Busy. Working."

Younger turned all the way around, back to the window. "That's good. Keeps 'im outta trouble, I bet."

"Brey's not the kind to make trouble."

Younger's smile was a grimace. "I wasn't thinking of Brey."

Hank knew Younger was looking at Brian and resisted looking around until the sound of heavy bootsteps filled the room. Brian's friends—half a dozen. Josh was looking backward too, then up front again, a look of distance sweeping quickly across his face. Hank gave him a small nod, and Josh got up and went to Brian's side.

"We almost ready?" Younger asked.

"Just waiting on Issa."

Younger nodded and Hank went over to the table to sit down. Men arrived by the handful then Issa. She sat beside Hank, windswept strands of her silver blonde hair pulled out of her topknot of a ponytail. Younger sat down too, and Issa pulled off her mittens with a flustered quickness. Hank frowned at her, and she pursed her lips and jerked her chin at the door. Brey stood just inside, leaning against the wall. He gave Hank a blank stare, then moved to one of the chairs and sat down.

"Sorry, Hank," said Issa. "I never thought he'd want to come."

Hank shrugged. "I wasn't trying to keep him away."

But he could tell Brey was angry, just from the blankness of his face—a blankness that disappeared when his gaze lit on the pillar behind the table Hank sat at. There were two pillars in a centerline, one near the front doors and the one behind him. On the one behind him there were hooks for cuffs to attach to—a slave's cuffs. Hank warned Brey, wanted him to be aware, even though he'd never seen a slave attached to the post. Brey stared for a long time, then he swallowed and looked away.

Nate rapped the table with his knuckles. "Okay. I think we can start. I'll go over last month's items then we can move on..."

Hank tuned him out. He saw Brey glance at Josh, a smile softening his face. Josh smiled back at him. Hank frowned until he caught Josh's eyes. Josh flushed slightly, looking embarrassed, then gave him an imperceptible nod before he leaned closer to Brian and whispered something to him. Brian shook his head. They both sat with their arms crossed in front of them. Both big. Same hair and eyes. Connected. Hank remembered families he met on his calls, poor often, with little to give but giving it anyway. A mix of relatives and outsiders pulled into their circles. Family wasn't always about blood, and blood didn't always connect.

He looked at Brey looking back at him.

Fuck. He'd do anything for him.

"An' that," said Nate, "leads into today. Any new business before the agenda items?"

Brian stood. "Two things. First," he said, pointing back at Brey. "That doesn't belong here."

Issa glared at him. "Brey belongs with Hank. And Hank, as you can see, is here."

"That slave went past the post-line. I didn't see it on the agenda last time or this time. I never heard of anything being done about the attack on Pete Sawyer either."

"Christ," muttered Younger.

"The whole point of the Slave Laws is that they're consistent an' just for every slave."

"You aren't concerned about the slaves," said Issa.

"Pete never made a complaint," said Younger.

"I don't think Pete really wants to go up against Hank. I didn't say anything about that. Not my business. This time that slave went right past the post-line with no consequences."

"Your own son was there," said Issa.

"I don't—an' my kid doesn't change this—show favoritism to anybody."

Hank was looking at Brey, whose face had gone bloodless.

"You can't manufacture a problem where there isn't one," said Younger. "The law addresses deliberate excursion. Hank's slave was pulled past that line. Injured too," he added, looking mildly at Brian, who stared at him with a sort of stunned bafflement.

"Good," said Issa. "I don't want to talk about this anymore."

Nate rapped his knuckles again. "We have other topics anyway. Our waste collection problems, the Summer Park calendar, conservation—"

"That's me too," Brian broke in. "I need water for my crops—"

"We all do," said Issa. "We need to conserve for that reason."

"We need to collect."

"I agree with that," said Paul.

"I agree to both," said Issa.

"We're already bare bones up at our place," said Younger. "I don't see us able to contribute that way."

"You can collect," said Brian. "We can help with that. Build cisterns, tanks, the canal..."

"Those are big projects," said Issa. "You're talking years."

"I'm talking slaves. You don't like that talk, I get it. But slaves are here. You have a slave working for you, Issa. We need to make tough decisions."

"We don't need—"

A sudden thunderous clap shook the building, and a deluge of rain began to pour down on the roof. Everybody looked up. The windows darkened, sheets of gray slashing down. Lightening flashed, brightness exploding. The air smelled of ozone and wet cement. The splashing sounds of water grew louder. Rain spilled over the eaves, slapping loudly on the walkways, rushing through the gutters.

"That," said Brian, "is a fucking waste."

Issa rolled her eyes.

Younger gave Hank a wry smile. "You sure you're on the side of the angels?"

Hank laughed. After a few minutes people moved away from the windows and sat back down. Hank's gaze swept the seats in back, but Brey's stayed empty.

* * * *

Brey meant it about playing in the rain. He took off his jacket and let it drench him. He splashed in the gutters, soaking his shoes. The icy shock invigorated him.

He steeled himself against his fear. He wouldn't feel it. He wouldn't imagine that whip against his back, worse than Thom's belt.

He let the rain plaster his hair to his head and felt it run down his back. It smelled like metal and beaded like oil on his skin. He licked it off his upper lip, and it tasted salty and sweet. Like tears. Life. The taste of Hank's cum.

It rained day after day.

A few people came into the library, slopped mud across the floors.

Brey mopped.

The next day he mopped again.

He didn't take any pictures, but he didn't want to either. He didn't want to use up all his film. He took a chair in one of the random reading clusters and sketched on his old sketchpad. He drew while the rain came down—the statues in the library, copies of the pictures on the wall, one or two people. And he was good at it and he liked the lost feeling it gave him. He floated off into the pictures—safe and absorbed. Only the darkening of the light brought him back, surprised at where he'd gone.

He could do that, he thought. He could draw instead of take photos.

A strange feeling of relief came over him. He wasn't sure where it came from or what it meant. It had something of gratitude in it, a feeling that he wasn't entirely alone.

The rain poured. Slowed. Stopped and came again. Sprinkled. Clouds clotted the sky. Grew thin and blew away in wispy patches, letting the pale sun shine through. The light glittered. The air tingled with damp and sweetness. Sprinkles showered. Showers poured again. Clouds filled the sky, drifted away.

Brey mopped.

And sketched.

Mopped again.

The sun came out. A bright yellow sun. The muddy ground steamed. The rain stayed away.

He stood on the library steps, waiting for Hank. The park was green with weeds. It was time. Time to go.

And he didn't want to.

Panic filled him. Afraid to run. Afraid to stay.

Hank said nothing, and Brey grew angry. Maybe Hank wasn't going to keep his promise.

Even if Brey didn't want him to.

He drew a picture of the interstate stretching far away into nothing. Outlying houses. The rough hills and the mountains. The road that wound away to the garage. Cars in parking lots with hillocks of dead leaves against deflated tires. He found a bleached out candy bar wrapper. His sketches had nothing to do with anything he pretended to care about.

Everything to do with those orange posts.

The sun came out, drying the mud to thick, friable crusts. Clouds whipped by, shadows skating across the ground, making the pale sun flash and burn.

The dark came quickly, a descent of sudden, starless black.

He flirted with that dark, dashing back into town with the last of the gray light. A burn of cold air in his lungs. A stitch in his side. The sharp jangle of fear. He was always back in time, but he played with the fear that he wasn't—a fantasy fear that wouldn't ever really come true because he wouldn't let it. The real fear burrowed deep, lived in anger. He never took it out to look at it, flared with rage when it peeked out anyway.

Coming into town this time, he saw Hank walking toward him and sweated in the cold air. A shiver ran through him.

"Hey."

"Almost curfew, Brey."

Hank's voice was neutral, meaning he was waiting on Brey's mood. Brey's voice challenged him. "Almost."

Hank sighed, turned when he reached him to walk at his side. "You know Issa wanted you to close up."

"Fuck."

Jack's birthday. She was cooking dinner for him. "I forgot."

Hank nodded. "Get any good pictures?"

"I wasn't taking pictures."

Waspish. *Fuck, what an asshole.* He could imagine the clenching in Hank's jaw.

"That wasn't what I meant. I meant draw."

"You didn't say draw."

"Okay, Brey."

This time Brey's jaw clenched. He felt the jostle of Hank's shoulder as they walked. A strange ache grew inside him. At home he lay on the bed, reading from his stack of books. At night, mist crept up against the windows. His eyes drifted to it. He watched it bead the glass, seal him in, as secure as bars. He imagined that he'd never escape. That this was life. Warm. Comfortable. With the puttering sounds of Hank in the living room.

His head throbbed. He looked at his book, and the words swam. He wanted a drink. A glass of beer. He brought it back to bed, sank back against the pillows. The beer eased the throb in his head, but every time he looked at the window, he wished for bars. He drank, read, set his book and empty glass down.

"Hank!"

"What?"

"You comin' to bed?" He was restless.

"In a bit."

Fuck.

He switched off the light, squirmed down under the covers and stared at the ceiling. Slept. He woke up to the sounds of Hank in the dark and rolled away. There was a quiet quieter than before. A hesitation. Then the creaking drop of the mattress as Hank lay down. Brey kept his eyes open, staring out of the dark windows. The mist was gone, just darkness outside. Brey wasn't surprised to feel Hank's hand on his hip, a gentle squeeze before he rolled away too.

* * * *

The alcove pulled his eyes over. He frowned, staring at a place in the hall he passed every day without seeing it anymore. A corner of the bed peeked through the gap between the wall and the curtain. A place he didn't sleep in, didn't want to sleep in. He remembered slamming like a crazed thing in Hank's arms, flooded with fears that were formless and not, rocked on the floor, Hank's gentle whispers seeping through the terror-filled dark.

Only anger now. Just anger.

He was a fuck. Only that probably. Always that. Only the world changed.

He went into the kitchen, and Hank looked up. "Chico?"

That's all it took. A chink he could squeeze through. Chico — not coffee.

"Oh yeah. Gee, thanks. Fake shit."

A slow flush started up Hank's neck. "You know, Brey, I come from a family of fighters. You ain't got nothin' on us."

Brey flushed too. "I don't want your shitty chico."

"You want a fight instead?"

If he wanted to, he could fight about anything. It didn't matter what Hank said. He could drive a wedge, push it wider and wider. His nerves drove panic skittering through him. His stomach clenched, rolled over.

"I feel sick."

Saying that surprised him. He guessed it was his body usurping his stupid brain, trying to put an end to this.

Hank came over quickly, gripped him by an arm. "Come lie down."

There were sick people at Younger's. Jack kept going up. A cold that was worse than a cold at first. Then a flu-like sickness.

"I just have a stomachache."

They were getting better at Younger's, and Jack didn't have it. Jack wasn't worried either. He even grinned. "Germs abhor a vacuum."

So people were getting sick again, just like before. Except nothing else was like before, and his stomach clenched in another angry wave.

"I feel sick talkin' about your fucking chico."

"*My* chico?"

The word came out through gritted teeth. Brey was almost fascinated by Hank's anger. Leery too, though, because this was an almost scary Hank. The blood in his cheeks, a flush across his forehead. Hank's lips thinned, waiting.

Brey spoke carefully. "I don't really care about chico—yours or anybody's. I just don't want it. I don't want chico or tea or any of that." There was almost a taunt in his voice, edged by a barely contained fury. Brey put his face up close, spoke through his teeth because he wasn't really afraid of Hank. He couldn't ever be. "I want you to let me go!"

Liar! Liar!

Hank spoke carefully too. "I...don't...welch."

That panicked him. Inexplicably.

Sweat broke out. His heart raced. Almost against his will, his finger rose, hooked in his collar, yanked and twisted at it. The metal bit into his skin, pinched it, cut off his air. That was good, a thing to focus on, a thing that didn't tear him apart inside.

God, I can't... I can't....

Then Hank's fingers gripped him by the hair and his wrist, yanking his head back and trying to pull his fingers loose. "God damn it, Brey. Knock it off!" Light sparked in his eyes. He let go and stumbled back. "God damn it," Hank said again, huffing out frustrated breaths.

"Fuck it," said Brey, glaring at him.

But he wasn't angry anymore. He was disoriented, felt like a top spinning in the open, nothing to grab onto. He almost laughed at Hank's wary look, the way he was sliding back over, palms up, face flushed.

Angry.

Brey let out a gust of pent-up air. "I can fight too."

The minute he said that, he shivered, suddenly clear-headed. Hank straightened too, and Brey saw pity bloom in his eyes because Brey was thinking of Patric—of anger, of one stupid, mindless second in time, and Hank would know that. The enormity washed over him like icy water. He felt his scalp prickle and went suddenly around the table, out of Hank's way.

"Brey—"

"I'm okay. I just have to go."

He grabbed his bag out of the bedroom and headed back for the door.

"You don't have to, Brey."

His steps faltered. He felt a presence behind him, not pressing, not pushing. A wall, a pillar to grab onto. Without looking back, he went out the door, slamming it behind him.

Chapter Seventeen

The interstate stretched away to nothing. The two-lane to Thom's garage cut across dark, barren soil until it met the hills below Younger's. The mountains were a dark, faraway ridge.

A few miles outside the post-line Brey wouldn't even be a speck. His collar just a flashing red blip on a radar in a room in Hank's station.

At least it wouldn't shock him.

But they'd run him down anyway, cuff him. Take him back. Whip him.

He breathed. The air was damp, sweet. He was following the interstate up to the crossroads to Thom's, Waterfall mostly behind him, those peculiarly situated outlying buildings taking shape up ahead of him. An empty repair shop. The Water Spout with its unlit neon sign in the window. The bar was set back from the road, taller than the repair shop. It was two stories but didn't look tall enough for that to Brey. Maybe it wasn't even a bar before. He was curious about the inside, but once he saw the people on the front porch, he stopped, sat down and took out his sketchpad.

As he drew, an awareness of beauty stole over him. It wasn't that way with the photographs. Taking pictures, he concentrated on the things people kept around them. Drawing pictures, the empty buildings took on fragile and lonely outlines. The whistle of the wind through windows, down empty aisles was the sound of unquiet voices.

Permanence was built into girders and struts. Structures made to outlive time.

But they didn't. Their walls resonated with echoes. Everything decayed, and leaves collected — orange and yellow and honey-gold.

In his lonely thoughts, Patric was smiling at him again. His gentle fingers drew upon Brey's face.

"I love you, Brey."

A flutter moved under eyelids that would never open again.

Brey drew, let his fingers sketch the bar, the people, let his eyes stray past the orange posts.

In his imaginings, time looped back and Patric sprawled on the club floor, beet red and furiously alive. He got up and pushed Brey away. Time wobbled. And all the things in real life that came after that moment never did. Everything pivoted on that second of time. Pushing Patric tore a hole in some invisible fabric, and Eve came through.

His thinking was childish. He knew that. To blame himself for this new world was ludicrous. Arrogant. It wasn't about him. Children died. Good people. Kind people. People he breezed by every day before. Unseeing. Still — the belief was there, an ache inside. All he had to do was love Patric. Give. Give in. But he was selfish. Greedy. Even Hank said he was selfish.

And he was.

He wanted happiness.

He wanted to run. Run past those posts.

Run away.

His fingers trembled, and he looked up again and saw her. She was out on the gravel lot beside the bar, standing by a sun-bleached blue pickup, waving her arms at him. He almost looked behind him. Then her arm came down, and she shielded her eyes, bouncing on her toes.

The wind flattened her skirt against her, blew at her hair. The pages of his sketchpad slapped, and the currents pulled at his jacket. Just a moment ago, it was almost still. But it was a good reason to get up, to walk away, just in case anybody on the porch was looking at him.

He crossed the asphalt over to the repair shop. The building blocked him from view. Out back was just broken asphalt and clumps of soggy dead weeds. He went over to the bar, coming up in back. The building was angled from this direction, part back porch, part side wall. A stretch of empty, dark windows.

Inside, people drank. An ordinary, everyday activity.

Except here. Except in Brey's life. He wasn't ordinary. He was a slave, beginning to run, bag thumping against him, running to a woman his family used to employ. Not ordinary. But he was grinning, and she looked around quickly, then ran over to meet him, arms open, wrapping around him as he hugged her back.

He swung her up with a laugh.

"I can't believe I get to see you again."

"You scared me that last time."

He set her down, and she pulled him under the back eaves. At the top of the porch, a door was open. He could smell food cooking inside. Heavy screens covered the bottom windows.

"Younger promised you were okay," she said. "You weren't hurt?"

He shook his head, saw her fingers come up to touch his collar.

"I'm okay. I knew Hank from before. Are you okay?"

She smiled ruefully. "I'm married. That protects me." Then she shrugged. "I don't love 'im. I don't hate 'im."

"We're lucky, I guess."

She was thin, and the sparkle that always danced in her eyes didn't rise to the surface anymore. But she was smiling, and she wasn't giving up.

Then her face turned suddenly impish, and she said, "You sure are a gorgeous thing."

"Christ."

His cheeks burned, and she laughed, glancing back quickly. "I can't stay, Brey." She took a hold of his jacket and pulled him close. "But I wanted you to tell you that your family didn't leave you—"

"I know."

"They wanted to come back. People were crazy."

He nodded. "I saw a little of it. I went to the house."

"Your dad flew your family to Big Sur."

He choked. "God, I knew it. I knew it."

"I don't think your dad came back, though. I didn't stay. I went home too. I don't think he had time to come back. It was so fast, Brey. The world just fell apart."

"I know. I don't blame anybody. I just need to get home."

"Brey, you can't." She whipped another quick glance behind her before she reached up to cup his face.

"Honey, you can't go anywhere. I just wanted you to know that they didn't leave you."

The restless whipping of the wind made him anxious, nervous, like a sign.

"Come with me," he said.

She shook her head and frowned, and there was regret in her expression. She was already backing up. "I have to go back inside. We're having a birthday party. I even made a cake."

"Molly—"

"Go on, Brey."

"Yeah. Go on, Brey."

Molly spun.

A man with long brown hair and a beard stood in the back doorway. He drank out of a beer mug, eyes on Brey. Molly swiped her palms on her skirt, the hem blowing around her ankles.

The man lifted his chin at Brey.

"You have a curfew, don't you?"

It wasn't even close to dark, but Brey nodded, looking into eyes that warned him to remember he was a slave—with rules, not rights. Curfews. Cause to worry.

The man on the porch slid a boot down to the next step, and Brey backed up.

"Bye, Molly."

The sound of his voice was off. He wished he could pull his words back. He was supposed to skulk off silently. He knew that. The familiarity in his voice brought the man bristling down the steps.

"Are you deaf? A little dense, maybe?"

The chance of just walking away diminished. Molly saw it too, put herself in the way of the man walking across the gravel. He veered around her without touching, dodging as she darted back at him. The man bellowed, "Hey, Frank!"

Brey hitched up his bag. "The fuck is your problem?"

The man blinked, amazed, slowed his steps as he came up. "Pretty boy's got a pair, eh?"

"Fuck you."

The man bellowed out a laugh. "Oh, yeah. This is gonna be fun."

Gravel crunched. Footsteps. Brey looked sideways into a glare. One man was dragging a cue stick on the ground. All of them had beer mugs, grins on their faces. Molly went over to the man Brey knew was her husband. Frank—red hair, freckled face, smashed nose.

A voice from in back said, "Hey. It's that slave."

"What slave?"

"Hank's. You remember. Chattin' up Molly then, too."

Frank scowled and said, "My wife can talk to whoever she wants."

"Oh, yeah?" said the man with the cue stick.

"I tol' 'im to fuck off," said the brown-haired man.

Molly pulled away from Frank and said, "You better lay off, Mel. Brey's my friend."

"Kinda friend?" asked Mel.

"Hey," yelled Frank.

Mel shrugged. "I don't care anyway. I care about teachin' that mouth a lesson."

Brey felt something splinter in him. That thin shell he formed against the horror that the world became around him. "You fuckers. You love this world, don't you? You must've been jumpin' for joy knowing you were gonna get set loose. You goddamn throwbacks.

A million fuckin' years of evolution pissed away. Fuckin' morons!"

Mostly they gaped. The one with the cue stick gave a half laugh of disbelief then Brey bolted.

Confusion slowed him at the front of the bar. They'd run him down. He wasn't getting away. But that thought filled him with a strange euphoria. He couldn't escape, wasn't going to waste any time wondering where to run. He was going home. That was his fantasy anyway. He set off and ran toward the interstate, kicking up dirt and debris on his way. He pounded up onto the pavement, clutching the strap of his bag, a line of orange posts wavering up ahead. His lungs labored, dragging in cold, sharp air. He raced off the pavement, slowing and stumbling in the dirt, picking up speed again. Under the sound of the blood in his ears, footsteps thudded audibly behind him. Boots, heavy. He pushed ahead, kicking up dirt, sprinting past the posts. Laughter burst out of him, gusting chortles of happiness. He was a little red dot zigzagging across a radar screen. His freedom already ticking away.

But he was free.

Stumbling. Slowing on wobbly legs. Wheezing happily.

Clomping boots came closer and closer. His lungs burned, aching. He couldn't run anymore, spun around and threw his fist through the air. The sight of it, the motion, the blur of faces exhilarated him. Raced through him like lightening. Burned out all his fear. Pain exploded in his knuckles, and he yelped in surprise.

His fist had connected with a nose, and the man with the cue stick stumbled back, clamping his hands over his face.

"Fuck!"

Brey snatched up the cue stick and dropped his bag. He jabbed out and stabbed Mel in the collarbone. Excitement jangled through him. He swung the cue stick through the air and said, "Fuck off."

Frank and Molly ran up, Frank flushed and sweaty, Molly's hair a wild halo. Frank raised his hands, stepping into the space between Brey and the others.

"Okay, guys. We're supposed to be celebratin' a birthday here."

"Fucker broke my nose."

"You were ugly anyway."

"Fuck you, Frank."

"Lookit. C'mon back. Cops are gonna be here any minute."

"I don't care about any fuckin' cops."

"C'mon. I wanna eat," said Frank.

"Gimme that cue stick," said the brown-haired man.

Brey laughed and swung it in a whistling arc. "Come an' get it."

He was floating on a strange feeling of lightness, like ether was flowing through his veins. Energy tingled in his fingertips. The sky was a clear pure blue. The wind was cold and sharp, scented like weeds. Everything he sensed was acute. His heart pounded without fear.

They weren't going to hurt him.

This time he fought back. He smiled, whipping the cue stick through the air again.

"Crazy bastard."

Molly said, "Look," and they followed her finger, pointing at the Jeep flying across the ground. It bounced, tires churning back clots of dirt. "Are you happy?"

Frank tugged on her. "C'mon."

She pulled her arm away, and Brey felt his energy running out of him. He set the bottom of the cue stick into the ground and waited for the Jeep. Eyes fixed on him. He stared back. Sweat matted his hair. He took a breath and licked salt off his upper lip.

The Jeep pulled up. *Vince and Anderson again, for godsakes.*

He grimaced. Vince frowned at him. Molly said, "They chased Brey out here."

"You know better 'n that, Molly. We were tryin' to catch 'im."

That was from Mel, and Brey gave him a grim smile.

"Dude just bolted," said a man with grizzled stubble on his skull and jowls.

Frank said, "We probably scared 'im" and Molly said, "You chased 'im," her eyes on Frank.

Frank shrugged. "Could be. I didn't see it all."

Anderson took the cue stick, and a muffled voice said, "Gimme that."

Frank grabbed Molly before she could say anything else and pulled her away. "We're goin' now. C'mon."

Molly just looked at him, and he let her go. Then she ran to Brey and hugged him, whispering, "I'm sorry, Brey."

He hugged her back. "I'm not. I'm happy. I got to see you again."

"Molly…"

She let go and backed away with a small wave. He felt his heart grip. But it wasn't panic, even though he felt nerves squirming in his belly. He looked at Vince. Vince pulled out a pair of cuffs, and Brey said, "C'mon."

But Anderson picked up his duffel bag, and Vince put the cuffs on anyway.

* * * *

It was an ordinary room with a heavy mesh screen on its only window now. An office once, before the screen. It was dark out, a light in the hall was on and it spread across the floor of the little room.

Hank looked in, and Brey stared at him. He didn't make a move to get up off the cot he was sitting on. It wasn't really a cell, just a place to sleep off a drunk or a fight, but maybe Brey thought it was. No reason not to, Hank guessed.

"C'mon," he said, stepping back.

"Are… Are they going to whip me?"

"The Council meets in three days."

"I have to wait?"

"Get up, Brey. We can talk at home."

The cot creaked. Brey rose slowly, jaw gritted, angry. A smile quirked Hank's lips. Brey walked out, and Hank followed him. He was bothered by Brey's pallor, though. Too pale.

"You want a drink?" Hank asked.

"Fuck, yeah."

Brey's voice was gravelly. There was nobody on the street. Hank jostled him gently and murmured, "Don't worry, Brey."

Brey stared at him, trying to get a read, but Hank just kept walking. At home he poured whiskey into two glasses and went to Brey in the living room. He sat on the coffee table across from him.

"Here you go."

He watched Brey drink, watched him thinking, emotions playing across his face.

"I ran, yeah, but I wasn't trying to run away. I knew I couldn't't."

"You were chased."

"By a lotta things."

"I know you have your demons," Hank said after a moment, and a smile worked up Brey's lips.

"A couple."

Hank swirled his drink, watching it glow around the ice cubes. The aroma was warm and sweet and familiar, like the way things used to be.

"You won't be whipped, Brey. I will kill anyone who tries to touch you."

His voice sounded perfectly normal, even to him, though the promise was contrary to everything he had ever lived for. He took a swallow of his drink then looked at Brey, who was staring at him in shock.

"I promise," he added.

Brey swallowed and shook his head. "You don't have to, Hank. I can take it."

"I can't." He gestured at Brey's glass. "Drink."

He watched Brey try to puzzle him out. His eyes darted all around Hank's face then he frowned and drank the rest of his whiskey. Hank took the empty glass, then brought it back full, sitting back down.

"I made a promise to you. I mean to keep it. We won't make it to the Council meeting, Brey."

"What are you talking about?"

"Brian an' a couple others from Waterfall along with a faction from Younger's group are going to attack us in two days. The day before the Council meeting."

"Attack us? Like a war?"

Hank nodded. "A lot of people secretly side with Brian."

"That's crazy."

"They have weapons. Bombs. I suspect they were stockpiling materials at the pumping station. You surprised one of them."

"Bombs?" Brey echoed.

Hank nodded. "I want you to run, Brey. You can get away. I want that for you."

But Brey seemed dazed. He drank his whiskey then stared at his glass. "I don't... I don't... I can't." He shook his head. "I won't."

"You have to, Brey. Brian can win."

He let that sink in, and Brey's gaze turned glittery, inward. Hank didn't know what he was seeing, but it made him pale. Then he was angry, flushing with it. "Arrest 'im!"

"We have no evidence. Anything we do now will tip 'im off."

"Jesus Christ! This isn't right. I'm sick of this. This isn't fucking right."

"Not even a little. Which is why you need to go, an' I need to see this through."

"You? Just you?"

Hank took the glass out of Brey's hands. "Give me this, Brey. I can't walk away from people who need me."

"Oh, yeah, sure. You don't have to walk away. You just make me run away."

His voice was bitter. He stared at Hank for a moment longer then got up and went down the hall.

* * * *

Jack gave him a bigger duffel bag.

Brey took it back upstairs with him then he sat on the side of the bed with a few of the books Hank gave him for Christmas on his lap. His favorites. Taking them made no sense, though. He'd read them. They were things—things that could take up the space for food and water. Sentimental things. He put clothes in the pack. Water bottles. His compass. A knife. A sketchpad. His razor. His blades. He rubbed his stubbly chin and got up. He was on house arrest and wasn't supposed to go out.

He went out anyway.

Walking through the cool air, he thought about water. That was his worry, even though he'd come this far alone and didn't die of thirst. He could do it again.

Even if he didn't want to.

He went into the library and let his eyes follow the rays of light through the high windows. Cool, pale... The kind that let the dust and dirt show on the floors he waxed. Voices murmured. People he didn't know. Younger's people. His heart sputtered. Hank was right. He felt eyes on him, speculative, following. They sat at one of the reading clusters, perched on the edge of their chairs, leaning in, elbows on their knees.

He passed by. Went into the reference room where Issa was working on the card catalog. She gave him a startled stare, then a frown of censure.

"Brey."

"You know?"

"Hank stopped by."

"I'm grounded."

She made a show of grinding her teeth at him, got up and hugged him. "I'm glad to see you. You'll be okay in here."

"I like it here."

He didn't wax or dust. He went into the building next door and looked at the pictures he'd taken and the items Issa collected before they'd decided to leave everything where they found it. He took his sketchpad back outside and sat on the edge of the cement walkway and sketched the outside of the library. Heavy. Permanent.

Out of the corner of his eye, he saw Younger's people go by. He liked it here. He could make a life here. No cars. No clubs. No drugs. No school. No classrooms to teach in, but there was this library. Hank, Issa, Jack, and Josh. He could write his own history. A book of the new world. There were reams of paper in the library. He'd just be careful and not waste any of it. This was a real place with real lives. Every other place else was a horror story. Ghost cities. Empty stores. Drained water pipes.

People who hurt other people.

Not like his family.

His family. Waiting. Mourning him.

Issa brought out cups of tea, and they drank together quietly. Hank came in after work and said, "C'mon, brat."

He went, hands in his pockets. The weather was cool but his sweater was enough.

Inside the apartment, Hank stopped him with a hand on his elbow, pulled him over and hugged him. It was a warm, chaste hug, and he relaxed into it, resting his forehead on Hank's shoulder.

"This is fucked," he said.

Warm air gusted against the side of his neck, then Hank let go.

"We're supposed to have a drink with Jack."

Brey nodded. "I would love a drink."

They played *Sorry*, a game Brey hadn't seen in years. The pain inside him was a brittle thing, about to shatter. But he drank and laughed. Hank nudged him with his shoulder, and Jack just shook his head at him.

"You suck at this."

He lost every game and laughed around a sense of doom that burned like acid in his belly.

* * * *

Hank didn't wait long after Brey had gone upstairs. He finished his drink, looking pensively into his empty glass. Jack's living room was one of the old clinic rooms, windowless, stuffed with two leather couches, a coffee table and a liquor cabinet.

Hank set his glass down, his fingers lingering on the edge, and said, "I want this over. Fuckers anyway."

"You only have a day to wait."

Hank glared at him. "I'm not wishing this."

"You're wishing for a bloodless victory."

"You bet I am."

"You have a vision, Hank, an' Brian an' his crew are walking right into it."

"You make it sound like I set it up."

"You're just on the right side of history."

"I don't want people to die."

"An' yet they do," Jack mused into his drink.

"I want Brey free."

"You'll get that. You have Younger on your side. A chance to free every slave. You want that too."

"I want that too," he agreed quietly.

And Brey. He wanted Brey, a man he thought he'd never see again. A man he couldn't separate from the worst days of his life. Part and parcel of all the good he lost that day outside the sliding glass doors of the house he lived in with Beth and the girls. A part of the job he loved, of his convictions and beliefs. Of his desires. His passion. His confusion. His hope.

He accepted another slosh of whiskey and clicked his glass against Jack's.

"To a bloodless victory."

Jack snorted. "Go on. Get upstairs."

He swallowed the whiskey and went.

* * * *

The air smelled of steam. Brey's shower. Lavender and verbena soap. A dark hall drew him on to dull lamplight in the bedroom where he stopped in the doorway in shock, and his lungs pulled in a silent gasp. Dizziness struck him, blood rushing to his dick. *Fuck!*

His lips moved. He licked them. Swallowed. This was his dream of Brey. That sick, shameful dream he could never tell him about. He wanted him like this, knees spread, ass up, face on the mattress. The way he saw him at Thom's. The way Brey didn't like to be anymore. Hank went across the carpet, a shaky hand rising, palm settling on Brey's hip, sliding down and under to cup his heated balls. Brey shifted, knees pushing wider.

He spoke into the sheets. "You want me like this." Knowing him.

"Yes," Hank agreed.

He pulled his hand away and kicked his shoes off, unbuttoned his shirt. Brey looked back, cheek resting on the mattress. His eyes were heavy, skin rosy.

Hank couldn't explain the strange panic that tingled through him. He fumbled at his clothes, fingers clumsy. Brey sighed, digging his fingers into the sheets. A shiver ran through him.

"You like this?" Hank asked. "Me looking at you?"

"Yeah."

Hank got onto the bed and ran his fingers down Brey's ribs, traced his snake tattoo, rubbing a circle where the tail curled up toward Brey's back. His skin was still moist from his shower. Hank cupped the cheeks of his ass, thumbs pulling down the crease, rasping against the soft hairs around his hole. Brey's ribs expanded, back arching. Hank kissed the delicate nub of bone at the top of Brey's ass before he sat back on his heels, feasting on Brey's body.

Drowning.

Lost in him.

He loved Brey's hole—puffy, loose, red, seeping cum. Pink, fluttery, a knot against his thumb. All ways. He dug his fingers into him and bit, suckled, licked, wanting, needing to reclaim him, obliterate Brey's memories of pain and fear, renew him with worship.

He circled Brey's rim with his tongue, poked at his pucker, bit and sucked out whimpers at porn star volume. Brey bucked, humped the air, fucked his ass on Hank's tongue. Gasps rolled out of him, and he gnawed at the sheets. Hank inhaled—lavender, lemons, the scent of Brey.

He needed to remember Brey's smell, his taste, the heat of his balls, that hot, silky prick sliding through his fingers... Those noises.

"You like this, Aubrey?"

He bucked back. "Yeah."

"Want me to keep eating your ass?"

"Yeah... Yeah... Please..."

Brey rocked back, and Hank pushed his tongue inside him and loosened his fingers on Brey's cock.

Brey whined too loud to be real. All for Hank. "C'mon, Hank. Fuck me. Stick your dick in me. C'mon."

Hank rose up and dug his thumbs into Brey's ass, and Brey lunged up on his elbows, throwing a look behind him.

"Lube. Next to you. Please."

The bottle was already there on the bedside table. Hank reached for it, and Brey dropped his cheek back onto the mattress, fluttering the sheets with his breath. His legs shook, and Hank slipped an arm around his waist as he pushed in.

"Oh, God," Brey muttered.

A low, throaty voice. His real voice.

Hank squeezed his eyes shut, sinking into heat and bliss. Pleasure tingled in his cock, tantalizing, electric shocks. His blood was liquid fire. Brey rocked, fucking his cock into Hank's fingers again. Hot, sweaty skin slid against his, slippery, sparking like static electricity.

His whole world, emotions, thoughts of Brey, loss, loneliness swirled in the far reaches of Hank's consciousness.

"Aubrey..."

Here, in this place, there was just Brey, just white, hot, incandescent pleasure, happiness, joy...

His cock ignited in the sudden clench of Brey's ass and shock waves raced up his spine and out of his prick in wave after wave of pleasure. Brey spasmed underneath him, shook and went limp.

Hank's arm relaxed. He let Brey go and collapsed beside him. His chest heaved. Heat rolled off Brey, sinking into his weary muscles.

His eyes were heavy, daylight coming too quickly.

He wanted to stay awake, but then Brey came to lie against him and he pulled him in and slipped away.

* * * *

Brey woke up to Hank's lips scraping across his, stubble, fingers on his dick, jerking him quietly. He shot silently, Hank's mouth over his, swallowing his air.

A warm, damp cloth wiped his skin. He took it and sat up.

Hank was dressed, jeans, khaki shirt, badge, gun in the holster he almost never wore in Waterfall.

Brey looked up into the coolness of Hank's stare. He was pulling away from him already. Then regret flickered in Hank's eyes. He got onto the bed and lay down beside him, pulling him into his arms.

"You have to go, Brey. You wanted this, now I need you to do it. Run away for me. Go home."

"I am home."

Hank breathed into his neck, kissed him gently. "I need you safe."

His hands roamed, sliding against Brey's skin. Then he got up, bent back down again slowly, put his lips against Brey's, not kissing, just touching, warm breath meeting warm breath.

"I love you, Brey."

"Hank—"

Then Hank pushed up, abruptly, wheeling away, out into the hall, the front door slamming behind him with a bang.

Brey fell back, staring for a long time at the ceiling and thought about the first time he lay like this, looking up at shadows flowing across the plaster like water.

Getting up, he took a shower, letting the hot water run for a long time. He stayed naked because dressing was paramount to functioning, and he didn't want to function. He wanted to list quietly through the day, let it uneventfully pass him by. Bombs. War. His brain stalled on that the way it did on the evidence of Patric's dead body. His drunken, addled brain spun off into some altered reality where Patric sat up again, but Patric didn't. And Brey was desperate and looked around in a panic for salvation.

In prison, he dreamed of Patric's groggy return from the dead. In the club, he had fixed on Hank. Hank, who had materialized in the swirl of panic. Whose arms supported him in warm water, washing away sweat and grime and grief. Speaking his name from the same fantastical place where Patric lived again— *"Aubrey..."*

Solace in his loneliness.

He took a T-shirt out of Hank's drawer and put it on, finally climbed into a pair of jeans and stood at the window. Two men crossed the park, not talking. Shadows stretched, and the light sky grew a darker blue.

Maybe there'd be no war. No attack.

Maybe Brey could put his things away. Check out new library books. Would he read everything one day? Maybe Hank could take him on a trip to that college and he could find new books, sketchpads, colored pencils. Maybe Issa would marry Jack. Maybe Chrissy would fall in love and have a baby—a chubby girl baby. Maybe they'd name her Eve.

Maybe he'd never leave Hank, wrap around him like the snake wrapped around his ribs.

He pressed his forehead against the windowpane, saw the edge of his reflection, then turned suddenly, stepped into his shoes and ran downstairs. The clinic was dark. Outside, he bolted down the street, shadows out of the corner of his eye, men going in the opposite direction. He dashed across the intersection and down the other block to the library.

Lights glowed in the soft gloom, but he didn't see anybody. The sky was darkening out of the high windows.

"Issa!"

Something thumped then she was coming out of the far corridor and he ran over and pulled her into a hug. She stroked his hair. She was warm and soft, and he thought of his mother.

"I love you, Issa."

"Oh, sweetheart. I love you too."

"Jack isn't home."

"I know."

"Say goodbye for me?"

"I will."

"I don't want to go, Issa."

"You are a joy, Brey. You deserve to be happy."

"Without Hank?"

She pulled back and cupped his face. "Sweetie. You won't be without Hank. You know that."

He swallowed. He wanted to believe that. Believe in the man who was there for the worst times of his life. He wanted him for the good times, too, though. He wanted him forever.

Issa let him go, and he backed away. Shadows grew thick as smoke.

Outside, he was alone. He didn't see anyone. A light popped on, though. A warm, yellow square in a building across the park. In the houses outside of town, other windows lit up, sending a dim glow into the sky.

A normal day.

A normal night.

Then a shock wave hit him, a cacophony of noise, a whoosh, orange flames. An arc of color rose behind a wall of buildings across town, not near him. A sound of water or wind. Shouts, distant, rolling over each other.

He began to run.

Another explosion. Closer. He stumbled, hit a wall beside him. The noise was ricocheting through his head. *Fuck!* He bolted across the park. Not home. His breath wheezed. *No! No fucking panic attack!* He made it to the far corner, saw shapes running against the backdrop of fire. A burning truck. Patches of flames on the ground.

Then the pop-pop of gunshots.

Engines. A pickup squealed out of the dark and barreled past him. He fell back and stumbled over the curb, landing on his rump and palms. The impact on his spine sent sparks of light shooting through his head. He blinked and got back up.

A high-pitched whine ebbed and flowed. A siren. He ran toward the fire. Behind him, he heard another explosion. Smaller. He looked back. A single column of flame rose, then descended. He started to turn. A body slammed into him, and he fell back. The man ran on.

Plaster spat.

Another pop-pop.

Startled, Brey ran to the other side of the street, fetching into a doorway.

The sound of the siren blared louder and louder. His ears rang, and his head pounded. His breath choked him, but he stepped out again.

A man yelled, "That way! That way!"

The shadows up ahead of him collected, broke apart again. He stood in the middle of the street and looked back. Heavy footsteps thudded by. Then another shape came to a stop. "Brey! Jesus Christ!"

Josh ran over. He went to him, shaky, felt Josh drag him away. Resisted once, pulling back at him. Josh jerked him up the curb and around the corner.

"Fuck. I thought I lost you. Hank sent me."

"Sent? I don't —"

"We didn't tell anybody. Couldn't take a chance." Josh's head whipped around. "C'mon. We don't have a lot of time. Things are already settling down. Fuckers."

"We?" He couldn't grasp that. Josh's voice came through the ringing in his ears and didn't make any sense to him.

"I was passing on info about my dad's plans. Fuckin' loser. No wonder my mother divorced 'im. I knew a couple locations the bombs were gonna be set, an' Hank already took those fuckers out."

Brey stared into Josh's face — stony, strong. *Fuck.* His surprise numbed him. They were half running now, Josh pushing him through the door of his building.

"You're packed, right? Go get your stuff."

Brey went upstairs. His resistance evaporated. Hank had sent Josh, determined to make Brey go. A blip of nervous energy made him start to rush. He was going. Going without Hank. Going alone. Going home.

Orange light swelled against the windowpanes.

He grabbed his coat and duffel bag and ran downstairs. The lobby was ghostly, a gleam at the glass doors, Josh a dark shadow below him. Then Josh came up a step and took Brey's collar in both hands. The raspy feel of Josh's fingers sent a jolt through him.

"I have the key," Josh said. "I'm gonna lock it back up the minute I get it off. Nobody's gonna be at the radar right now, an' if we lose — which we won't — nobody's gonna notice that it's not on you anymore anyway. You can get away."

Brey nodded. The scrape of the collar made him flinch. His collar. The collar Hank put on him. Josh let go of him and dug in his pocket. A faint light flashed against the key.

No.

The click of the lock made him jump. The collar slipped off, and Josh snapped it shut again, and Brey felt a strange surge of anger at a betrayal that made no sense. He was confused. Nobody betrayed him.

He stared at Josh, back at the doors, looking out.

A clump of darkness at the corner of a building across the street broke apart, people running. Popping sounds again. Gunfire.

Brey's fingers felt at his bare neck. Friends, family, ties. Ties that he took for granted. Lust that he mistook for love. Insecurity. Fear. He always ran.

"Fuck," he said.

Standing with his face pressed to the glass, Josh looked back at him. "Go out the back way."

"No." Without the collar he was free to stay, too.

"Whadda you mean, no? You have to. I promised Hank."

"Come with me."

"I can't. I have to make up for that asshole dad of mine. I need to make things right again."

A man flashed past the door, startling Josh back a step. Another man was barreling after him across the park. Orange light undulated in the sky.

Josh whirled.

"Brey! Go!"

Then Brey went, skidding to a stop at the end of the hall, looking back at Josh's shape in the lobby before he pushed through the door to the parking garage below.

His steps thudded.

He thought about his old house, the emptiness of it, the pool he swam in, half-believing the fantasy that if he lived as if everybody was still there, they'd suddenly appear again. But they didn't. He went to sleep and woke to an empty house. Wanting wasn't enough.

Downstairs, he ran across the garage and up the incline out of the building. He stopped at the exit and peered out. The air smelled of smoke. There were houses on fire in the residential section. All those homes, the ones he walked through. Anger surged through him. A flare-like energy.

Fuck Brian. Fuck Younger.

Nothing ever changed.

He ran again, farther and farther until the lights fell away behind him, and all he heard was the pounding of his steps on the interstate.

Away.

Free.

Alone.

Chapter Eighteen

Smoke rose in thin tendrils. A bitter, acrid scent clung to the air.

The sun was up, the sky a cloudless blue.

At the end of the street, a body lay under a tarp beside a burnt-out Jeep. The wall of an office building bore the sooty arc of an explosion on its surface.

Another vehicle had crashed into the cannery before it exploded.

Curtains had been set alight in a row of houses, and the flames had leaped into the dark sky. Now there was just sooty rubble in the daylight. Arcs of water spilled from the old fire hoses.

A strange quiet filled the air.

The aftermath of crazy.

People went in and out of the buildings looking for Brian and Pete. Hank kept moving. *That fucker!* He knew Brian wasn't here, that he was out there wherever Brey was.

He picked up his pace, heading for the station. All of Younger's people were here. Except for Pete and Brian, Brian's faction was jailed or dead. Earlier he saw Josh at the burnt-out Jeep, his gaze sweeping across the horizon with a bitter humor.

Seeing Hank, Josh laughed. "That bastard just up an' left me, not that I'd go with 'im. Stupid waste of time lookin' for 'im, though."

Hank gave no sign that he'd heard Josh's hurt.

"You're better off here."

"I plan on staying. Younger too," he said pointedly. Because Waterfall didn't need Hank anymore. Because Josh wanted him to go. His eyes had turned implacable, and Hank knew that he was thinking about Brey and Brian, and the nature of luck. Brey had a way with bad luck.

Before he could leave, Josh stopped him again. "Here," he said.

His fingers unfolded, Brey's collar hanging from his palm.

Hank took it, a useless rope of metal. But the feel of it reminded him of the feel of Brey's skin, the weight of despair bending his neck when Hank attached it. And he realized that something had cracked in him that first day with Brey, a break in the ideals that had risen up and surrounded his heart. Everything good he'd ever wanted to do appeared in Brey — in Brey's anguish. In that torment that beat at his hope. In the will that braved his hopelessness. The passion that fired him. Crumbling was every certainty that Hank had ever had that he wouldn't just give up all his visions of the future for one man's salvation. Brey had run, but he hadn't wanted to. He'd run because Hank wanted him to. Hank knew the transformation in Brey's heart. The unwillingness to leave him for the memory of love, because it was Hank's transformation too.

There was no contest between the past and the future. No way to measure one life saved against a hundred others.

It was Brey's life in his hands. Brey, who'd bent his neck and given Hank power over him. Brey, he owed his heart and soul to.

On his way across the park, he pulled off his badge and clutched it in the hand with Brey's collar. Useless things to him now. He dropped them on his desk in the station where Younger was sitting in Hank's chair with a cup of chico he sipped reflectively. He eyed the badge, the collar then Hank.

"You leavin' us, Hank?"

Hank took off his holster. Then he thought about that and clipped it back onto his belt. He wanted that, his gun too.

"You need me for anything?"

"Nope."

"Good."

"Doc was lookin' for you. Packed you up," Hank started. Humor played across Younger's face, then he said, "You better get goin'."

Hank turned for the door.

"An' Hank..." He looked back. "Have a good life. You an' your boy."

"You too, Younger."

Younger nodded then went back to drinking his chico.

Outside, the wind came up, stirring leaves, blowing at the bitter fumes in the air.

At home, Jack pushed a duffel bag at him and headed for the door. "I have people to check on. I can do that. I can't do this. I don't fuckin' know myself without you, Hank."

"Jack... Fuck. Come with us."

"Issa's safe here." Then he was pushing the door open, and Hank felt the bottom of the world drop out from under him.

"Jack—"

"Nine o'clock on April second, Hank. I'll be drinking with you."

Then Jack went out the door, and it swung back, flashing light into the lobby. The air stuck in Hank's lungs and the pain of it swelled his chest. April second. Lacy's birthday. He exhaled, sucked in a bitter plastic smell.

"Fuck," he whispered.

Then he picked up the duffel bag and swung it over his shoulder. Liquid sloshed. He set the bag back down and opened it. Water and Jack Daniel's. He laughed, and the laugh stuck like the air.

It hurt.

But he picked the duffel bag back up again and walked outside.

Shade angled across the sidewalks. The sun glittered on windows, then rocks, occasional bits of glass, the rough surface of the interstate. The pavement stretched into the distance, cracks looking like wide rivers. The sun was cool and bright.

Night came. He slept.

The cold grew, and by dawn he felt damp. Walking again warmed him up. The land stretched out flat and dry. A small town studded the horizon. Before he came to it, he clipped his holster and gun back onto his belt. A faint, almost musical creak met his ear.

A bird sang in a tree by an empty house. A single song until he passed, and a sudden chorus of happy singing followed him away. The creaking continued, intermittent, sweet-sounding. He never saw what it was. Brey wasn't here. The short buildings of the town collected along the interstate. Brown and unimaginative. Charming, homey houses stretched along side streets.

The sun rose up and began to sink again.

He walked into the dark. Then he lay down and conjured Brey against his sleepless eyelids, a sinuous, pale body swaying to some strange, creaky music. He thought of Brian, and his heart clenched. He was empty without Brey, like the lifeless houses.

He woke at first light, walking again, keeping to the interstate.

Another little town stretched out like a patchwork quilt, colorful grids of homes, blue and red and purple storefronts. A brick school house with bright yellow and white trim.

A happy place once.

He liked to think about places like that. Picnics and block parties. His girls. Bicycles and soccer practices. Sleepovers. Beth's potato salad. His neighbors, Scott and Ellen. People like Jack. People who never turned into monsters like Brian.

He stopped halfway through the storybook town.

"Brey! Brey!"

He rotated in every direction, waited, began to walk again.

The sun grew warm, and he felt lazy in it. Tired. His feet hurt.

Then a hazy, ragged range of mountains appeared far away and closer to him were high rises, smudged by a bluish blur. He walked faster. Occasionally a sharp splinter of glass flashed ahead of him. Light on a window. The sun rose higher. The shape of the high rises sharpened, angles, occasional curves, needle-thin, bulky and columnar. Other buildings separated out of the blurry distance. Short, white, gray, beige.

Industrial and office complexes. He was hot in the sun. He ran, walked, ran again. The buildings loomed above him. Empty neighborhoods collected on the outskirts of the city.

The sun blazed down, then started to sink.

He slowed and stopped and waited. He scanned windows he couldn't see into, let his eyes roam over cars and buses and semis. The vehicles looked eerily ordinary, parked against curbs, frozen in motion on the freeways. He set the duffel bag down and climbed up onto the hood of a black Tundra.

Shadows angled. The sun was a polished gold.

Sweat ran down his spine.

He tugged at his shirt.

The sound came, more musical than birdsong or creaky metal. *"Haaaank!"*

He appeared out of the shade of a building, running toward him. Baggy gray trousers, T-shirt, and sneakers. He ran, lean, strong limbs pumping. Hank jumped down in a shaky leap, dizzy with relief, gratitude. Brey was laughing as he ran, and Hank started laughing too. He opened his arms and steeled himself as Brey flung himself into the air. Hank caught him, staggering back against the Tundra's grill until he could right himself again. Brey wrapped around him, cheek against his, laughing a giddy, almost hysterical laugh.

"You found me!"

"I found you, sweetheart. I found you."

A place opened up in him. A place that was Brey's from the moment Hank had seen him. Brey's legs squeezed Hank's hips, Hank's arms like girders against Brey's back, holding him up. Brey's forehead clunked Hank's.

"I fucking love you, Hank."

"I love you too, sweetheart."

And he wasn't afraid of that anymore. Wasn't afraid of losing all the things that were always his. Jack had packed Hank's pictures of Beth and the girls. Pictures he never showed Brey before, but would now, because he saw the way that all their faces blurred and overlay each other, a composite of his life, of him. A feeling of perfect peace came over him, inexplicably, in this dead city with the steel remnants of the old world rising against the sky and the lonely silence.

But here he was with Brey's wondrous blue eyes smiling into his, everything he ever wanted in the world in his arms.

Chapter Nineteen

At night there was a light, a dim and wavering glow they couldn't account for.

Hank ascribed the light to the reflection of the sun on ocean waves, a lingering luminosity, but the glow hung over the dark silhouette of distant hills.

They heard hidden rumbles like motors.

In the day, the ocean was a shimmer of lights that gave way to murky shadow under clouds or soft blankets of fog. Mists clung to cypress, then oaks and pines and redwoods. Then came the day that Brey walked head of him, anxious and short-tempered. This was his moment of truth. His family was here or nowhere. He was walking toward the possibility of death—his father's, his mother's, his sister's. All the desperation he put into this one goal grew inside him.

He shot glances at Hank as they walked. Brey's pale blue gaze begging, but Hank wouldn't give him hope he couldn't promise him.

"I hate this fucking walking," Brey said, day after day until Hank felt his nerves grate.

"We can stop, Brey. Rest a while."

"Good idea, Hank. Why don't we wait until fucking winter?"

Hank gritted his teeth.

He bit him and stroked him and fucked him gently every night. Slow slides. Deep thrusts inside. The clamp of Brey's thighs, the shine of his eyes, reminders of Brey's fragility.

Hank prayed silent prayers.

Please give him this. Please...

The air was heavy with damp. The smell of wood smoke drifted by, wisps of it. The ocean pounded in the distance. They were following a paved strip that wound off the highway. Then Brey began to disappear into the mist.

"Hey! Wait up!"

But Brey didn't slow. He ran. Redwoods and mist swallowed him. Hank ran too.

Then— *"Dad! Dad!"*

The road descended in a slow curve. Wooded hills sloped down to a wide expanse of water. Gray and flat in the stillness. And behind that, built into the hills was a golden house—golden windows, golden wood.

Light. Electricity.

A generator. Hank remembered all the depleted oil fields in California that had once been used to store surpluses of gas.

Then Brey came into view again, running out of a grove of redwoods. A man stood on the lawn, golden in the scoop of light out of the house, dark in the shadows, running toward him. His voice rose too— "Brey!"

The man opened his arms, and Brey ran full force into them. Laughter—both of them. The man was rocking Brey side to side, stroking his head, hugging him, leaning away again to cup his face.

The door to the house flew open and a woman ran down the steps. "Brey!"

Another woman with a toddler in her arms emerged too, a man behind her.

Brey was in his mother's arms now, his father's arm around his back. The younger woman, Brey's sister, hugged him from the other side. The toddler wailed. The woman set the little boy down, and the boy backed up and sat on the grass. Through all this, Brey continued to laugh, giddy and breathless. "I always believed you'd be here. I always believed. I never stopped. I love you. I love you."

Clambering slowly down the porch steps was a big, golden dog, plumed tail wagging.

"Brey... Sweetheart." His mother kissed him and rubbed his shoulders, his cheeks. "My beautiful boy."

Brey laughed again, clapped his hands to his face, hugged his father, his mother, picked his sister up, swung her in a circle, let her go. Then he yelled, "Goldy!" and they all stood aside and Brey collapsed onto the grass beside the old dog, hugging her around the neck. Her tongue lolled, her tail thumped the grass and she gazed up at everyone in bewildered happiness.

Then Brey got back up and they were all hugging and laughing again. His sister picked up her little boy, the boy gave Brey a shy palm slap and they all laughed again. Then Brey's eyes roamed, met his brother-in-law's, who grinned at him.

"Hey, Brey."

"Evan. How are you?"

Evan laughed. "Good. I'm good."

Brey's chest heaved. He looked sideways and a smile split his face again. He laughed, eyes glittering in the dimming light.

"Hank!"

Then he was running back to Hank, who stood on the lawn nearby. He flung himself into Hank's arms, clasped his legs around his waist and kissed him, whispering, "I love you, I love you," between kisses.

Hank hugged him tightly, feeling the vibrations in his body.

"Okay? You're okay now?"

"I'm happy," he said, sliding his legs down. "I'm so fucking happy!"

A moment later he was pushing away again, running back, swinging an arm around his father, hugging his mother. She pulled him closer, and his father stepped sideways, looking over at Hank.

Then he approached, smiling at every burst of Brey's laughter and Goldy's sudden joyful barks. Up close he stopped smiling and stared thoughtfully for a moment. Hank watched the memories shift across his face as he tried to place him. Then he smiled again, slowly.

"Hello, Officer."

"It's just Hank now."

"Hank."

They stared at each other for a moment. In the background, Brey was holding his nephew, bouncing him, giggling, eyes flashing to every smiling face. They leaned in to kiss him, rub his back, stroke his hair. Brey's father looked over, back at Hank again then he held out his hand and gave Hank a smile like Brey's, and Hank remembered the faith in Brey's eyes all those years ago, a faith he finally shared.

Only love and hope put him here.

He took the hand Brey's father stretched out to him and saw Brey look over, grin at him and mouth, "I love you," before his family's arms enveloped him again and his laughter, disembodied, happy, rose in the misty, salty air.

Brey's father grinned too.

"Welcome home, Hank."

About the Author

Kayleigh Sky is a writer of M/M erotica romance. Kayleigh's stories are tales of struggle and pain, loss and despair. Love is won in the battle to rise out of the depths of darkness. Victory is in the sweet bliss of happily ever after.

Once upon a time, Kayleigh hid out in a cold, dark garage reading a book her parents had just told her she wasn't old enough to read. She was nine. The book? *Giovanni's Room* by James Baldwin, a story of love between two men—well, actually the story was a little more complicated than that, but hey, she was nine

And then? A light, a passion, a sheer joy for love in all its manifestations awoke. And love between two men—hot! Kayleigh's men are often broken, always brave and always memorable.

Kayleigh Sky loves to hear from readers. You can find her contact information, website and author biography at http://www.pride-publishing.com.

www.ingramcontent.com/pod-product-compliance
Lightning Source LLC
Chambersburg PA
CBHW031940260626
47157CB00016B/695